for Lori —

Matt Phelad
2012

THE DREAM SEEKER
by
Matthew S. Field

THE DREAM SEEKER
Matting Leah Publishing Company/November 2010

Published by Matting Leah Publishing Company
Warwick, New York.

Printed in China

All rights reserved
Copyright © 2010 by Thomas A. Mattingly II

Book Design by Tom Lennon

No part of this book may be reproduced or transmitted in any form or by any means, electronic or mechanical, including photocopying, recording, or by any information or storage retrieval system, without the written permission of the publisher except where permitted by law.

Cataloging-in-Publication Data
Field, Matthew S.
The Dream Seeker / by Matthew S. Field. – 1st ed. – Warwick, NY: Matting Leah Pub. Co., c2010.
   p. ; cm.
   ISBN: 13-digit: 978-0-9761528-2-8; 10-digit: 0 -9761528-2-7
   1. Dreams – Fiction. 2. Lucid dreams – Fiction. 3. Widowers Fiction. 4. Cancer Patients – Fiction. 5. Mate selection Fiction. 6. Life-change events – Fiction. I. Title.

PS3606.I335 D74 2010
813.6 – dc22   1011.

www.MattingLeahPublishing.com

For Amy

Prologue

The security guards at the Milstein Pavilion knew Quinn. They'd seen and spoken with him when he and Gina made their many visits or during one of Quinn's food runs. After Quinn passed through the electric rotating door, the on-duty guard waived him past.

With a throng of doctors, nurses, candy stripers, patients, hospital administrators, visitors, and pharmaceutical reps, Quinn waited for one of the four oversized elevators. He didn't need to press the number 5, because every number was already lit. One passenger made the same tired joke at the mezzanine. "This was the local! I thought I boarded the *express*!" He thought he was the funniest man in New York since Jerry Seinfeld. A few of the passengers sniggered, but most rolled their eyes or just continued to look blankly at the illuminated numbers. As Quinn waited for his floor, he couldn't help but wonder what had awakened him just before six o'clock. He would've sworn he heard Gina's voice.

When the door opened on the fifth floor a few minutes before nine o'clock, Quinn saw Sandy waiting for the staff elevator.

"Good morning, Sandy," Quinn offered.

Startled, Sandy answered, "Oh, Quinn! We've been trying to call you."

"Did you try my cell? It didn't ring." Then Quinn connected the dots. "Is Gina okay?"

Sandy was in crisis mode. "Gina's in ICU. She went down a few minutes ago. We wanted to talk with you because we needed to know if you wanted to resuscitate."

"Resuscitate?"

Sandy gave Quinn a little hope when she said, "Let's go Quinn. I'll take you to see her." Quinn followed Sandy into the elevator. It was the express.

"See her," Quinn silently rationalized. "See her. That implies that she is there to see—that she'll be there to see me. See her. Come on. Give me a happy ending here."

"What happened, Sandy?"

"She crashed this morning, Quinn. We had to make the decision without you. They worked on her in the room, but then she flatlined and we moved her downstairs."

Still hoping to see his wife, Quinn asked "What? Why? What happened?"

"It could have been a lot of things, Quinn. Decreased liver function or the shock as the antibiotics were introduced for the pneumocystic pneumonia could have spurred some reaction. The heart was already weakened after the heart attack last summer." Sandy paused. "It was just a perfect storm."

As the elevator doors opened to the ICU, Quinn asked, "When did it start?"

"I got the call at about five minutes to six this morning."

The intensive care unit at New York Presbyterian Hospital is below street level. There is no natural light. The fluorescent tubes were supposed to provide illumination, but many were off, and the relative darkness was disquieting. If the ICU's subterranean twilight was not disturbing enough, then the doctors and nurses who worked there were.

In contrast to their counterparts on the surface who wore slacks, button-down shirts, and, in the case of the male doctors, a tie under a pressed, white, monogrammed lab coat, ICU staff wore nondescript, bluish-gray scrubs from head to toe. They congregated at command posts spaced through the center of the rectangular room. Glass-front rooms spanned the perimeter where the workers tended their patients.

Sandy led Quinn to the rear, and the two of them stood between the nurses' station and a room where at least a half-dozen doctors and nurses surrounded a bed. Quinn could not see his wife, but one of the nurses in the room noticed the new observers and pulled the curtain closed.

"What are they doing?" Quinn asked.

Sandy answered, "They're trying to to save her."

"Jesus, Sandy," Quinn said, putting is hand to his mouth.

Medicine, like other professions, has its own collection of idioms that illustrate the truth in the most favorable context. The vernacular is not necessarily untrue, but, to preserve a person's dignity, special words and phrases are used instead the blunt truth. In Corporate America when an executive is fired, an official communication may read that the executive "left the company to pursue other opportunities." In accounting, cash businesses that do not report cash transactions, Gina often joked, "liberally interpret the tax code."

Even as Quinn asked the question, Sandy knew the answer but knew better than to tell Quinn the stark, honest truth. She said simply to the frightened young man standing, staring, at her side, "It's too early to tell."

A doctor not much older than Quinn noticed the curtain closed and walked over. He recognized Sandy as a fellow hospital employee, if not as Dr. Reinsdorf's assistant, and asked abstractly, "Is this the husband?"

Quinn answered the question that hadn't been directed to him, "I am."

The doctor didn't introduce himself. Quinn assumed he was a resident and probably better at saving lives than he was with interpersonal skills. Based on the doctor's tone and demeanor, Quinn also guessed that the man, who might have been a student in an auditorium survey of American history ten years earlier, believed himself a weathered veteran who'd already seen it all.

In a feeble attempt at sincerity, the doctor looked over at the room and said, as if reciting a statement he and some of his fellow medical school students had disingenuously memorized over beer and pizza, "We're doing all we can." Then, after a brief pause, "But, I'm afraid there is nothing you can do here. Can I suggest that you wait upstairs?"

Sandy didn't think Quinn saw the irritated look she shot at the self-satisfied resident. Then she looked up at Quinn and said, "Come on up to the fourth floor. There is a nice place for you to wait."

A conflagration of about two dozen people spoke in hushed tones, watched the television, or just sat quietly alone. Vainly, he tried to imagine the reasons and paths that brought each of these others to this place with him. He wondered whether the others asked themselves the same question about him. He walked over to a window and looked out, but there was no diversion there. Having no other place to go, his thoughts returned to Gina, who was lying in a bed five stories below.

"It's too early to tell." Quinn considered Sandy's answer and the resident's insincerity. "That doesn't sound very good. If Sandy thought Gina would be all right, she would've told me. What should I do? What should I do right now if Gina's not all right? If Gina isn't going to be all right, maybe I should call someone. Who should I call? Maybe I should call Gina's family. Yes, that's a good idea."

Quinn had kept Gina's little brother well informed about his sister's progress and setbacks during the past year. Although Quinn spoke occasionally with Gina's parents, Mike was most often Quinn's conduit to the rest of the family. The call was brief, so the diversion was short lived. After all, what could Quinn say? What he did say was, "Look, Mike, your sister is really sick. The doctors have her in intensive care. I'll call you when I hear anything new. Please let your mom and dad know."

Quinn felt satisfied as if he'd accomplished something. He didn't feel like making any more calls, though, so he was right back to where he started, anxious, concerned, uncomfortable, and now, nauseous. All he wanted to do was to be with Gina and all he wanted for Gina was her smile and her life back. Minutes passed slowly. Mercifully, Sandy appeared in front of him after about ninety minutes, but Quinn easily established by the look on her face that she had nothing good to report.

"Hey, Quinn. Why don't we start back downstairs to see Gina," Sandy spared the inconsequential. "We can talk while we walk."

In the hallway, Quinn's tone was hushed as he spoke. "Give me some good news, Sandy."

"Quinn, Gina is not good," Sandy said. "Between the metastases, the liver, the treatments, and her heart, she's not good. Here's the thing, Quinn. She is stable, but she's on a respirator. I'm not sure she'll be stable for long."

The doors to the elevator opened. Quinn listened to the nurse without saying a word or betraying his emotions with an expression. The elevator started its descent.

"This may be the last chance you'll have with her," Sandy admitted.

Quinn still hadn't as much as uttered a syllable and hardly blinked. Sandy asked, "Are you all right, Quinn?"

"I want to be with her," was Quinn's simple response.

Quinn entered Gina's room. Tubes seemed to be connected to every limb of her body and emerged from beneath the sheets. The young resident with whom Quinn had earlier spoken asked a question for which Quinn was wholly unprepared. This time the doctor's tone had manifestly transformed.

"Excuse me, Mr. Powers," the young doctor began contritely, "My name is Dr. Trainer."

Even under the inconceivable circumstances, the irony of the doctor's name was not lost on Quinn.

Dr. Trainer continued, "We needed to know, if your wife goes into arrest again, well, we need to know if you want us to resuscitate."

Quinn paused for a moment as he looked at the bed. "Thank you for asking me that question. Can you tell me why you should resuscitate or why you shouldn't?"

The young doctor stopped for a moment as if he was surprised by the direct, honest question. "Well, Mr. Powers, I guess I'll start by telling the reasons I would not suggest resuscitation. First, your wife's situation is dire. She's unable to breathe on her own. If she arrests, it will be unlikely we can stabilize her again. More than that, and I guess there is no easy way to say this, if we attempt to resuscitate, well, because of all those tubes connected to her arms and legs and stomach, things will get very messy."

Still looking at Gina, Quinn asked Dr. Trainer, "And why would you think it might be a good idea to do it, Doctor?"

"Well, Mr. Powers," Dr. Trainer said as he winced and rubbed his chin, "I really can't think of one."

Tears welled in Quinn's eyes. His own breathing was troubled. He understood. It was all he could do to manage the four words he spoke before he walked the rest of the way into the room and sat down on the chair next to Gina's bed.

"Leave her alone then."

Quinn's gaze turned toward Gina so he didn't see the young doctor look down knowingly toward the floor before he closed the door.

Quinn pulled a chair from the corner of the room to Gina's bedside. He sat down, gently took Gina's arm from beneath the sheet, and held her hand.

Sheets covered Gina to her chest. They were the same color as those worn by the nurses and doctors. Except for her left arm now, only Gina's shoulders, neck, and head were exposed. Taped to her face, a plastic tube trailed into her mouth. A respirator pumped a quantity of oxygen into Gina's lungs. Her chest rose and fell mechanically at precise intervals. From beneath the sheets, Quinn saw all manners of tubes and wires that connected to IV bags and machines that enveloped the bed like a semicircle of brooding judges. Not that it mattered much, but Quinn wasn't able or wasn't willing to determine whether tubes delivered fluids or relieved. However, he had no problem identifying the machine that monitored heart rate. Quinn had seen it a thousand times on hospital television dramas. He thought to himself that the machine was the only part of this that television and movies got right. The scriptwriters failed miserably with the rest.

Hollywood could never have captured the aura of impending death contrasted with the dispassionate medical staff. Television would disappoint in its inability to describe the smell of antiseptics, latex gloves, IV medicines, and detergents. No actor could reproduce the pallor, the loss of body fat and muscle, and the lifelessness that could transform a once-vigorous, spirited, beautiful woman into almost a skeleton, or a ghost. Not a single viewer of one of those hospital dramas would know the difference. Millions of people all over the world would turn on their televisions tonight or go to the local multiplex. They'd watch a sad, perhaps even tragic story about a young woman whose life was cut short by disease or accident. Then, as heroic doctors attempt to revive the patient, she briefly opens her eyes and with her last breath pledges her love to a distraught and frightened husband or boyfriend. The heart monitor flatlines, doctors, nurses, and the man hang their heads, knowing they and she had fought bravely and believing they'd done everything they could. But those people who watched that drama unfold wouldn't know the difference. Quinn hadn't known either, until now.

Quinn leaned over and kissed Gina on the forehead then on her cheek. Unless a doctor or a nurse watched on the monitor from the command center, no one saw and certainly no one heard Quinn as he moved his mouth over to Gina's ear. Tears welled in his eyes and fell down onto Gina's face. Quinn placed his hand on her cheek and with his thumb wiped away the tears. He whispered, "Gina, come back." Quinn lifted his head and waited. No response. Then, Quinn leaned toward Gina again and said, "I'll switch places with you right now. How do I switch places with you?"

For a long time, he kept his face next to Gina's before he finally sat back in the chair and found her hand again. It struck Quinn how cold it was in spite of the blankets. He tried his best not to cry even as tears collected on his eyelids and roll down his face.

A moment later, a machine started to beep loudly. Another produced a single-pitched tone. The judges had rendered a decision. Dr. Trainer opened the door abruptly. A nurse stood just behind him.

"She's arresting, Quinn," Dr. Trainer declared.

Quinn breathed deeply and barely managed as he exhaled, "I know." And then, reaffirming, "Leave her be."

Dr. Trainer nodded as the nurse walked around to the machines and silenced the alarms. The room was quiet once again. For what seemed like a lifetime, Quinn held Gina's hand as the number of blips that the monitor registered became less frequent. 67. 42. Quinn was completely helpless as it declined to 35, where it plateaued for a few minutes before falling in regular, spaced intervals descending to 15 beats per minute. Twenty minutes after Dr. Trainer left the room for the second time, the numbers on the monitor clicked downward like some perverse countdown, three...two...one. The line on the monitor was flat.

It was not like the movies.

"Eventually, enough will be known about science that there will be a single event that can't be predicted. We'll know when it will rain, when a tragic accident will happen, or when someone will die. It may take thousands of years, but eventually there will be no natural event that can't be accurately predicted using some formula. In spite of all of this knowledge, though, there will still be nothing we can do about it. Based on variables input into the great equations that define the universe and those that continue to be input, nothing will change. The future will happen. Everything is predetermined, but there is no reason for anything that happens. How could there be? God is no one special; he just knows all the equations.

"Maybe there is no order to any of this. No plan. Maybe it is really just chaos. Why did it rain on Thanksgiving? It's that butterfly in China. Maybe there is no reason.

"Does it really matter?" Quinn asked himself as he emerged from Riverside Drive with the traffic from the West Side Highway onto the George Washington Bridge. That gray sky hadn't changed a bit as November yielded to December.

Random, disjointed, anxious thoughts reeled in his mind, "As much as Guiliani's done to make New York a better place to live, the ramp to enter the GWB still looks like a crumbling mess. What in the hell am I going to do? What am I going to do?"

Quinn turned north from the upper deck of the George Washington Bridge onto the Palisades Parkway. The weather sympathized. Quinn picked up his phone and used the speed dial to call Kelly.

Skylar Smart turned her blue Volvo S40 north onto Lake Shore Drive toward Lincoln Park. The recent graduate of Northwestern Law had almost every advantage, save for perhaps one. Although Skylar's physical features were striking, long blonde flowing hair, piercing emerald eyes, a figure painstakingly fashioned during long runs on the Lake Michigan shoreline, beach volleyball, and a gym membership, she was strangely unpretentious.

The fact that Skylar was humble was not unusual in the Windy City. Because Chicago attracted so many pretty country girls from Upper Midwest farmland and because there always seemed to be more women in the city than men, snobby girls, even gorgeous snobby girls, found themselves without much attention from the opposite sex. Being a decent person was a necessity for a woman to function among all of that Midwestern hospitality. Pretty girls who had a great smile, who could turn a double play during a coed softball game, and who knew the difference between Cubby Bear and Murphy's Bleachers in Wrigleyville had become part of the culture.

As she approached the exit onto West LaSalle toward Taylor Kerr's high-rise on North Lincoln Park, Skylar still wasn't sure how to tell him the answer to his question.

She'd met Taylor just after she moved back to Chicago from Champaign. Skylar just started law school at Northwestern and blew off steam one night at Durkins, a great little hole-in-the-wall on Diversey. She was immediately attracted to Taylor, whose blond curly hair, boyish good looks, and naturally muscular physique were hard to miss. She walked right up to him and began a stormy, three-year relationship. Had she known more about him then, maybe Skylar would only have approached Taylor for some one-night company. Maybe two nights.

Taylor's father, Dean, had been a successful tort lawyer during the era of cocaine, junk bonds, and big hair. As a personal injury lawyer in the Roaring Eighties, Dean had been influential in establishing benchmarks for absurd personal injury awards. He had been a below-average student, and most people believed his legal practice benefited from being at the right place at the right time. This belief was buttressed when his luck changed. Dean was convicted of securities fraud and sentenced to ten years in a minimum-security federal prison. He'd taken a mining company public by claiming to have found vast gold deposits in the Arkansas Ozarks. It had turned out that Dean salted the samples with gold from jewelry and falsified the geologic reports. He served three years.

The apple doesn't fall far from the tree, and such was the case with Taylor Kerr, who benefited from his father's wealth, but he had none of the discipline associated with its attainment. By the time Taylor reached high school, he'd already gotten used to having things his way. During the years he attended private boarding school in Connecticut, no one was willing to stand up to Taylor and risk losing a benefactor. Fortunately for Taylor, his father's securities fraud conviction wasn't finalized until after the first semester of Taylor's senior year. In spite of the last semester's tuition being unpaid, the school allowed Taylor to graduate with the understanding that the school's magnanimity would be repaid during better days.

Taylor had little chance for the Ivy League education his father envisioned. The Kerr name had become synonymous with white-collar crime, and Taylor's academic effort accurately reflected his intellect. Neither boded well for the young Kerr, and Taylor found a spot at Hamilton College in Clinton, New York, where he majored in biology. His grade-point average was not distinguished, but he did manage to graduate. By that time, Dean was out of prison and accessed assets set aside prior to his incarceration to influence the University of Chicago of Medicine to accept Taylor into their program. While Dean convinced the admissions committee, he had little sway over the professors. Taylor was placed on probation after the first semester. After the second semester, he was expelled. Taylor was forced to find employment, but his father subsidized a luxury apartment in Lincoln Park.

It happened before Skylar was born. Nonetheless, when the United Express Delivery driver backed over her then five-year-old brother, Skylar's fate was shaped forever.

John survived, but he suffered significant injuries and was rendered quadriplegic. The first born, the boy had been his father's pride and his mother's joy. The accident devastated the young parents. Frank, a former Navy Seal who worked for a Missouri-based propane distributor, was shaken to the core. The incident transformed him from a life-loving man to a distant and detached husband and father. Tracy, a nurse, quit her job to care for the boy full time.

In contrast to the frivolous awards granted to some of Dean Kerr's clients, National Express Delivery was ordered to pay the Smarts $2.3 million. Frank and Tracy used the money to provide the care their son would need for the rest of his life. Tracy never returned to work and Frank was never the same. However, Frank invested part of the award in a couple of McDonald's restaurants in suburban Chicago and continued to do so as Chicagoland sprawled westward.

When a daughter, Skylar, was born five years later, the little girl didn't have quite the same childhood as most other upper middle-class children had. Tracy was rarely able to give the little girl the attention that she wanted, and Frank could not provide the intimate, loving relationship every young girl needs from her father. While Skylar grew into a wonderful, well-rounded young woman, some of her most basic emotional needs were never fully met. Perhaps those missing pieces in her childhood made Skylar believe she could change Taylor Kerr. She desperately hoped the love of a good woman would convince Taylor to be a good man. Then he could be all the things and they would be all the things together that Skylar so much wanted in her life.

She parallel parked her car on a quiet, tree-lined cross street. After taking the elevator to Taylor's apartment, she let herself in with the key he'd given her.

Fortunately for Taylor, the doorman in the building called up a warning. He'd barely had time to get the young woman out of the apartment and into the other elevator going down. Unfortunately for Skylar, she hadn't gotten out of her elevator soon enough. If she had, Skylar may have changed her mind.

As it was, Skylar found Taylor on the couch watching CNN with seeming indifference. He'd had just enough time to hurriedly make his bed, clean up, and dispose of all evidence of the tryst as he casually turned toward the front door, smiled, and said, "Hi, honey! What a nice surprise."

Skylar walked over to Taylor, sat on the couch, and turned to him deliberately and began, "I'm sorry I made you wait, Taylor. I should have told you right away, but I love you. And, yes, I would love to be your wife."

CHAPTER 1

A warm Christmas Eve sun illuminated the smallish, gold, bronze, and silver casket, which in a peculiar way, complemented the spirit of the season while making a statement about the life of its permanent resident. Only a few minutes earlier, a group of solemn men had carefully removed the container from the Mercedes hearse. Younger women wept, while others, self-conscious and too naïve to fully comprehend the fragility of life, looked around nervously for cues from the older women about how to act. Some *jovensitas* mistook the funeral for a social event and made misguided fashion statements in their skimpy black dresses. Older women dressed in traditional full-length black sobbed audibly as the container was placed next to a rectangular hole in the ground. Men milled, occasionally sharing a sympathetic look or whispering respectfully a direction or observation. Puzzled children occasionally raised their voices in playful laughter only to be corrected by their parents with a stern look or measured word.

The burial plot was located in a newer area of the memorial park far away from the frequented sections. The line of limousines, late-model European imports, and sports cars wove its way through the cemetery past the mausoleums built atop hillocks. The procession continued over stone bridges under which ran a small brook and past ponds where wing-clipped waterfowl gracefully glided. The motorcade encountered an area of manicured, eighteen-foot shrubs behind an eight-foot fence. The gate, which was wide enough for just one car to pass, was open. The procession led by the hearse entered slowly. In contrast to the meandering roads inside the rest of the memorial garden, the only road traced the oval created by the shrubs. The entire enclosure sloped gently toward the center, where a sparkling pond spouted a fountain and golden, white, black, and spotted koi congregated under the cool splashing water. A man-made waterfall babbled through a small channeled stream that fed and circulated the perennial pond. Interspersed among the plots were well-tended gardens and decorative trees of varieties atypical of the region.

To provide enough space for the queue, the hearse navigated the entire span, passed the gate, and then stopped just past the entrance. Dutiful funeral home employees quickly exited and pall bearers descended on the lead vehicle. Park workers, also dressed in conservative black, waited with hands folded at the belt to provide instructions to pall bearers and mourners. A small silver-haired priest in full vestments stood holding a Catholic Bible aside the open plot.

Quinn Powers's rented Volvo S80 was the motorcade's last car.

An assemblage had already congregated around the casket containing the remains of singer, actor, and international superstar, Noelia Vega. Immediate family including her father, older brother, and younger sister sat on a bench under a small open tent that was set up in front of the casket. Behind and surrounding the Vega family stood the throng.

Quinn reached into the left breast pocket of his coat, found his sunglasses, and nattily placed them on the bridge of his nose. The glasses were Quinn's way to keep in as much as to keep out. As many of life's tragedies as Quinn had endured, he never quite achieved full command of his emotions as a tear formed in his weathered, hazel eyes.

Quinn casually maneuvered his left hand under his suit coat into his pants pocket. He walked from the car to a discrete spot near the rear of the nearly complete circle. Other than his slightly lighter hair and skin, Quinn's appearance was consistent with that of the other men who came to say good-bye to Noelia Vega, who, everyone agreed, was as influential as any other Latina performer, including Selena.

The priest spoke in an elegant Mexican-Spanish accent. Quinn recognized Noelia Vega's ex-husband, record producer El Gordo, Porfirio Machado. At Machado's side was his new, beautiful, and talented singer, who hoped El Gordo would make her into a superstar the same as he'd done for Noelia. Quinn wondered whether the girl understood the cost of fame and whether she would be able to pay the tab.

When Machado discovered Noelia Vega, she was the talented twenty-year-old singer of the band, El Galipote, named for an urban legend among the Latin-Caribbean islanders. Not unlike the New Jersey "devil" or the Mexican *chupacabra*, *el galipote* can assume any shape to hide as it terrorizes *el campo*, the countryside.

There was nothing for Machado not to like about the fresh and beautiful Noelia Vega. Her voice both had a sultry, innocent timber and a five-octave range. She was tiny, although her figure was characteristically Latin. Her full and pert breasts, firm flat stomach, and an ample shapely back side endeared her to fans of El Galipote. Vega's long, straight, black hair flowed as she effortlessly sang the band's original songs through a tender, comely smile. In short, she was what El Gordo would call *una cosa segura*, a sure thing.

Quinn then glanced over toward Noelia's brother, sister, and seemingly grieving father. Noelia's siblings, her stoic brother and weeping sister sat on each side of him. Just behind the bench where family mourned stood Mexico's president, who, Quinn speculated with some derision, knew neither the decedent nor the family, but wanted to be seen participating in his country's most noteworthy social event. "El Presidente," to whom the rest of the world sardonically referred, wasted no time making his presence known to some of the luminaries. He stood next to Latin music's most successful cross-over couple, a beautiful New Yorker of Puerto Rican descent and her Colombian-born pop-singer husband.

Like most people, Vega longed for real love and companionship. She'd agreed to become Machado's wife, but Vega soon realized that the life was nothing like the one she'd imagined. It had been no music industry secret that El Gordo liked younger women and had, for all intents and purposes, bound his talent to him with a recording contract and intimidation. The latter wasn't difficult considering his quarry had always been young women who usually had little formal education and almost no experience in the ways of the unforgiving world of music. His appetite for sex was eclipsed only by his appetite for food, although not by much. Machado never failed to take exactly what he wanted. He sexually degraded the young women millions of men desired. Although he did not physically abuse Vega in any traditional sense, Machado often used demeaning sex as a way to demoralize, punish, and maintain his dominance.

So, quietly, Vega resolved to finish her legal commitment to Machado, which was only for a couple more years. Then, she would leave, strike out on her own, and try to find real love in her life.

The commercial success of her work continued while she upheld a façade of a perfect marriage. As the end of her contract approached, Machado began to discuss a new agreement. Just as Machado was drafting the contract, Vega exaggerated the importance of a personal issue pertaining to her brother and insisted on returning to Mexico City. Machado grudgingly agreed but assigned a private investigator to observe her and report to him.

Machado's detective reported that Vega visited a local gynecologist and then a series of other visits to other doctors. What the investigator failed to report, however, was a stealthy meeting with a well-known divorce attorney who had an office in New York, Mexico City, and Los Angeles. It was a complete surprise when, during lunch while in the company of a young woman at his favorite restaurant, Machado was served with divorce papers.

Disappointment did not even begin to describe Machado's reaction. He promised he'd get back at her. At the very least, he would make sure she'd never work in the music business again.

For her part, Vega learned her lessons as they pertained to Machado and planned well for any contingency. She knew her future ex-husband was capable of anything from intimidation to kidnapping, so Vega had surreptitiously coordinated press releases to every major English and Spanish newspaper in the United States, Latin America, and Europe. The releases were neither salacious nor uncomplimentary of Machado. Rather, Vega believed, if the whole world knew that she had initiated divorce, the whole world would dissuade Machado from making any overt attempts at harassment.

Vega's efforts achieved their ends. In spite of Machado's bruised ego, he left Vega alone. When speaking with his music business colleagues, he discouraged relationships with Vega. Soon, Machado found other distractions to help him put that *pecena perra* out of his mind.

Noelia Vega reunited El Galipote. In spite of Machado's efforts to freeze her out of the recording industry, she'd made plenty of friends during her tours and recording sessions and didn't think she'd have any difficulty finding a studio. By that time, she could handle the production herself.

Of course, there was something else, not music, not El Galipote, and not even Machado, more urgent on her mind. Her visits to the gynecologist and other specialists yielded some terrifying news. Noelia Vega did not include in the press releases the fact that she had an advanced stage of uterine cancer.

CHAPTER 2

"Hello. This is Life Dreams. My name is Amelie. May I help you?" Amelie Dawud answered the telephone in her home office at her luxury apartment on Central Park West.

Amelie heard nothing on the other end. Although calls to the business phone were infrequent, essentially every call began the same way, with silence. Amelie didn't repeat her greeting. She knew that the caller would either respond after a moment or hang up without saying a word. Considering she already received a call during the previous afternoon in which the caller had, in fact, ended the call before speaking, Amelie believed that there were better than even odds that the caller would reply.

"Hello," the female caller answered tentatively. Amelie thought she detected a Spanish accent in the single-word acknowledgment.

"Hello," Amelie compassionately responded.

"Um, hi. I heard about you from a friend," the caller hesitantly said. "Is it true what you do?"

Because her employer never advertised, the caller could only have gotten the phone number from some exponent of a friend of a friend. Amelie answered with warmth and understanding, "Well, yes, I think so, even though I really don't do anything except answer the phone and take care of a few things around the office," Amelie understated. "Do you want to tell me what you think we do?"

Amelie was right. The caller's second language was English. She was Hispanic, most likely from Mexico. Amelie added, *"Puede hablar en Espanol, si quiere."* "You can speak Spanish if you want to."

Silence again. Then in her native language, the caller began, "I heard from my friend that you...that someone...provides a very unique and a very discrete service to very unique and discrete clients. I understand that you are sort of a dream-come-true service for terminally ill, adult women. Is that really true?"

"Yes, that's mostly it," Amelie answered in fluent Spanish. "And I talk to people like you and tell you what we do and how we do it. It is important for me and for my employer to know that this is really right for you. We can talk for a while on the phone. This is a secure line, so what we discuss will go no further than my ears. I will not even discuss our conversation with my employer unless you decide to proceed. That's his rule, not mine. If you want to continue, then I will tell you about the secure Web site that you may access with a unique password. Using the site, you can give me more information. Again, all the information you give me will be for my eyes only. My employer will not know anything about you. Only after you and I speak and you tell me you want to take the next step will I talk with him. If for any reason you don't want to continue, all records of our conversations and access to our Web site will be destroyed by a reliable third party. You'll have the ability to anonymously verify with that organization that all hard copy and all electronic records relating to your inquiry to us have been destroyed. Are you all right with this so far?"

A sweet, timid voice replied, *"Si."*

"Okay. After all that, my employer will want to meet you personally. At that meeting, he'll explain to you who he is and he'll want to know who you are. By that time, he will have spoken to me and seen the information you and I discussed, but he'll also want to know who you really are inside and what you really want from him. Believe me, my employer is extraordinary in ways you can't imagine. You will be completely comfortable with him, the meeting, and the questions he'll ask.

"At any time, you may stop the process. If you do, the only people who will know you've contacted Life Dreams will be you, me, and my employer. The same records disposal service will be provided, and you will have the ability to verify custody. You're in complete control. If you do choose to continue, however, he will make arrangements for those things you want him to provide.

"I know this is a lot of information. I also know you're probably already overwhelmed with many things in your life, but can I answer any questions about any of this?"

The caller answered, *"No, gracias. Entiendo todo."*

Amelie asked, "Do you want to start now?"

"Si. Si podemos, señora," the voice shyly said.

"Sure," Amelie responded, "May I have your name please?"

"Si. Mi nombre es Noelia Vega."

CHAPTER 3

After the priest concluded the Sacrament, many of the people who'd gathered to pay their last respects lingered and whispered solemnly to one another. Women dried tears. Men provided comforting shoulders. Quinn walked to the Volvo to avoid speaking to anyone. He pulled past the line and out through the gate between perpetually green cover that would provide Noelia privacy *por eternidad*, for eternity.

"This never gets any easier."

He pulled from his soft, black leather brief case a compact disc case that contained Noelia Vega's final recordings. The demo, which had been recorded with El Galipote just a month earlier, would be released later in the year. Quinn's eyes misted as the stereo speakers delivered first a melody and then the pure, sultry voice. No one would see the tear Quinn shed behind his sunglasses. The first was for Noelia. Those which followed were all for Gina.

Having no other place that he had to be, Quinn remained in Mexico City that night. While he slept, he had the recurring dream about Gina. For Quinn, the only times this dream came to him were shortly after, as Quinn euphemistically referred, "a relationship with a Dream Seeker has ended."

It was a short dream, but it was a very nice one. It was not a dream about the past, but rather about the present, and it seemed very real. Quinn needed it to be.

Gina looked as vibrant and healthy as she did before she learned she was sick. The two were at home, just sitting on the couch on a Saturday afternoon watching a nationally televised Tigers football game. She was adorable in her jeans, jersey, and pony-tailed hair.

It was a slight exaggeration to describe Gina as "sitting on the couch." In the dream, she mostly fluttered. Apparently, Quinn had moved some things since she'd last been home and Gina was busy putting everything back where she wanted them. Quinn kept the afghan folded twice and draped over the

17

cushion on the couch when he wasn't using it. Gina insisted that it be kept under the coffee-table folded in eighths. Gina had finally sat for a minute. Then, she noticed something else. She got up, smiled, rolled her eyes, and made it the way she liked it.

Quinn finally said to her, "Would you please sit down? I haven't seen you for such a long time." Gina finally joined Quinn on the couch, and she held him lovingly, familiarly.

"Please don't leave again."

"I won't," Gina promised.

Gina knew what Quinn meant and Quinn understood Gina, too. Quinn knew when he woke up, Gina would not be there. Gina knew when he woke up, she would be.

Quinn continued to say, "Don't leave. Don't leave again."

"I won't, QuickPick," Gina whispered. "I won't"

CHAPTER 4

The vibrating phone on the nightstand startled him awake. Disoriented, Quinn still felt Gina's aura all around him. In fact, he could almost smell her. After ten years, he still remembered how she smelled.

Quinn may have been disappointed about being awakened by the phone, but the dream was over anyway. It always ended the same way. Besides, there were only a few people who had Quinn's phone number, including his parents, his sister, Jordan, Kelly Hill, Bob and Lina, Mike Sparvieri, and Amelie. Any one of those people who would call him at—Quinn looked over at the digital alarm clock on the nightstand—7:01 AM, was a person with whom Quinn would want to speak.

"Hullo," Quinn answered.

"Hey, sleepyhead." was Amelie's perky greeting. After having worked with Quinn for a baker's dozen years, Amelie knew Quinn as well as anyone did. She understood the last thing Quinn wanted was pity. It was a character trait that both amazed and mystified her, but "Quinn is Quinn," she'd remind herself.

"*Miércoles, Amie! Sabe qué hora es?*" The synapses in Quinn's brain began to fire.

"It's only an hour difference, and you should be out of bed anyway. Besides, I just wanted to call to wish you a Merry Christmas, you knucklehead. So, Merry Christmas, you knucklehead."

"Gee thanks, Amie. Merry Christmas to you, too," Quinn replied.

"You've made this little French-Tunisian girl very happy with your heartfelt sentiment. I wanted you to know, though, that I've gotten a couple of hang-ups in the last week. One was yesterday. I think you might have a Dream Seeker in the not-too-distant future."

"Great. I hope she gives me a few weeks," Quinn lied.

In a peculiar way, Quinn thrived on relationships with Dream Seekers.

It had little to do with sex, although his clients had generally been emotionally mature people. The screening process assured him of that. Considering both Quinn and Dream Seekers were responsible adults, physical intimacy was sometimes a part of it. In practice, however, fewer than one in three had the interest in going there. Frankly, the women for whom Quinn provided his service gave something to Quinn. His clients provided him with the closest thing on Earth, Quinn believed, to Gina and the things that Gina endured while he walked, stood, and sat by her side. Quinn understood that much. Quinn may not have realized that with each one of his clients—there had now been eleven in all—he himself had subconsciously hoped that he could actually change fate and save these women's lives. Deep in a place where he himself was not allowed to go, Quinn believed he could change the outcome of a Dream Seeker's illness.

"We'll see. In the meantime, Quinn, please try to have a nice Christmas."
"Thanks, Amie. You, too."

Quinn pressed the "End" button on his phone, rolled over and, reaching for no one, whispered, "Gina."

CHAPTER 5

Amelie had known Quinn virtually all of her adult life. Her first job after getting her degree from the State University of New York at New Paltz was Merrill Lynch. Soon after she had started, she was assigned to Quinn. She remembered Quinn before he lost his wife as a caring, friendly, and charming friend and financial adviser. After Gina died, however, perhaps no one was as close as she was to see the dramatic change Quinn had undergone.

Yes, he was still caring. He also had more empathy for other peoples' suffering than anyone else Amelie had ever known. However, the charming part of Quinn that won him the immediate friendship and respect of others almost immediately melted away. He had never and, Amelie hoped, would never turn his back or hide himself from his family and his many friends. Still, Quinn rarely offered that side of himself now to people he did not already know.

The only exceptions to what had appeared to be Quinn's new rule for strangers were Dream Seekers. Quinn made Dream Seekers believe that he cared about them, Amelie was sure, because he did. He was meticulous about understanding Dream Seekers, their illnesses, and their personal situations. He memorized the histories clients provided during the screening process. Quinn obsessively studied the diagnoses and treatments and soon became capable of discussing detection, medication, therapy, and prognosis of many illnesses with specialists in the respective fields.

Because Quinn was Quinn, Dream Seekers felt comfortable that he was not just anyone else, or everyone else as the case may be, who would in the end be another disappointment. When Quinn discovered a unique event or circumstance in the life of a Dream Seeker, like growing up in a family without a mother or growing up in a family without a father or enduring emotional or sexual abuse, he studied the likely results of that situation in the Dream Seeker's life. Quinn read. He attended survivor support groups. He met with experts in the fields of psychology and psychiatry. Given the special needs of the person, Quinn understood what he might do and what he could not do. While he learned about healing and how to help a person get past an anxiety, he wasn't surprised to learn that just taking the time to listen was often almost enough.

In the context of Quinn's evolution, advising people about investments no longer held any appeal. He sold his considerable book of business to Kelly, who by that time had left professional baseball, and to Amelie who managed it for a couple of years before Quinn asked her to work for him again. For Amelie, it wasn't a tough decision to make. Amelie received a windfall upon the sale of her book that was already half again as large as the original stake. Quinn's admittedly unusual offer would both pay well and offer her extraordinary freedom. At the same time, Amelie was a little more than curious about the idea to be a part of something that could make a person unimaginably happy when it could be the person's last chance to feel happiness.

Quinn was still physically fit when Amelie saw him again three years after Gina's death, but his face was more weathered. There were crow's feet at the corners of his eyes. His hair had grayed just a little at his temples. He was no longer clean shaven. He wore a beard most people call a goatee, although in fact, it was a Van Dyke. His eyes were darker and somehow more perceptive.

As Quinn explained Life Dreams, he wasn't at all self-conscious about discussing the fact that he believed such a purpose would fulfill an essential, personal longing inside of him and would provide an income. Quinn volunteered that an outsider could misunderstand the arrangement. He explained that he'd be no more likely to have an intimate, sexual relationship with a Dream Seeker than any other man would with any other woman between whom mutual attraction existed. In addition, Quinn understood that the Dream Seekers would almost certainly be in vulnerable situations. There would be a cost for the service, which would be part of Amelie's responsibility. Quinn would never discuss it. However, it would be tantamount that the Life Dreams agreement would stipulate that no gifts or bequests of any kind be accepted beyond the original, rather considerable fee.

"Finally, Life Dreams will not be advertised. My service will be certain to be discussed as urban legend. However, you're the only person who I've even considered to be a part of this with me, Amelie. If you decline, I will not pursue it. However, if you agree, then you may not discuss what you do or what I do," Quinn stressed.

After hearing the specifics of Life Dreams, Amelie agreed to Quinn's conditions and sold her business to Kelly. Kelly took a loan, which Merrell Lynch was only too happy to write. Kelly was by that time generating more than $10 million in commissions annually. His clients were more than happy to pay given the personal and profitable service Kelly provided. For Amelie's part, she left Merrill and the only job she'd known for a secure satellite phone and a secret.

During the two years after he'd sold or given away his clients, Quinn was almost completely off the radar. Sure, he called his parents every week or two and spoke to his friends occasionally, but he always responded ambiguously to questions relating to where he was and what he was doing. The best Amelie could determine Quinn spent little time in Warwick anymore. She knew Quinn had asked Kelly's father to be caretaker for his house. Because he was never home and because he unconsciously sprinkled his occasional telephone conversations with European idioms and dialects, Amelie correctly assumed that Quinn was in a semipermanent state of mobility. She could only imagine what other things Quinn was doing.

Amelie was sure Quinn felt an incredible loneliness on that Christmas morning. Like a child of an intact family can only presume to understand the life of an orphan, Amelie could not fully comprehend the need that Quinn's work filled in him. She wondered how long Quinn could continue to do what he did. "He seems impervious to disappointment, but how long will it be before he experiences an overwhelming letdown or the cumulative effects of this work catch up to him?"

CHAPTER 6

"How much more of this can I take?" Skylar Smart-Kerr asked herself. She began to cry. "God-damned it! Why me? Why? I'm a good person! I have never, not even once mistreated or abused anyone! I have not even been nasty to anyone unless they really deserved it! Why? Why!"

Skylar Smart-Kerr sat alone in the oncologist's office. During this follow-up to a routine visit for the cervical cancer her gynecologist diagnosed two and a half years earlier, the oncologist just told her it had returned in a different form. The blood screen provided the circumstantial evidence, but the MRI confirmed that cancerous lesions had adhered to the bone on the lower part of her spine.

When Skylar was first diagnosed a couple years earlier, her mind raced. In addition to considering for the first time the more profound philosophical questions associated with her own mortality, Skylar was troubled by the prospect of losing her reproductive organs. At the time, she still had hoped a child might change things and Taylor would understand she loved him and that their marriage was something to cherish. "That's rich! He's the prick who gave me HPV in the first place!" Skylar thought to herself. "He got it from some slut."

Dr. Walter had ordered an aggressive treatment plan. "It's lucky for us that your gynecologist found this so early. I'm almost sure that it's stage IA2, which means you have a great chance to beat this," Skylar remembered her oncologist telling her after the original diagnosis.

First, Skylar endured what was in the surgeon's words, "a fairly simple surgery" known as a LEEP, which is short for "loop electrosurgical excision procedure." She had told Skylar that "It's a procedure in which the surgeon slices out a circumference of the cervix, or the area around the cancer tissue in the shape of a doughnut to confirm beyond a doubt the diagnosis." There was no surprise when Skylar heard the results, but again her oncologist was almost certain "the barn door would be closed before the horses ran out."

Because Skylar placed a priority on preserving her uterus, her doctor suggested a treatment used at the best research hospitals. While the standard treatment for cervical cancer had previously been radical hysterectomy, the new treatment was known as a radical trachelectomy and involved only the removal of the cervix and the lymph nodes in the pelvis. At the same time, a cerclage, or a reconnection, of the area where the cervix had been is performed. The uterus is left unmolested, although natural child birth could no longer be an option. In the event that Skylar would have become pregnant, she would have had to deliver by Caesarean.

Skylar agreed to the surgery. Unfortunately, the choice was made without much input from her husband, who provided the least possible amount of emotional support. So, he was nowhere to be found when Skylar started to feel like something had gone wrong. While she recovered in her hospital room, Skylar's temperature spiked to 105 degrees. She was delirious. The surgeon who performed the resections told Skylar she contracted sepsis, a bacterial infection that entered the blood stream during the surgery. During a lucid moment when the infection-related delirium subsided, she almost wished that the infection would just take her already. "Wasn't it bad enough that the Little Bastard," Skylar's name for it, "Wanted to rape her? It wanted to kill her, too?"

Skylar remained in the hospital for more than two weeks as she recovered from the surgery and from the infection. Although not every patient who contracts a postsurgical infection survives, Skylar did. For a time, she tired easily. Eventually, she regained her strength and returned to work. Later she resumed her regular visits to the gym and her runs along Lake Shore Drive.

After a series of weekly examinations that started after she'd finally been discharged, the doctor pronounced, "It looks like the cancer is in remission. You have a better than average chance of being able to conceive once your body gets back to normal."

Three months later, Skylar's cycle resumed and she still held some hope that a child might bring some comfort to a man who hadn't yet found any solace in marriage.

"A lot of good that did," Skylar angrily thought. "A working reproductive system is about as much good to me as tits on a boar. Christ on a cracker! What have I done to deserve this? I've been the good girl. I did my work. I did my best to understand my parents. I helped with John and didn't bother my father with, 'Daddy, look at my spelling test,' or 'Daddy, will you take me to play miniature golf?' or 'Daddy, how do I look today?' Jesus, he had checked-out before I was even born!"

John had caught pneumonia and died. Almost as if their purpose on this earth had been to care for their son, Skylar's parents died six weeks after John's funeral. Their car drifted across the double yellow lines and struck a loaded garbage truck. Skylar facetiously reflected, "Damned bad luck with trucks for my family."

"Jesus! I'm alone! At least now that Dad's gone, there's one less person in this world in whom I need to be disappointed," Skylar allowed herself some self-pity. "It certainly was gracious of him to leave me the restaurants, though. What will I do with those now? Huh? Then, who knows why I even married Taylor. Maybe I thought the love I could give would make him change. How stupid could I be? He couldn't keep his prick out of other women if I had a gun to his head. The reasons I've stayed with that man, I'll never understand. He always has something better to do. He works. Yeah. Right. He sells just enough and plays the game enough to keep his job. He entertains clients, which typically means if he's not getting loaded with his friends, he's seducing some waitress or dull-eyed bimbo. Seriously? I have not been happy with Taylor for one full day since we married, and now I have terminal cancer? Is this some sort of joke?"

Skylar stopped. Then, in a moment of clarity, Skylar thought to herself, "Well, I guess that barn door was not closed quite fast enough, Doc. But, that's it. I'm finished. No surgery. No drugs. No radiation. No Taylor. No anything. Merry Christmas to me! The time I have left is my time."

Just then, the oncologist reentered the examining room, but Skylar already had put on her jacket, slung her purse over her shoulder, and started for the door. "Skylar, we should talk about treatment options."

"Look. Thanks. I'm sorry, but I am done with all of this. I really have to go now," answered Skylar.

Surprised, the doctor rejoined, "Skylar, I am not sure that I was clear enough before. The metastasis of your disease is very serious. Without treatment, well, your condition is almost certainly terminal."

"Look, Doc, you were plenty clear, but let's be frank. My condition is terminal regardless of treatment. It seems to me that I can live miserably, sick and tired and puking my guts out every day for a few months? A year, maybe?

Or I can live for just a few months less and do what I want to do. Am I right?" Dr. Walters was silent.

"I'm right. Thanks Doc, but I am out of here."

As soon as Skylar sat down on the leather car seat, she picked up her phone and dialed. She did not wait for an answer, "Where are you?"

"Working," Taylor lied.

"Cut the shit, Taylor," Skylar abruptly responded. "It's three o'clock on a Friday afternoon. I know you're not working. I need to see you. Now!"

Taylor felt the hair on his neck stand up. "I'm at Kirkwood's with some friends."

"Don't go anywhere," Skylar ordered. "I'll be there in fifteen minutes."

"This should be interesting," Taylor thought as he emptied his fourth beer.

CHAPTER

Skylar found a parking spot a half block from North Sheffield on Oakdale and walked with purpose into the Kirkwood Bar & Grill. Parking was not an easy ticket on the busy Northside streets. Finding Taylor was not as difficult. He and his friends, including low-life Charlie Mazzola and four twenty-somethings, whose busts were bigger than their brains, had chosen a table near the entrance in front of the window. It was too early in the day for a big crowd at one of the more popular bars on the Chicago's trendy north side.

"Hi, Honey," Taylor slurred. "I want you to meet my friends. You already know Charlie. And these are, uh, my new clients. We're going to the Blackhawks game tonight. Want to come?"

"That's enough, Taylor," Skylar said abruptly. "I need to talk to you. Alone."

Taylor smiled, "Look, these are my friends. You can say to them what you have to say to me."

Skylar declined to play his game, "Fine. If that's what you want, Taylor, then that's just fine." Skylar looked at each one of the girls at the table, then to Charlie, and finally back to Taylor.

"Here's the deal, Taylor. We're done. This charade is over. I loved you once, but it has been a long time since I've felt anything. I know you don't love me, not that I'm complaining. You weren't there for me when I was sick. You didn't have my back and I did it alone. I knew what you were doing. I looked the other way because I loved you once and I hoped that my love, which was more than you deserved, would somehow change you. How naïve? Now we're done, Taylor. It's over. Jesus, look at you. You're not even trying to pretend. An attorney in my office specializes in divorce. You'll meet her soon. In the meantime, I'm leaving."

The smirk on Taylor's face slowly changed to a spiteful scowl. Skylar had embarrassed him in front of the gargoyle and the girls, who squirmed uncomfortably on their stools. "Newsflash, you stupid nasty cunt, I never loved you. I only married you because you were a great piece of ass and your daddy had money. The day you came over to tell me that you'd marry me? I had to sneak a little bitch I'd been fucking out of the apartment. It was nice for a while, but then it wasn't. The money was great. Good work on that. But look at you now. You're thirty-four years old and just look at you!"

Taylor paused as if he suddenly realized something. Then, as an aside, he asked, "You're sick aren't you? You had appointment today with your doctor and she gave you bad news, didn't she? You're sick again, and, and you're dying, aren't you? Yeah. That's it."

Skylar listened as Taylor's words cut into her like tiny shards of glass, but she was past feeling anything but scorn for the man she thought she once loved.

Gaining an impious confidence, Taylor stood and approached Skylar. Charlie leered. The girls, whose skirts were too short for a December day in Chicago, looked away. "Hah! I got it. You're dying and, and you're filing for divorce? Oh, that's amusing. Get this. I will fight it tooth and nail. I will draw out the process as long as I have to. Guess what? You'll die and I'll get everything: your money, your car, and your restaurants. Everything. You'll die knowing I'm living and fucking on your daddy's dime! Hah! You're a loser, you know that?"

"Are you finished?" Skylar shook, struggling to control her emotions.

"I'm not even getting started," Taylor answered so everyone at the table could hear.

"You are finished." Skylar retorted, "And you will listen to me, you little man. That goes twice for you, Charlie."

Taylor was visibly surprised by Skylar's confident response. Charlie shrunk, but the eye candy now sat at rapt attention. Taylor stood but unconsciously took a half a step backward. The barmaid heard Skylar and walked from the server's station to the other end of the bar.

"Taylor, you are right about few things. I have been stupid. I married you because I wanted something I never had at home. I knew who you were, but I thought I could change you. That was stupid. I thought if I gave you unconditional love, then you'd see how much better it would be for us together. I should've known. Are you getting all this, ladies?" Skylar asked the girls as they nervously picked at the labels off their beer bottles. "I just want you to know what you're getting yourselves into if you intend to invest another minute with Taylor Kerr."

"Shut up, Skylar," Taylor uttered through gritted teeth. "I'm warning you."

"You're also right that I'm sick, although you certainly would never have known. You never did give a rat's ass about me. The cancer is back, and, yes, I am dying." Skylar paused as much for affect as her surprise at the frank admission. "I'll be damned if I waste another minute, or very soon, another breath on you. The sham is over and, so help me, I'll do everything I can to prevent you from getting a nickel. I hope I can live long enough to see the divorce come through. Don't worry. I know plenty of people who'd be more than happy to tell the court just how much of a son-of-a-bitch you really are. I've carried your ass since the day we said, 'I do,' and I can prove it."

Taylor sensed that he was losing the hearts and minds of the ladies at the table and his chance at some freak sex with one or two of them or, at the very least, a blowjob.

"Listen, bitch, this is your last chance," he growled. "You better shut the fuck up, Skylar."

The barmaid had been watching as the drama intensified. She sensed that things were just about to get out of control, backtracked, and came around the bar.

"Don't worry, Taylor. I'm almost done," Skylar continued. "Besides, you are far from any place where you can tell me anything I should do or shouldn't do. In about sixty seconds I will walk out of here, and you'll never see me again. But that's not the end of it. Yes, it is possible I won't be here and you will get a nice payday. You've heard the one about the boy who got caught smoking his uncle's cigars? He had to sit in a closet and smoke a whole box! As likely as not, if you do get the money, it will kill you. Either way, you lose and the world will thank me. But in the meantime, I'm out of the house. It's your responsibility. No more money from Skylar, baby. My salary and the distributions from the business all go to my account. You think you can get some cash from the stocks? You can't get a penny from our joint accounts, you dumbass, unless I agree to the transactions. While I'm on this planet, you'll have to make your own way. You have to live on your salary, and something tells me that you'll be eating a lot of macaroni, cheese, and old-fashioned Illinois crow."

Taylor started toward her, "That's it, bitch."

"Hey!" There, just a few feet behind Skylar stood a petite woman with hands on hips, her highlighted brown hair hung over her shoulders and her pretty brown eyes were despoiled by her fierce expression. The woman wore a white, button-down shirt with sleeves rolled to the elbows, "Kirkwood Bar

& Grill" was embroidered above the left breast pocket. She stood like an angry badger staring down a den of snakes.

"Is this your first time off the playground, kiddies, or just your first time in a bar?" the woman glared at Taylor. "Why don't you take the field trip someplace else?"

"Wah, what? We're not leaving," Taylor managed to answer as he felt what remained of his dignity melt away.

One of the girls, who had just a few minutes earlier enjoyed a few laughs and beers with a couple of guys who she thought were cute and funny, stood up and announced, "We are." The other three grabbed their purses and walked two-by-two toward the door, whispering and giggling on the way. "Yeah, I mean, what an ass," one said to another. "C'mon, let's go to happy hour someplace and then go dancing," another added. "Can you believe that girl? Wow!" said a third as the door closed behind them and they walked north on Addison, past the window in front of the table where Taylor, Charlie, Skylar, and the barmaid still stood. One of the girls must have said something riotously funny because the girls doubled over in laughter as they passed.

"Yeah, Biff, I think you are," said the barmaid again as an identically dressed coworker built like a Chicago Bears' defensive back emerged from the back bar. "Everything all right here, Katie?"

"Sure, Wave, everything here is just fine. Isn't it, Biff?" said the barmaid sarcastically.

Wave looked at Taylor and asked dryly, "Well, Biff? Everything okay?"

Looking down and then over to Charlie, Taylor responded, "Uh, yes. Everything's fine. Let's get out of here, Charlie." Taylor and Charlie slunk dejectedly out of the bar.

Once outside, Taylor said to his sidekick, "I'm going to get her for this. I really am."

Like a good minion, Charlie uttered his first syllables in the context of the entire ordeal. "Uh huh," was his supportive response.

"Thanks, Wave," Katie called over, but he already started back to the other room, where he was icing up for the big Friday, which would start in just a couple of hours.

He responded over his shoulder as he walked through the door to the other room, "No problem, Kate."

Katie turned to Skylar, whose composure had begun to erode a little.

"Men like that aren't worth the breath we waste on them. They're certainly not worth any of our tears," said the barmaid as she put her arm around Skylar. "You must be Skylar."

Skylar looked at Katie with surprise.

Smiling, Katie explained, "I was pretty sure your name was not, 'Bitch,' 'Cunt,' or 'Loser.' I took a shot." Skylar laughed and Katie introduced herself, "I'm Katie. Katie Novac."

"Hi, Katie," Skylar, looking down, almost whispered.

Katie turned around and then turned back to Skylar again, "There's no one at the bar yet. Why don't you sit down and have a drink. You can relax a little and we can talk."

"Thank you," Skylar said. "I need a drink."

CHAPTER 8

Skylar freshened up. An Absolut and tonic waited for her as she grabbed a stool. Skylar inhaled a deep breath and started to talk while Katie stocked liquor, iced beer, loaded pint glasses, shot glasses, old-fashioned glasses, martini glasses, Manhattan glasses, highball glasses, wine glasses, and port glasses on the racks. Katie listened to Skylar's story, which began with her brother's accident and its effect on her parents. When she'd finished, Katie had heard all about Skylar's immersion in her job, the emptiness in her marriage, and finally, the cancer.

After about an hour, Skylar finished her second drink. Young professionals started to arrive to play with their disposable income. As the bar filled, Skylar decided it was time to call it a day. "Katie, thank you for your help with, well, you know, and for listening."

As Skylar stood up and reached for her purse, Katie reached out, touched Skylar on her arm, and said, "Wait a second." Katie turned around, picked up a pen, a small piece of paper, and her Blackberry. "Look, Skylar, the first number is mine. If you need anything, if you need to talk, if you want to get out for a drink, if you want anything, you call me," Katie ordered.

After Katie had surfed for a moment through the phone, she continued, "Okay, look. This second number is the one that might help you. This sounds crazy, but I heard about some guy who has started sort of a Don Imus Ranch, you know, like a wish-come-true thing. Instead of working with kids, though, he makes grown-ups' dreams come true. You know, like real adult fantasies, but supposedly not sordid or unseemly. I haven't called, I don't know the specifics, and I do not even know if it's real, but I heard what you told Taylor. My brother's girlfriend said her friend's friend said it was more than worthwhile. A better, more compelling recommendation, you cannot wish to hear, a bartender's brother's girlfriend's friend's friend, huh? Anyway, the important thing is, call me if you need anything. Okay?"

Just then, a nice-looking, athletic-type guy pulled up a stool two places away from Skylar. He'd seen Katie give the paper with the numbers on them and asked, "Hey, Sweetie, can I get your phone number, too?"

Katie looked over and replied, "Sorry friend. I'm not sure you could handle me."

"That's too bad," he said, "Because you and I will share a name and a bedroom in six-months' time."

"You're sure about that? I'm not that easy."

"Don't I know it?" said the man.

Katie turned back to Skylar, "Skylar, this is my fiancé, Chase."

Katie continued, "Chase is one of the few exceptions to the rule that all men are spineless, slimy piles of cat puke."

"Thanks, Skippy. That's quite an endorsement." Then to Skylar, Chase added, "Actually, she's being kind. I can only aspire to be a spineless, slimy pile of cat puke."

Skylar let herself laugh just a little. She needed to.

Then aside to Skylar again, Katie said, "Listen. Check this out if you want to, if you think it might help you. Heck. I'd be interested to know whether it's the real deal. Regardless, please call me if you need anything."

"I can't thank you enough Katie, or would you prefer Skippy," Skylar smiled. "Anyway, I'll call you. As far as the other thing goes, well, I'm not sure that's my style. Good night, Katie. Nice to meet you, Chase."

CHAPTER

As Skylar rounded the corner and headed west the half-block on Oakdale to her car, reality pressed down on her like the yoke on the horse at a one-horse farm. The sun set on the charming old brownstones. Wind blew in her face, and she walked alone on the sidewalk under the bare scrub oak and elm trees. She considered how little she'd done in her life as she faced the end of it. She thought about Katie and Chase. "How lucky were they to be truly in love? Why couldn't I have had that?" Skylar asked herself as she opened her car door and sat down.

Although the day had been long enough, Skylar picked up her telephone and called one of the partners at the law firm. She gave no reason, but resigned from the firm effective immediately. She'd send a fax for confirmation. She stopped at a liquor store for a fifth of Absolut, a couple of limes from the wicker basket at the checkout, and a couple of quarts of tonic. Twenty minutes later, Skylar pulled into a Courtyard at Hubbard and State. She'd worry about a change of clothes and long-term accommodations later. For the moment, complementary toiletries and a cocktail in a plastic cup would have to do. She grabbed the ice trays in the refrigerator, cracked out a few cubes, and put a hand full in a glass. After she poured the Absolut, she placed the bottle in the freezer next to the ice, splashed in some tonic, sliced a lime with a plastic knife, and started a bath.

While water filled the tub, she took the paper Katie had written her number on. Below Katie's number, Skylar read, "DREAM-COME-TRUE?" She picked up her cell and dialed. A woman's voice answered, "Hello. This is Life Dreams. My name is Amelie. May I help you?"

Skylar hung up before saying a word.

CHAPTER 10

"Thanks again, Kelly," Quinn said to his friend as he took his dog's lead.

At seventy-seven dog years, Dierdorf had lived a lot of life with his master. The animal heeled at Quinn's left hip with or without a lead. Nonetheless, Quinn well understood that animals, especially older animals, could be unpredictable. Even though Kelly was nearly as much Dierdorf's alpha male as Quinn was, Quinn never took chances, especially when Kelly's children were around. Quinn walked Dierdorf onto the front porch of Kelly's center-hall colonial. Kelly trailed behind his seven-year-old twin boys, Kelvin and Melvin, who followed their favorite "uncle."

Powdered sugar snow dusted Kelly's one-acre lot. Quinn admired Kelly's meticulously manicured lawn. Quinn called back, "Thanks, Marisol. You're a saint to put up with Dierdorf, but you're more of a saint to put up with Kelly!"

"You're welcome, Quinn," Kelly's wife answered from the top of the stairs. "You're right about Kelly, but Dierdorf is never any trouble. Happy New Year."

"Thanks, Buddy," Kelly followed as he closed the door. "She already likes your dog more than she likes me."

Dierdorf stood regally and looked out over the yard like a medieval lord might have done from a castle upon his conquered lands. Kelvin and Melvin scratched the dog under his ears. Periodically, Dierdorf looked back at one or both of the boys like he needed to be reminded who was behind him before he returned a gaze to his empire. "Can't he stay a little longer, Uncle Quinn? Please?" the boys looked up hopefully.

"No, guys. Uncle Quinn wants to hang out with Dierdorf for a while. Besides, I think he might miss his own bed," Quinn responded. "But, hey. Did you guys help your mom and dad take care of Dierdorf?"

"Oh, we did! We did." Kelvin enthusiastically answered.

"I fed him!" Melvin replied.

Kelvin added, "So did I! So did I!"

"Well, thanks for helping and for being such good boys for your mom and dad. I got these for you." Quinn pulled four Knicks tickets out of his jacket pocket.

"Awesome! The Knicks! Thanks, Uncle Quinn!" the boys took the tickets. Upon a closer inspection of the tickets, Kelvin screamed, "Melvin! Melvin! Look. It's the Cavaliers! We get to see LeBron!"

"Oh, no way! Oh! That is sick!" Melvin malapropped. "Thanks, Uncle Quinn!"

"Jeez, you didn't have to do that." said Kelly as he looked at the tickets. "Man, you really didn't have to do this. Thanks. These are right behind the Cavs' bench."

Quinn explained, "Kelly, look. First of all, I can't let down my favorite nephews after they helped with Dierdorf, right guys?"

Kelvin and Melvin nodded enthusiastically, "That's right. Uh huh."

"And, you and Marisol are always great. Not just with the dog, but I'd agonize thinking about Dierdorf in a kennel. He's just too old for that now," Quinn persisted. "I wanted to. Besides, the money goes to charity. My alma mater has this auction every year around Christmastime. The money goes to scholarships for disadvantaged kids. Well, you know Donnie David and I went to the same high school. He donated these tickets. It was only natural considering it's only a sixty-minute drive to The Garden, how could I pass them up? Before I left, I put in a sealed bid."

"Well, thanks, Quinn. Thanks. Donnie David, huh? I sure would like to have his portfolio," Kelly mused. "He's good now. He stands out like a one-eyed man in a kingdom of the blind. He's bright and level headed. Can you imagine what he'll do when he matures a little? He'll be a Bill Lambeer or a Kevin McHale, except pretty. What will happen to him when he gets a ring? In New York? Jeez. 'Bo knows' jack, brother! 'Be like Mike?' 'Bend it like Beckham?' You kidding me? Donnie David will be selling everything. It'll be all, 'Do It Like Donnie.' You think you can introduce me?"

Quinn joked, "I said he graduated from the same high school that I did... about ten years later! But yes, I'd bet that I could probably find someone who can get me in touch. It'll be my New Year's gift."

Melvin and Kelvin were still bouncing around the front porch like a bonus on a pinball machine.

"Hey, guys," Kelly said to his sons. "Daddy wants to talk with Uncle Quinn for a minute. Why don't you go inside and help set the table?"

"Yeeessss siiirrrr," the boys obediently but disappointedly replied. "Thanks, Uncle Quinn!" they said before starting for the door. Then, as if they remembered a wonderful secret, their energy renewed, "Let's go show Mom!" They bolted through the door before it slammed shut.

CHAPTER 11

Kelly and Quinn first met in Williamsport when the both were eleven years old. The boys played baseball and represented their hometowns, Warwick, New York and St. Charles, Missouri, respectively, at the Little League World Series. Most people would probably think it would have been unlikely for two boys who seemed to have little other than baseball in common to become such good friends. Quinn's father was a real estate broker. Kelly's father was a local cop in what was, at the time, an afterthought upstate village. Quinn was raised in a homogeneous community that included almost exclusively white Catholics and Protestants. Kelly's parents were mixed race; his father, Bob, was black and his mother was Mexican and had come to Warwick as a migrant worker in the local orchards and nearby black dirt onion farms.

However, most people are not like Quinn and Kelly. Both were friendly, outgoing, and adventurous. During a pre-tournament party, the boys became immediate friends. From that day, Quinn and Kelly were inseparable except when the teams were practicing or playing. Even then, Quinn watched the Warwick team play and Kelly watched the team from Missouri. Quinn was impressed by his tall, lanky friend's speed and cannon arm from centerfield. Not a single runner went from first to third base on a hit up the middle. At the same time, Kelly could only wish to hit a baseball like the more compact and muscular Quinn. During the three games the St. Charles team played, Quinn had seven hits in thirteen at-bats, including two home runs and two doubles.

After the third game, Quinn's team had lost two games in the double-elimination tournament. The team from Warwick, however, won the Northeastern bracket, but lost in the semifinals to the eventual U.S. winner, Belmont Heights, Florida.

After the tournament, the two remained friends and wrote regularly. Once during the next seven years Kelly visited Quinn in Missouri and one time Quinn made it to Warwick to spend a week with Kelly the summer before their senior years in high school. It was the one week of the year after baseball had ended for the season and before summer football camp began. During that week in August, Quinn stayed with the Hills at their modest home in Warwick's west side. During the day, the two walked to Stanley Deming Park and played pickup baseball. Not knowing better, the other kids allowed Quinn and Kelly to play on the same team, an obvious mistake. At night, the two went to one of the orchards where the other high school kids made a bonfire or to one of the coffee shops in the village and talked to girls. Quinn was impressed when he discovered that Kelly could speak fluent Spanish. Kelly's language abilities opened up an entirely new "market" of pretty young ladies for him that was largely out of reach for the monolingual.

Among the many things that Quinn remembered about his visit to Warwick and his stay with the Hills was the reverence Kelly held for his parents. Although Quinn loved and respected his parents, he had a rebellious streak and would occasionally challenge Mr. and Mrs. Powers. It was not so much insolence as it was testing boundaries. With Kelly, however, his respect was sincere and absolute. When Mr. or Mrs. Hill asked Kelly a question, Kelly responded or complied without debate or resentment. Quinn knew Kelly did the things he did not from fear, but from sincere love for his father and mother.

It hadn't registered at the time, but a few years later it would click. The secret about Warwick was out. It seemed to Quinn more than sheer luck, though, when the Yankees picked the "brothers from different mothers" during the 1991 amateur baseball draft. The big-fish-in-a-small-pond Brown University centerfielder, Kelly was the 88th player chosen, while his pal who was a Tiger at the University of Missouri was the 403rd.

CHAPTER 12

"You're doing a great job with them," Quinn observed. "They're terrific kids."

"They are, I know, and I'm a very lucky man. I have two wonderful boys; I have a wonderful wife," Kelly almost imperceptibly paused, "and I have the best friend a guy could have. I'm not sure I deserve all this."

"Look, Kelly, if anyone deserves it, it's you," Quinn assured him. "I know no one is perfect, but you're one of the good guys. When life gives you a soup sandwich, when you have some kind of moral dilemma, you always go the right way. Remember Joan Ziegfeld, that girl I met when I was here the summer before we graduated high school? She wasn't hard to look at and she threw herself at you. You're not a prude and I know you've always done well with the ladies, but you knew that Joanie didn't feel good about herself and gave it away. Well, you didn't take it, but you said it in a way that made her feel better. You talked to her. You told what that sort of stuff meant to you. The way you handled it I'm sure helped Joanie see things differently.

"When things don't go right for you, you don't blame anyone. After you got beaned, you didn't get angry or throw in the towel. Sure, that asshole took a cheap shot, but you understood it's part of the game. You got yourself better and you went back. When you realized that you couldn't be the same player, you used the talents and made the most of them. Jeez! Now look at you!" Quinn added.

"I had a little help with that, Quinn," Kelly clarified.

"Very little. You made the decision to do it, and you did it. You wouldn't say, 'shit,' if you had a mouth full of it. You are the real deal, man," Quinn continued before Kelly interrupted.

"Okay! Okay. Thanks, Quinn. Thanks. Without making this a meeting of the mutual admiration society, you know I feel the same way about you," Kelly answered. "But, look, it's not me that I want to talk about."

"What is it?" Quinn asked with a genuine concern.

Kelly continued, "It's you, Quinn. I'm really worried about you. So is Marisol. So are Bob and Lina. So are the Sparvieris, I'm sure. I'd know for sure if I talked with them. I'd bet your friends' and family's concern would increase geometrically if they knew the things that I know."

"Come on, Kelly," Quinn said.

"No. Not come on, Kelly," Kelly answered. "Look, we're a lot alike. I believe that a man should do in his life the things that he wants to do as long as that man's pursuits do not intrude on someone else's ability to do the same. I'm not making value judgments about your choices. In fact, even though you haven't told me much about your individual clients—"

Quinn corrected, "Dream Seekers. They're Dream Seekers, Kelly."

"Okay, Dream Seekers," Kelly conceded. "Even though you have not told me much about the Dream Seekers, you have told me that every one of them dies."

"You haven't told me about a single relationship with a real future you've had since, well, since your wife died." Kelly paused for a moment. "This stuff has to take a toll on you, Quinn. It's almost like you are reliving Gina's death over and over."

"Look, Kelly, you're only one of two people who know anything about what I do," Quinn began. "I can't begin to make you understand the reasons I do it. It's not almost like I am reliving those last days I had with Gina. It's exactly like it. I can't explain it. I can't justify it. I will not apologize for it. One-sided self-interest doesn't even begin to explain it, but it is what it is."

"Quinn, I know. I don't understand it. I can't understand it, but I know. That's why I'm worried," Kelly finished.

"Do you know why Gina died?" Quinn asked his friend.

"Well, I know Gina had cancer, Quinn. But if you're asking me a larger question, like the reason she got sick in the first place, I can't tell you that."

"Kelly, the more I live and the more I see, the more I believe that there is just no reason for the things that happen. People who I know, or more accurately, used to know, ask me, 'Aren't you angry with God?' I say, 'No,' and it's the truth. What I don't say, Kelly, is how could I be angry with God? I'm not really an atheist. I'm not against God. In a funny way I can understand that a sort of god is all around, like in a child's laughter or in the young couples holding hands and giggling as they window shop in the Village. To think there is a caring, omnipotent God who looks down on the Earth, listens to our prayers, and grants miracles to those who are in need, though, is simply a fantasy. Think about the children in the world who are born with terminal illnesses or addicted to drugs or without enough food to eat. We don't even have to travel to the third world to see that. How about the woman who buckled her sons, put the car in neutral, and rolled it into a lake? How about the mother who drowned her six children in her bathtub, one after the other? Really? What happened to me is not even that bad in comparison. I lost my wife, who was an incredible, beautiful woman, who I loved, and who did nothing but make the world a better place for everyone she knew. What did those little boys in the car do to deserve not being allowed to grow up and not being able to look over to the sidelines on the soccer field and see their mother smiling and waving back at them? What did those little girls do to deserve not being able to shop with moms for school clothes or talk about boys or ask about the changes in their bodies? If there is a God, he's either forgotten about us or He has a severely perverted sense of humor. Given the choices, I prefer to believe that there is no God.

"Back to the question, Kelly, there is no reason. There's no reason Gina died. It just happened. And, to bring this conversation back full circle, why Life Dreams? Why do I have to do what I do for the Dream Seekers? Why do I have to relive Gina dying again and again? I don't know, Kelly. I just do. There is no reason for it. It's not a good thing. It's not a bad thing. It just is."

Neither man spoke, but rather both looked out over the railing of the front porch and looked past Kelly's front lawn and past the neighbors' houses toward the foothills that surrounded the valley. Dierdorf, still on his lead, sat at Quinn's foot.

In the silence Kelly thought, "There are just some things I can't understand unless I experience them myself. I've seen Kelvin and Melvin born. I've been told a thousand times the pain of childbirth, but I can never understand it. Quinn doesn't know what it's like to step back in the batter's box after being hit in the face by a ninety-six-mile per hour fastball. I don't understand what it's like to lose my wife. I hope I never do."

Kelly began, "Quinn. I'm sorry. I don't mean to pry. I know I can't understand those things. All I'm saying is that I'm worried. I've known you for almost three decades. You are my oldest and best friend, and I don't want anything to happen to you."

"I know. I know that and I hope I didn't sound like I was lecturing," Quinn replied. "If it makes you feel any better, I am who I am and, for better or worse, I'm okay with it."

"All right," Kelly relented. "You know if you need anything, I mean anything, I'll be there for you."

"I know. You're on the B-Team," Quinn paused and smiled. "You were there at the beginning of all this and you'll *be* there when it's all over."

"That's right," Kelly laughed with his friend.

"Thanks again. I appreciate your help with Dierdorf," Quinn repeated as he walked to the car. "You tell him, Dierdorf. Speak!"

Obediently, the animal barked two times.

"Thanks again for the Knicks ticks. There are four seats. Wanna come with?"

"No, man." said Quinn. "You'd better take that smokin' hot wife of yours."

"Hey. Watch it," Kelly warned as Quinn opened the passenger door of the Triumph. Dierdorf climbed rather than jumped in and sat on the old towel Quinn put on the passenger seat.

Quinn came around to the driver's side, opened the door, and called to Kelly, "Be good, brother."

Before Quinn closed the door, Kelly called, "Hey! Don't forget about Donnie David!"

Quinn smiled, nodded, started the car, and pulled away.

CHAPTER

Dierdorf had always slept in the king-size bed between Gina's and Quinn's feet. Dierdorf was Gina's dog. When Quinn rolled over during the night and threw his arm or leg over his wife, he always had to nudge the eighty-pound animal to gain access. Gina was not quite as tall and didn't have the same problem when she reciprocated.

When Gina died, Dierdorf didn't sleep with Quinn. For days, Quinn was too distracted to wonder or care where Dierdorf slept. All Quinn knew was that Dierdorf had made other arrangements.

It wasn't until late one night when Quinn, unable to sleep, got up and didn't see the dog and decided to look around. After checking the first floor, Quinn crept up the back stairs. When he reached the landing and walked down the hall, he looked into the first of the three spare bedrooms and saw nothing. Dierdorf wasn't in the second either. When Quinn looked in the last bedroom decorated with the Dali, Chagall, and Elias Grossman prints Gina had bought at auction, he found Dierdorf sleeping on the empty twin-size bed. When the animal saw Quinn, Dierdorf lifted his head and perked up his ears and looked at Quinn curiously as if to say, "Well, where did you expect to find me?"

Quinn returned downstairs and poured a glass of water from the spring water dispenser. He walked into the family room, flipped on the television, and watched the overnight loop of SportsCenter. Eventually, Quinn fell asleep on the couch. Dierdorf didn't come down until morning.

CHAPTER

Middletown, New York is not a center of financial activity, but location wasn't very relevant to Quinn's specialty practice. Quinn received referrals from Eastern League players who began to make real money in the Majors. Rich and famous begets the rich and famous, so it was not long before actors' and musicians' agents caught wind of the uniquely talented broker in Orange County, New York. He quickly became known in not just baseball circles, but in other sports as well. It was a shock to the local vice president of investments that Quinn built a portfolio of nearly $125 million during the next year. After his second year, his assets-under-management ballooned to nearly $375 million and continued to increase exponentially. Considering the broker's annual commission is typically a half of 1 percent of the total dollar value of the book, Quinn earned more than a comfortable income for himself and for his beautiful wife.

Long-time, small-town residents aren't always quick to embrace newcomers. Warwick, for all its charm, is no exception. At the same time, it wouldn't be every day even long-time residents encountered someone as genuinely warm and caring as Gina Powers. The effect she had on people was easier experienced than it was explained. Far from self-important or high-handed, Gina commanded a room when she entered. She simply exuded equal parts confidence and sensitivity that was palpable to anyone within her wide aura. When she smiled and said, "Hello," the object of her attention was lost or, more accurately, won. As a result, Gina quickly earned accounting clients among Warwick's close-knit business community.

When a woman who owned one of the two liquor stores in the village, began to lose market share to its competition, Gina suggested that her client offer through direct mail and personal visits gift baskets of wine and liquor to all of the area businesses during the various holidays throughout the year: everything from Thanksgiving to Hanukkah to Christmas to Secretary's Day. As a result, the store increased market share by a third and booked a number of wine-tasting events as a bonus. For Gina, such success stories bred word-of-mouth referrals. So, while Quinn conquered the financial portfolios of the rich and famous, Gina built a clientele to more than fifty businesses and individuals.

Each night, Quinn made the twenty-five-minute drive back to Warwick shortly after the markets closed while Gina made the fifteen-second walk from her home office to the kitchen, where she'd start the meal she and Quinn would eat together. If the weather was nice, Gina sat on the patio with a glass of wine and watched Quinn cook on the grill. If the weather was less agreeable, the two flickered about the kitchen like a couple of butterflies in a flower bed.

The one thing Gina and Quinn were most proud of was the house they'd together transformed into a home. The place on Grand Street that looked like Herman Munster's house on Mockingbird Lane became a great example of period architecture and a showcase home among the other beautiful homes in the village. When there had been some of the more difficult repairs like the roof, plumbing, electric, and masonry, the Powers' subcontracted. As much as they could, Gina and Quinn wanted to maintain the original appearance. Although it wasn't inexpensive, the original slate roof, which had been cracking and flaking and revealed large enough holes that sunshine could be seen from inside the walk-up attic, was replaced with new slate, including French gutters and copper troughs and downspouts. The dry-rotting front porch was removed and rebuilt in the same "tongue-n-groove" style. Much of the plumbing had been replaced when a new gas furnace and tankless water heater were installed. The wiring, the electrician explained, had been done in three stages dating back nearly a hundred years. The bricks that composed each of the three chimneys and that vented the three working fireplaces in the house had begun to crumble in their old age. Although an addition had been made to the house around 1920, the style of the craftsmanship and materials used suggested the oldest part of the house was built at about the time James Garfield sat in the Oval Office. After all that time, no one could blame the chimneys for having to be rebuilt above the roof line.

In the meantime, Gina poured over swatches of colors and chose the perfect family of colors for the interiors. After getting Quinn's mostly symbolic approval, they went to work. Gina and Quinn painted room after room after covering or moving furniture from one place to another. The various shades of tan or beige that Gina claimed to be related to the various shades of a very subtle greenish blue really clicked as they moved from one end of the house to the other. Working most evenings and at least a part of many weekends, the painting was finished after about three months and could not have looked better if it had been done by a professional. Their reward was to refinish the hardwood floors.

There were only two things missing from Quinn and Gina's idea of the perfect home. In the spring, the Powers drove to Pawcatuck, Rhode Island, a beach community and a summer tourist destination just down the road from West Greenwich where the couple lived when Quinn played for the Norwich 'Gators. Quinn navigated from I-95 onto an exit and eventually onto ocean front strip. Gina imagined the hot dog and ice cream stands, clubs whose dated neon signs had long been burned out, restaurants, bicycle rentals, arcades, and shops whose sole purpose was to separate beachgoers from their money, had not changed in fifty years. Finally, Quinn turned the car onto a poorly marked, unpaved country road. While avoiding ruts and potholes, Quinn read a hastily painted, plywood sign that read, "AKC GERMAN SHEPHERD PUPPYS." He hoped the owners were better dog breeders than the were spellers, and turned into the driveway.

Quinn wanted a basset hound, the same breed that his family had when Quinn was growing up. Gina didn't really like bassets' long ears and the saggy, bloodshot eyes. Gina wanted a German shepherd, and there was no argument. German shepherd would be the breed, but Quinn would pick the name. Gina agreed, but Quinn wouldn't have cared if she didn't. He just wanted a dog.

There was a litter of six, romping, four-week-old puppies whose parents were on site. The sire was kenneled in the yard while the female watched buyers as they played with her yipping, furry balls of energy. Gina was surprised how calm and comfortable the mother was with her and Quinn.

After rolling around on the floor with the puppies for a few minutes, occasionally offering an opinion to the other, asking a question or acknowledging a comment made by the breeders, Quinn and Gina agreed on the puppy. Quinn paid in cash half of the $600 fee. The owner grabbed the animal, took out a bottle of red nail polish, painted the puppy's middle claw on its left paw, and blew the polish dry. "So I know which one is yours," was the woman's only explanation.

Four Saturdays later, Quinn and Gina once again made the drive to southwestern Rhode Island and returned to Warwick with their new puppy.

CHAPTER

The fire Quinn made in the master bedroom fireplace the previous night was nothing more than ash that covered a few warm embers. Even though the old Victorian's windows had been replaced years earlier, the place was drafty. As he and Gina had remodeled and improved the house when they bought the old place nearly a decade earlier, there was just no way to completely weatherproof the antique.

Quinn preferred to keep warm under his flannel sheets, a thick, goose-down comforter and an auburn bedspread. The temperature in the two-zone heating system was set to 63 degrees on the first floor and 55 degrees for the seldom-used upstairs. Quinn sometimes wondered about the reasons he'd kept the enormous house considering its only residents were he and an old dog.

For quite a while, Dierdorf slept in the room Quinn eventually named the "Gina Room." One cold night, Dierdorf showed up and curled up in front of the fireplace. It was just as likely that Dierdorf had grown tired of sleeping in the cold upstairs, preferring the relative warmth in Quinn's bedroom as it was he realized that Gina wouldn't be coming back. Either way, Dierdorf slept on the floor, most of his body resting just beyond the rust-red masonry on the wide-plank pine hardwood floor. Only his snout, resting on his front paws, his front legs, and about half of his perpetually shedding tail infringed on the relatively warmer bricks that expanded out beneath the mantle.

Quinn didn't need an alarm clock. Dierdorf woke Quinn every morning at six, give or take a couple of minutes, which was when Dierdorf's biological clock told him it was time to answer the call of nature. Quinn rarely had any reason to wake up earlier.

At two minutes before six, Dierdorf raised his head and looked around for a moment before he pulled himself to his paws. Then, he looked straight ahead toward the two windows in Quinn's bedroom that faced the front and shook his body as if he had taken a swim in the pond across the street. Dust and dander flew from his body and fell gently to the floor. To get blood moving through the tiny capillaries to his muscles, Dierdorf tensed, shivered, and stretched each of his back legs, one after the other. Properly awake, Dierdorf walked to the side of the bed, cautiously jumped up, and rested his front paws next to Quinn's head. Then, he nosed and licked Quinn's face. Quinn's head twitched back, he opened his eyes, and he saw the familiar frame of a sideways dog face.

"Good morning, Dog," Quinn managed, groggily. Then, tilting his head slightly to see the digital clock on the nightstand, he said, "You're early this morning."

Dierdorf whined slightly as if to say, "A little less talk and a lot more action. I have to pee."

"All right, all right! I'm getting up."

Quinn pulled the sheet, comforter, and bedspread down, yanked his legs up, flipped them around Dierdorf, and let the momentum pull him to his feet. As carefully as Dierdorf put his paws and head on the bed, he was more careful to get himself down. Quinn grabbed the four king-size pillows and tossed them toward the foot of the bed. Then he quickly pulled the bed clothes back up, tugged at the side and corners until the bedspread was relatively unwrinkled. Then, he grabbed each of the four pillows one by one tossed them against the headboard.

Dierdorf was familiar with the procedure. He didn't even bother to follow Quinn into the bathroom, because he knew that Quinn would only be there for a minute. While Dierdorf sat patiently next to bathroom door, Quinn emerged from the bathroom and said, "Okay, I did my business. Now, you can do yours. Let's go."

Quinn pulled on a vintage pair of gray sweatpants and a matching hoodie over two other layers of clothing. The silk-screened letters on the front of the sweatshirt, which had faded, said TIGERS. Quinn smiled distantly as he considered how much times had changed, marked in a small way by the fortunes of his favorite football team. Dierdorf cocked his head to the side as Quinn asked aloud, "Who'd have thought it?"

After tying his shoes and putting on a black stocking cap and matching gloves, he walked back through the dining room, through the living room to the front door, where Dierdorf's lead hung on a hook. Quinn attached the lead as man and dog left the house for a brisk winter walk. Quinn didn't bother to lock the door.

At the sidewalk, Quinn turned right and walked Dierdorf the quarter mile or so on Grand Street toward Main. Dierdorf hadn't waited long to mark a tuft of grass between the sidewalk and the road just past Cherry Street. On Main, Quinn walked past the Sunoco Station and jaywalked Main Street onto Kings Highway and past the library. After walking barely the distance from home plate to third base, Quinn turned right and continued down Forrester. They crossed the railroad tracks, which still carried freight on trains that unloaded lumber at the yard in town. Dierdorf marked again.

Dog and master approached the back side of the Park Avenue Elementary School. It occurred to Quinn, as it did every day when he and Dierdorf walked past the playground, that Park Avenue was the school his and Gina's child would have gone. Quinn lamented to no one that this year his baby would have been in fifth grade. He wondered how his life might have been different.

CHAPTER 16

Gina tolerated the chemotherapy well. She was strong and young and if anyone could handle medications and have a healthy child, it was Gina.

Each time she sat down in the chemo chair among the twenty or so other cancer patients in the room, Quinn retrieved crackers, cookies, and juice the hospital offered. When Gina tired of chemo-room fare, Quinn trekked either to the hospital cafeteria or off the reservation to find a more exotic meal among the restaurants that catered to the hospital staff and visitors. Quinn was always pleased for the errand.

Gina used the time to speak with Sandy, who not only had a tolerance for ridiculously long hours and workload, but also an infinite capacity for empathy. Sometimes Gina and Sandy talked about the treatments or how Gina felt. Sometimes, the women discussed the baby and living with cancer in remission. Mostly, Sandy listened, but sometimes offered honest, compassionate answers.

During one of Quinn's sorties, Gina asked, "Sandy, why do I have cancer? I mean, what could possibly be a plan that might include a world in which a child does not have a mother and a good man doesn't have a wife?"

"Awe, Honey." Sandy whispered. "My eyes have seen a lot, but I don't know if there is a reason for something like this. I don't know how there can be. All I know is Quinn, your doctors, and I want you well and we're doing everything we know to make that happen."

Of course, she was nauseous shortly after chemo. As the bimonthly treatments continued, Gina's appetite declined. Less frequently Gina asked Quinn for an exotic lunch. More often, Gina was satisfied by the crackers and juice or a small salad or cottage cheese or soft-serve ice cream from the cafeteria.

The perinatalogist, Dr. MacVicar prescribed prenatal vitamins. As time passed and her appetite waned, MacVicar suggested that Gina have a high-protein, high-calorie, vitamin drink both for her sake and the sake of her unborn child. Still, the pharmacological cocktail her two doctors prescribed didn't help much. Gina took as many as fifteen prescription drugs to treat ailments that ranged from nausea to headaches to a weakened heart to constipation to declining red blood cells to her declining white blood cells. Sandy or William administered some of the medication intravenously after chemotherapy or during office visits. Others were taken orally once, twice, or even three times a day. Quinn made a spreadsheet to make sure Gina took the right drugs at the right times. Fortunately, the computer file was easy enough to update because the prescriptions changed weekly, if not more frequently.

Gina had never been anything but small. However, the drugs that dripped into her arm through the IV caused even more weight loss. By the time she had her final treatment, Gina was at the midpoint of her pregnancy but weighed no more than about 120 pounds.

Two weeks after what was supposed to have been Gina's eighth and final chemotherapy, the Powers met with William at his office on 165th Street. "One of the things my research suggests is some pregnant women who have cancer have something, I don't yet know what, that helps keep the disease in check," William said while Sandy stood in the doorway. "I don't want you to think that you are out of the woods, but the blood work indicates that there isn't any trace of the cancer in Gina's body."

Quinn looked at Gina, smiled, stood up, and hugged her. Quinn was barely able to contain his feelings. He looked at his wife, whose expression appeared to be one of both happiness and relief. "Thanks, William," managed Quinn.

"I'll continue to meet with you every two weeks through delivery. During that time, you will see Dr. MacVicar on alternate weeks. Then after delivery, which will be sometime after thirty-four weeks, we'll have had to make a difficult decision. We need to decide on either a unilateral mastectomy and radiation or just radiation. The cancer already metastasized, so the surgery wouldn't make as much sense as it would have if the disease had been identified prior to metastasis."

Gina's expression of relief suddenly contorted into distress. Quinn first assumed that her grief was the consequence of the subject William had broached. When Quinn saw the anguish in Gina's eyes, though, he felt the same sinking feeling he did when he heard the original diagnosis.

"Gina! What's the matter?"

"I don't know! I don't know, but, it hurts!" bleated Gina, holding the bulge that her belly had become.

It took a few moments for Quinn to realize what Sandy and William understood immediately.

Sandy knelt down next to Gina, noticing the spotting on the chair, "Oh, honey." A moment later, Sandy darted out of the room, calling over her shoulder, "I'll be right back."

William picked up the telephone on his desk and deftly dialed five numbers. Neither Quinn nor Gina heard the voice on the other line answer inquiringly, "Obstetric surgery?" The Powers' did hear, "This is William Reinsdorf. I need a room prepped immediately."

Only William heard the voice on the other end, "How soon, Dr. Reinsdorf?"

"Not now. Right now," William responded. "I'll be over in less than ten."

Sandy returned and helped Gina into the wheelchair she'd pushed into the room. "Are you okay, honey?" Sandy asked.

Gina was pale and frightened, "I don't know." Gina began to cry. Quinn stood helplessly, watching.

William got another dial tone and speed dialed again.

As Quinn followed Gina into the hallway to the room William had just ordered "prepped immediately," Quinn heard, "Paddy, it's William. Who's on call at the hospital today?" The procession turned the corner. He reached down and took Gina's hand.

The last thing Quinn heard William say was, "Gina Powers is miscarrying."

CHAPTER 17

When he walked through his front door, Quinn first noticed the temperature. It seemed to be quite a bit warmer than the 63 degrees he'd left. The second was the smell of bacon and coffee, which, Quinn assumed, emanated from the kitchen. Dierdorf's ears perked up as he processed new scents in the house. Quinn hadn't seen the red 2009 BMW 328i discretely parked on the far side of the garage next to the fence.

Keeping Dierdorf on his lead, Quinn quietly and curiously walked through the living room and dining room into the kitchen, where he discovered Amelie, who had her arms folded and was leaning against the counter and grinning.

"I thought you could use a good breakfast," she said.

CHAPTER

"Damn, boy, are you cold-blooded? This house was freezing." Amelie scolded. "You'll make yourself sick."

Ignoring Amelie's motherly rebuke, Quinn answered facetiously, "Well, make yourself right at home."

"I did," replied Amelie, who'd already moved her attention to the dog. "Hi, puppy! Aw, Dierdorf, good boy!" Amelie cooed as she scratched the dog under the ears.

"Some guard dog you are. Traitor." muttered Quinn in mock disgust.

"Oh, hush up," Amelie chided and, nodding toward the appreciative German shepherd. "If it were not for this guy taking care of you, Quinn, you'd be more of a disaster than you already are."

Dierdorf looked back at Quinn as if to say, "Yeah. You should listen to her."

"Okay. Okay. You're both turncoats." Quinn surrendered. "So, darling, did you make a wrong turn in Midtown?"

"That can wait, Mr. Powers," Amelie said, standing up. "First things first. Let me get you some coffee. Sit down."

Dierdorf walked over to his stainless steel water and food bowls next to the back door while Quinn obeyed Amelie's command. She washed her hands before pouring the coffee. Uncharacteristically, there was cream and a sugar bowl on the table, although Amelie didn't bring Quinn a spoon.

"I hope you don't mind that I used the brie," she said and returned with a plate containing two slices of bacon, a large omelet, and lightly buttered whole-wheat toast.

"Not at all," a wide-eyed and appreciative Quinn answered.

A moment later, Amelie returned again with a smaller plate with only one slice of bacon, a single piece of dry wheat toast, and a hard-boiled egg. She poured herself a cup of coffee, added a teaspoon of sugar and a little more than a splash of cream.

56

While Quinn knew that Amelie's appetite was only slightly larger than a humming bird's, he could not help but joke, "What? Did you poison these eggs?"

Amelie answered, "Yep. It has always been my plan to kill the goose that lays the golden eggs. In your case, the gander. Eat."

Quinn sat back. Amelie took the dishes to the sink. She warmed Quinn's coffee and hers. Quinn took a careful sip. As Amelie loaded the plates and silverware into the dishwasher, Quinn began, "I can guess the reason you broke in to my house this morning, Amie, and it wasn't to make me an omelet."

"To make an omelet, a girl has to break a few eggs," Amelie said as she segued into what she wanted to talk to him about. "First, I did not break in. You left the door open. Second, I actually did come here to make you breakfast. If that weren't true, I'd have come in the afternoon and made lunch, or maybe, I just would have called and you'd have been left to fend for yourself."

Amelie continued, "I know it's only been a few weeks since Noelia, Quinn, but I think you have a new Dream Seeker."

Although Quinn had never been abrupt with her, Amelie knew better than to actually tell Quinn he had a new Dream Seeker. The decision had been and would always be his. He could say, "No," and actually had declined prospective Dream Seekers who he believed either already had strong enough support or who called for the wrong reasons. Quinn never allowed a Dream Seeker to use him as a way to create suffering for others, like an ex-husband or even manipulative mother. Amelie knew Quinn did the things he did for intensely personal reasons she didn't fully comprehend, but she also knew he wanted only to add to the world's stores of goodwill, as inconsequential a deposit it may be. Taking a Dream Seeker whose motives were clouded would mean a withdrawal from that goodwill, which was contrary to Quinn's code. That code was one of the many reasons Amelie respected and loved Quinn. Still, Amelie had been through this enough to know when Quinn would agree to take a Dream Seeker.

"I'm almost positive it was the same caller who'd hung up a couple of times," Amelie said. "She finally got up the nerve to talk with me just before New Year's."

Quinn scooted the chair so his back would be against the wall. He sat back a little, crossed his legs, and said, "Tell me about her."

"Well, her name is Skylar Smart. Actually, Skylar Smart-Kerr. She's thirty-four years old, an attorney, and lives in Chicago. Metastatic cervical cancer, relapse. She doesn't plan to be treated. Before she was born, her brother was hit by a delivery truck. The accident left him a quadriplegic."

"Horrible for that kid," Quinn tried to empathize. "He was just a little boy, running, playing, riding his Big Wheel, terrorizing his parents, having fun. Then, boom! His body became his prison. I can't begin to imagine."

"Well, yeah. That was the environment Skylar experienced growing up. During our conversation, Skylar implied she believed her parents had her to recreate who and what her brother had been, but it really didn't work out. They were preoccupied with his care, and they detached from her, because, Skylar believes, deep down, they were unable to come to terms with their anger, or their guilt. There was a moderately significant settlement. Skylar's father used the money to buy a couple of McDonald's restaurants. As the Chicago suburbs pushed out, he used his profits to buy more restaurants. In spite of that emotionally sterile environment, Skylar grew up to be seemingly well adapted," Amelie explained as she referred to the private investigator's preliminary report. "In high school, she excelled academically. In the fall, she was a cheerleader. During the winter, she played volleyball. In the spring she played softball. She demonstrated a gift for music, particularly piano and flute, and was a member of the Chicago Youth Symphony. She had friends but none were particularly close."

"She was an overachiever. It seems that she worked really hard to get her parents' attention by trying to be the perfect child," Quinn observed. "I have to give her props. She could have gone the other way."

"You're right. She had no trouble with admissions at Illinois, where she excelled academically and participated in everything from Pan-Hellenic Council to intramurals. She was a Tri-Delt, by the way, and a varsity cheerleader. She had friends and dated, but mostly kept people at an arm's length."

"When she finished her undergrad, a B.A. in history, she went to Northwestern for law school. Consistent with her modus operandi, she did well and finished among the top of her class. She was on the staff of the school's law journal. Outside of school, she stayed active, joined a gym, played in various team sports leagues like beach volleyball."

"Skylar went to work for a leading firm in Chicago. No trouble with the bar exam. Two years ago, her gynecologist found something during a routine exam. It turned out to be early-stage cervical cancer. Surgery, chemo, and radiation put it into remission." Amelie added, "For a while at least."

Referring to the information Skylar provided on the secure web site, Amelie described Skylar in more detail. "She had an infection after the surgery, but she proved to be surprisingly resilient. After she recovered, she scheduled the treatments at times that would be the least distracting for her clients and coworkers. Her billed hours decreased, but only fractionally. The quality of her work didn't suffer. The partners took notice. She was on track to make partner, but after getting the news about relapse, she quit."

Quinn wrinkled his brow and leaned forward in his chair, "There has to be more to it, Amie."

"Interestingly," Amelie replied with tempered ambiguity, "there is."

"I knew you'd get to it eventually." Quinn answered.

"Skylar married the son of Dean Kerr," Amelie reported.

"Dean Kerr?" thought Quinn aloud. "Isn't he the lawyer who was disbarred for that bogus mining company?"

"The same. Skylar married Taylor Kerr because, she said, she thought she loved him and she thought she could change him. She knew he screwed around, but she would not let herself believe he was soulless."

"Skylar's quadriplegic brother contracted pneumonia shortly after Skylar received a clean bill of health the first time through. Then, two months later, her parents were killed in an automobile accident. Can you imagine the year this woman had?"

"No, I can't," Quinn answered as he took another sip of coffee.

"Not surprisingly, Skylar's parents weren't supportive during her treatments. Disappointingly, neither was Taylor. Then, apparently, when Skylar told Taylor she was sick again, the son-of-a-bitch told her he'd stopped loving her and was not sure he ever had. In a bar in front of a bunch of people, he told her he didn't care if she was sick again and hoped she'd die so he could inherit the restaurants and the money. She told him that she wanted a divorce, but, get this, he said that she couldn't divorce him before she died and he'd get everything and that she'd die knowing it!"

"That's cold. Can you believe that there are people who operate like that?" Quinn asked.

"I guess I can, but it's very sad."

"All right, Amie, you sold me. I know that's what you wanted to do and you did. Give me what you have and get me the full investigator's report. Make the arrangements. I'll meet her later this week."

Dierdorf looked up and groaned.

"Sorry, Buddy. Looks like you'll be spending some more time with Kelvin and Melvin." Dejectedly, Dierdorf replaced his head on the floor.

"Thanks, Quinn. I will," Amelie said. "I'd better be going. I'll call you later today with the itinerary."

After Quinn walked Amelie back to her car, Quinn returned to his coffee and the information about Skylar Smart-Kerr Amelie had left for him. Amelie thought to herself as she pulled out of the driveway how strange it was to feel so sad about doing something so good.

CHAPTER 19

Skylar looked at her reflection in the mirror. Katie stood behind and slightly to one side. "This is great, Katie. Thanks," said Skylar, with a sentiment far exceeding appreciation.

Katie rolled her eyes, "If you say it again, I'll throw your little ass out of here! Now hold up your hair so I can zip your Nicole Miller."

"Fine." Skylar conceded. Then, after a moment she said, "I promise, after this time, you can throw me out, but I have to say this."

"You don't, Skylar."

"No, I do. I've never really been close to anyone, I mean, any girls. You know, friends. When I met Taylor, I saw a great-looking, dangerous guy. Because I thought there was nothing I couldn't do; I thought I could change him. Just like I tried to please my parents, I tried to please Taylor. I just enabled him. Christ on a cracker. That doesn't really matter now, though. What I'm saying is I'm learning some pretty important things sort of late in the game." Skylar leaned back on the sink and started to cry. "What I'm saying is that I've never taken the time to be me or to give anything back."

"Aw, honey." Katie put her arms around her friend. "Come on. You're great. You're funny. You're tough. And gracious, girl, you are gorgeous." Katie stepped back to her arms' length and, like a lovingly admonishing mother, looked at Skylar and warned, "You'd better stop that crying right now or you'll mess up your makeup."

Skylar laughed.

"I can't imagine what you're going through now, but it's easy to be your friend. I'll be there, whatever you need."

The day after Skylar spent the night at the hotel, she called Katie to tell her about her call to Life Dreams or, more accurately, her attempted call. By the end of the conversation, Katie invited Skylar to stay. After almost two weeks, it was not a decision Katie regretted.

"One more thing," Katie said. "I don't want to hear about any of that it's-too-late shit, either. First of all, any time one person makes another person's life better, that's a good thing. Second, no one knows how much time we have. I'm not trying to sugarcoat this, but, no one knows. That's the reason that we need to make the most of every day."

Skylar didn't respond. She didn't have to.

"How are you feeling? You okay?" Katie asked.

"You know, it's sort of weird. I feel pretty good, but I still know something's not right. I don't feel sick like I had a cold. It's different. I feel a little stiff, and I have pain in my back when I exert. I have Percocet. When it bothers me, I just pop a couple. So far it hasn't stopped me from doing anything I want to do. That will change eventually."

Skylar saw Katie wrinkle her nose a little when Skylar mentioned the drugs. She was quick to reassure her. "What's the worst that can happen? I get addicted?"

"Well, anyway, I'm glad you're feeling good enough to stay active and go out and stuff. I'm glad that you finally talked to those people," Katie added.

Skylar agreed, with just a little apprehension. "Yeah, me too, but I'm nervous. Amelie was professional, and I have to say I think now she knows more about me than I do. She had me do this personality profile, you know, the 'what-would-you-do?' questions to the 'are-you-more-this-than-that' questions. There were some more direct questions, too, like, 'What foods or music or whatever do you like?'."

"Wow," Katie replied.

"Yeah, right?" Skylar affirmed. "That wasn't all, though. She also asked for a release for my medical records and a notarized health-care proxy. The guy, Quinn is named as proxy."

"That's a little bit of a concern, Skylar," Katie warned. "What if these people want to take advantage of you?"

"You know, I thought of that, too. I am aware that a person in my condition can be, well, vulnerable. I have you, though. You can help me keep my head straight. Second, Amelie didn't ask for money. I don't have to do this, and I do not give them anything up until I actually decide to do this. I'll meet Quinn tonight, and if I get cold feet, well, that's it. There's more. In the get-to-know-you stuff I did, one of the questions Amelie asked was about the thing in life that I most disliked." Skylar joked, "I was tempted to say Taylor Kerr, but I actually said death and the progressive income tax. She said she asked that question to make sure I didn't decide to name Quinn as a beneficiary in my will. Get this. The reason she asked was to let me know that if I did leave anything to Quinn, he would gift it to a place that supports those things I most despise. It would be in the agreement. In my case, Amelie told me that he would give my money to Jack Kervorkian or the Communist Party!" Skylar laughed. "I think she was only half joking."

"That is a great idea." Katie said. "I guess that makes a person feel better it's not a shakedown."

"Don't get me wrong. Life Dreams is not inexpensive by any stretch," Skylar said being careful not to breach her personal financial situation. "But, part of the dream or the wish or whatever is not only to have Quinn make those magical things happen, but he also is there for me as long as I want him to be. Kind of crazy, isn't it?"

"Well, it's very crazy, but it seems like the real thing," Katie affirmed.

"Seems like," Skylar repeated.

Then, Skylar qualified, "But, you know what? Even if isn't, it doesn't really matter. I'm realistic. The chances are I probably don't have a lot of time. I guess I'm lucky to know that. There are some things I really want while I still can walk, while my quality of life is still pretty good. If this guy is a stiff, I can always bail. Even if he is a complete ass, he's miles ahead of Taylor!"

Katie was as much awed by Skylar as she was terrified for her. Not two weeks earlier, Skylar received a death sentence. She really had no one else in the world she could count on. She endured the improprieties of a miserable husband and chose to try to fulfill her dreams. Katie wasn't sure she'd have the courage to handle such circumstances as well.

"So, I really want to know, what is your fantasy? What is the dream that you told Amelie?" Katie excitedly asked.

"It doesn't exactly work that way. Amelie didn't ask me anything like that. Amelie said Quinn would take care of that part. But, to answer your question, I want to feel warm. I want to feel the sun on my body. I want to lie on a beach, drink cocktails, and spend time with someone who knows how to communicate. I want to be with a person who cares for me and cares about me. I don't want to worry what the guy is doing when he's not with me. Other than that, I don't really have any specifics. Not much of a fantasy, huh?" Skylar said contritely.

"No, honey. It sounds perfectly wonderful."

"Of course, my other dream is to have a house that is as clean as yours, but I'm pretty sure Quinn won't be able to help with that." Skylar tried to lighten the conversation's ominous undertones.

Katie laughed, "Guilty. I sort of have an obsessive-compulsive thing about that. Speaking of obsessive, I'm also sort of fanatical about being on time. If you don't get going, you'll be late. Are you sure I can't drive you?"

"No, Katie, but thanks. I called a cab and it should be outside," Skylar answered. "You're right, though. I'd better get going."

Skylar grabbed a tissue and dabbed dry the mist before she retouched her makeup. Katie walked out to get Skylar's coat. A moment later, a horn sounded.

"Good luck tonight, Skylar. I hope things happen the way you want them to."

"Thanks, Katie," replied Skylar as she opened the door and started out.

"Call me if you need anything. Really, anything."

Skylar smiled and before closing the door she promised, "I will."

Katie bit her top lip, turned to the front windows. She watched Skylar cross the sidewalk and slide into the back of the waiting taxi. As soon as the car door closed, Katie broke into tears, which didn't stop for almost twenty minutes. When she stopped, Katie picked up her phone and pressed speed-dial number one.

Katie spoke into the phone, "Hi, Chase. I just called to let you know I love you."

CHAPTER 20

When he visited Chicago, Quinn preferred The Chicago Chop House on Ontario to Gibson's, which was more a place to see and be seen than to eat. In fact, Quinn preferred The Chop House to the Capital Grills, Ruth's Chris, and Rosebud Prime where Mayor Daly supposedly has his own table. The difference between The Chop House and the others was comparable to the difference between Albert Pujols and Derek Lee. Both are major leaguers, but the former will be a hall of famer.

Considering the biographical information Skylar provided, it was the obvious selection. Skylar also indicated she liked Japanese, but wasn't at all picky. Quinn found that last bit of information interesting, because it reinforced that Skylar was eager to please the people around her and regularly subordinated her own wishes.

"That is about to change," Quinn thought to himself.

After arriving via United at O'Hare, Quinn rented a black Ford Mustang hard top and drove to the Park Hyatt for a one-night reservation. He showered and dressed smartly but not too flashy.

As usual, he arrived early at the nineteenth-century Victorian brownstone to be sure he'd be waiting. Quinn walked from the street through the glass anteroom before opening the heavy oak door to the restaurant dining room. Inside the door to the right, an attractive Mediterranean-looking hostess smiled, "Good evening, sir. Welcome to The Chop House. My name is Marie." Then, she asked, "May I have your name please?"

"Hi. Quinn Powers."

"Welcome back, Mr. Powers. Table for two. Your table will be ready in just a few minutes," Marie stated politely, "You may sit at the bar and enjoy a cocktail. I will come for you when your table is ready."

"Thanks, Marie. Just to check, my table will have a view of the front window and the door?"

"Yes, Mr. Powers. Your table is the one that's ready to be bused, just on the back side of the bar," the hostess responded.

"Thanks. That's perfect."

Quinn walked down the stairs and angled 90 degrees left into the room. Three sides of the bar extended into the center. Quinn entered the bar corral past the dozen stools and took the second chair from the wait station. A small, brown-skinned man cleared the table on the other side of the rail behind him. Quinn didn't have to get the attention of the seasoned bartender.

"Good evening, sir," the bartender politely offered. "I'm Solly. What can I get you?"

"Club soda with bitters please," Quinn answered.

A moment later, Marie walked back down from her pulpit. "Your table is ready, Mr. Powers."

Quinn left a bill on the bar, said, "Thanks, Solly." He followed Marie around the rail and to his table only a few feet away.

Just before 7:30, Quinn watched through the glass as the exterior door opened. A moment later, the door swung open. A strikingly beautiful woman, who wore heels, an elegant wool coat, and leather gloves, walked through. Quinn could make out the sexy black dress with plunging neckline as she unbuttoned her coat. Just as the woman said to Marie, "I'm meeting Quinn Powers," Quinn stood in front of her with one foot on the bottom stair. He looked up, caught his breath, and said, "Hi, Skylar. I'm Quinn."

CHAPTER 21

Quinn was unprepared for the first impression. While many Dream Seekers had been physically attractive, Quinn had rarely met one who projected an aura that could not easily be captured in a picture or words.

As Skylar offered her coat, she looked back at him over her shoulder. She was at once confident and innocent, qualities that effectively balanced her striking looks. Her medium-long blonde hair was not unfamiliar with high-priced stylists. The cocktail dress suggested dedication to fitness, although her body was softly feminine rather than severe. Her green eyes imparted a sorrowful knowing, while her smile offered a perpetual optimism. Quinn tried very hard not to allow the thought into his head that he could count on one hand, perhaps a couple of fingers even, the number of women who, after a first meeting, had made anything approaching a similar impression.

As he hung her coat carefully in the coat closet, Quinn said, "I have our table right here by the bar. It may not seem terribly private, but you'd be surprised how well a couple of people can hide in the middle of a busy restaurant."

"Oh, that's fine, Quinn," Skylar answered. "I don't need to hide what I'm doing. After all, why should I care what anyone thinks? Especially now."

Quinn smiled and pulled out Skylar's chair. The table, roughly the same height as the railing around the bar, was a hybrid of a traditional dining table and a bar room high-top. As a result, the chairs' legs were so long that Skylar's feet could not quite reach the floor. As he adjusted Skylar's chair under her, Quinn observed she perched expectantly like a curious bird on a branch.

"This place is great," Skylar said. "Coming down the stairs into this big room with the bar and the tables is almost like walking down into one of Al Capone's speakeasies." Skylar looked around the room to look at the pictures and captions of all the Chicago mobsters dating back to the second half of the nineteenth century.

Quinn answered, "Yeah, and if you like the atmosphere, you'll love the food. You know, I shouldn't have assumed. Have you been here before?"

"Actually, no. I like to have a couple of drinks at Hugo's Frog Bar before dinner at Gibson's, but I have never been here. When I was a little younger, I spent some time up the street at Excalibur, though," Skylar explained.

Before Quinn could respond, a waiter approached, and after an introduction, he asked, "Can I bring you a cocktail?" Quinn deferred to Skylar.

"Absolut and tonic, please," she said.

"Aberlour rocks. Thank you."

"You're welcome, sir. I'll be right back with your drinks and the specials," the waiter said before he walked quickly away.

"So, thanks for meeting me," Quinn offered. "I'm glad you decided to talk with Amelie"

"Well, first of all, I'm a sucker for a gentleman who asks me to dinner. Of course, Amelie is delightful." Then abruptly, "Seriously, though, I am very curious about Life Dreams. What made you decide to do this sort of thing?"

Quinn appreciated the direct approach, which, he observed, was not uncommon among Dream Seekers. As much a consequence of the women as it was the screening process, a vast majority of Dream Seekers were candid and confident. By design, there was a considerable cost involved, which may have seemed exclusionary to an outsider. Quinn really had no interest in what an outsider thought. The fee screened all but the most sincere, determined, and in most cases, self-assured. As such, Dream Seekers were typically self-made women who were educated and unafraid to ask or say what was on their minds. Dream Seekers were also perceptive enough to realize questions to avoid.

"I'm glad you asked. Before I answer, I want you to know there is nothing you can't ask. I want you to feel comfortable about that. Several years ago I lost someone very close to me. When I was with her, I honestly felt lucky to be the person at her side when she needed someone the most. After I had put some time between me and her death, I realized how lucky she and I were to have had each other. We'd become even closer. Frankly, I know the experience of being together helped me, and I am just as certain it helped her. She knew she was loved and was able to actualize. At some point, it occurred to me other people who weren't as fortunate as we were or as she was," Quinn told a part of the truth. "I lamented the people who were alone under those circumstances. At the same time I wanted to sustain my own purpose. Considering I'm a man who has relatively normal preferences and natural desires, I thought I would be more helpful to the ladies."

The waiter brought their drinks, while Skylar understood a great deal more about Quinn from what he didn't say than from what he did. "Like spending time with interesting people, right? Like spending time with attractive women?"

The waiter stood patiently before he described the entrees until Quinn finished his thought.

"There's no question that women are more evolved creatures," Quinn answered. "And, yes, I prefer spending time with interesting, attractive people, but it's more than that."

Skylar ordered a petit filet done medium. Quinn chose the rib eye medium rare, which, the server explained, was sliced from a prime rib and grilled to order. The smaller, sixteen-ounce cut sounded like more than enough. Quinn suggested a half bottle of 1999 Bryant Family Vineyard Cab. Skylar wasn't familiar with the vineyard, but knew 1999 was a good year for Cabernets.

"I know all of this seems strange, artificial even," Quinn admitted after the waiter ambled sprightly toward the kitchen. "That feeling will be soon forgotten. I'm not here to convince you of anything. It's important you do the things that make you happy. There's been some formality so far, but the formal part is done. In fact, I don't even get involved with that stuff. If you're not completely comfortable with me, or this, or anything, all bets are off. In more ways you can imagine, I'm here or not here for you."

Skylar nodded.

"You know, I've read the stuff about you from Amelie, and, by the way, you are an extraordinary woman." Quinn didn't have to embellish.

Just then, the waiter arrived with the wine, opened the bottle, and poured a splash in Quinn's glass. After tasting the sample, Quinn announced, "That's great, thanks." The waiter poured Skylar's glass slightly less than half and repeated with Quinn's glass.

"Your dinners will be just a few minutes," said the waiter before he dashed away again.

Quinn continued after the welcome interruption, "You've accomplished a lot. You are a successful attorney. You've endured a difficult situation at home. You're a confident person who's dealing head-on with a serious medical condition. That and so much more, like the fact you're here, speak volumes about you. I hope you'll excuse me for wanting to know more about you and being straightforward about asking. Tell me about the things that make you happy."

Skylar paused for a moment. She expected Quinn to ask questions, but the questions she imagined were more direct and objective, which was ironic because Quinn asked in such a direct and objective way.

"Well," she began, "When I was about thirteen years old, I had a piano recital. It was December just before Christmas. I'd had private lessons since I was six from a teacher who had many students who eventually played professionally. She held a recital every year at the University of Chicago. Usually, some of the music school faculty attended and offered scholarships to some of the better high school students."

"I was pretty good. I could play technically correct and I could play with passion. I probably could've become a professional myself if I wanted to. Like just about everything I did, I worked hard, I think, for attention from my parents. I didn't realize that at the time, of course. It sounds kind of silly or maybe even a little sad, but my parents never came to the recitals. I think they had actually found these activities, like music, to occupy me so they didn't have to. You know about my brother, right?"

"Yes, I do."

"Well, I eventually learned my parents lost something more than a son when John was hurt. It may sound cruel and I say this without the least bit of jealousy, but it would have almost been better if John died in that accident. When someone dies, even a child, a person grieves and in most cases, moves on. With John, my parents were reminded about their loss every day," Skylar lamented.

Quinn nodded.

"Anyway, I'd become used to being on my own. Besides, I enjoyed playing. During the times I felt like I didn't have anyone or anything else, I always had music, you know?" asked Skylar. "As I warmed up in the sound-proof room backstage, my piece was the third movement of Beethoven's Fifth Piano Concerto, my Mom and my Dad came in! At first, I was scared because I thought something was wrong with John. When they told me everything was fine and that they had a nurse for the evening, I was thrilled! They wished me luck, you know, told me to break a leg and all that. I was so excited I almost forgot how to read music!"

"When I was finally called to go on stage, I was euphoric. I was not in the least bitter because they hadn't been there all the other times. As I sat down on the bench, I glanced into the audience and saw them smiling. I can hardly describe the way I felt and I know I can't describe what I was thinking. I guess there was a part of me that dared to hope that something had changed and I can remember having so much fun and feeling so happy as I played that night. It's sort of a short piece. The Allegro Rondo is only about eleven minutes, but it seemed like I finished in seconds. When I was done, I looked out, blushing, and saw my Mom and Dad standing and applauding. It was probably the most memorable moment in my life."

Quinn asked, "What happened then? I mean, did things change at all?"

Skylar frowned, "No. No they didn't. After the recital, my parents took me to a Buco di Beppo for dinner to celebrate. Seems kind of funny, now, but Buco was one of my dad's passions.

"Sounds like a true connoisseur of franchise restaurants," joked Quinn.

"No doubt about that, I guess," Skylar conceded. "It was wonderful, the attention, their interest in what I had worked so hard to do. But the next day, and it was almost that fast, it was back to business as usual. For a while, I'd get a smile or a pat as if to recall that night when my parents allowed their world and their pain to go away for a few hours, but it didn't take long for even those small tokens of affection to fade. Then, life was normal again. My parents disconnected from everything, everything but John."

It seemed like a pretty good time for Quinn to drain his scotch. Scotch influenced the palate and was supposed to detract from the flavor of a good wine, but it never bothered Quinn. He took a drink of water before sipping the Cabernet again.

"I'm sorry," Quinn said.

Skylar had long become used to the circumstances of her life and made the best of it. She hadn't had much experience with others expressing compassion, however, and had some difficulty checking her emotions. "Thank you, Quinn."

"This will sound sort of funny, for a girl anyway, but I had one guilty little pleasure," Skylar added shyly. "Yes, I had sports and piano. There were times, though, that I just needed down time."

"Yes," Quinn answered in a way that begged to extract the nugget of information.

"It was an accident, really," Skylar began. "Like a lot of kids, I had a healthy curiosity. Finding myself with nothing better do to one day, I was in the attic of the 1940-ish Colonial where we lived. The house had a walk-up attic and plank floor boards. I remember it was cold. There was no insulation in the roof. I wore a jacket. There were a bunch of wooden milk crates filled with old stuff. In a couple of boxes were some old seventy-eights, some big band, some classical. There were a few of those old box sets of LPs recorded from NBC Radio broadcasts of Mozart or Bach or Beethoven or Wagner. Before there was television, DVRs, satellite radio, and MP3 players, I guess radio and LPs were the cutting edge of entertainment media. In another box were old newspapers and a few *Saturday Evening Posts* from the forties and fifties,"

Quinn listened attentively as Skylar built anticipation.

"You'd have thought that I would've liked the old copies of the *Saturday Evening Post*. Some of them included some great short stories, "Skylar recalled.

Quinn's interest intensified, "Wow!"

"You should have seen those old magazines: cigarette ads selling health and gadgets to help women become better housewives. It was a riot! You might have even thought that I would have connected with the old vinyl, considering my music. Alas, no, it was the box of old comic books," Skylar confessed.

Quinn smiled. He enjoyed Skylar's story, and he was learning more about her. He reminded himself that the pleasure he drew from Skylar's stories was related strictly to his interest in her as a Dream Seeker.

"When I opened the box," Skylar spoke like a child on Christmas morning, "I found what must have been fifty or sixty comic books: Superman, Batman, Green Lantern, Hulk, and, of course, Spider-Man! I opened one and was fascinated by the colorful cartoon art. I began to read. I think the first one I opened was a Superman because he was the most recognizable. I loved it!"

"They must have belonged to my father, but they'd been long forgotten or at least long ignored. I carried the box down the stairs and into my room, where I stashed them in the back of my closet. I'm not sure why I did that. I don't think my parents would have cared if I'd wallpapered my room with them! Regardless, I read all of the comics during the next few days, but I really connected with Spidey."

"That's interesting," Quinn asked curiously. "Why do you think you connected with Spider-Man?"

"I don't know. I guess Superman was sort of the alpha male and knew it. No doubt his heart was in the right place, but it bothered me that he was always so squirrelly around Lois Lane. Come on, you're Superman! Just get the girl already, will you? I never was really much into muscle heads either, so Hulk was out. Batman was too much of a schizo. When Robin showed up, that was the least of the implications. I don't know. Peter Parker was just one of the good, decent, down-to-earth guys who just happened to get bitten by a radioactive spider. What could he do, you know? His respect for his Aunt Mae and for others was endearing. He learned the hard way from his mistakes. He found out that his Uncle Ben was killed by the same thief who he could have, but didn't stop, Peter resolved never to let that happen again. That's when he made the difficult decision to accept the responsibility of being Spidey. I sort of fell in love with Peter Parker and even had fantasies about him," Skylar confessed finally.

"There were some pretty old ones, but the earliest one was number fourteen. I still have it, The Grotesque Adventure of the Green Goblin. The plot line was sort of thin, but it was the first time the Green Goblin appeared in a Spidey comic, so it's pretty special."

"So, you must have been pretty charged when the movies were made, huh?" Quinn asked.

"Yes and no. The first two movies were pretty good even though they weren't completely true to the original character. The third was too Batman-ish considering the whole alter ego thing.

Quinn was delighted by the rapport he developed. Some people just have that "click," and, Quinn thought, that chemistry will be important later. He tried to guide Skylar further down the path, "Was there a time when you were happy just for happiness' sake? Something or someone made you happy and it still makes you happy now?"

"Spidey still makes me happy," Skylar asserted, "But yes, I know what you mean. A couple years after Taylor and I were married, he and I went to see Mark Burton at the United Center. Even though I was with Taylor, or should I say, in spite of the fact I was with Taylor, we had a great night. It was at a time I still had the fairytale image of what our lives could be together. Taylor was, well, Taylor, but we got along all right most of the time. I either didn't know or didn't want to believe what he was doing in his spare time. He was trying too, I guess, because he thought I was still worth the effort. So, it was nice. Ignorance is bliss, huh?"

Quinn assumed her question was rhetorical.

"The first song I really connected with was 'Bridge To My Heart.' It was the early nineties and everyone said that he wrote the song for his daughter, who had died. I know now it was true, but I didn't know then. I just loved the song. Like I said, I always had music and I sort of immersed myself in Burton's musical library. I started to buy his old music to get myself caught up. I didn't really like some of his early stuff, but I got there with his solo stuff during the seventies. I know he was writing and singing about his own life, but it was almost like he was singing those songs just for me. I saw him in 1994 on the Born Late tour."

"I remember that one," said Quinn. "I saw the same tour in Hartford."

"It wasn't long after that I really got involved in school, then law school, then the firm. Well, I guess you already know I am sort of obsessive when I put my mind to something. I will not say I focus on one thing to the exclusion of all else, but the truth is not far from there. I usually didn't take the time to indulge my interests if they weren't at least indirectly associated with my work. Later, I was the same with Taylor. To make a long story short—too late," Skylar said aside with a wry smile, "I continued to enjoy the music, but didn't get out much to concerts until 2001, which I read or heard somewhere that this might be Burton's last world tour. Of course, that was like The Who or The Rolling Stones farewell tours, which they do every three years. It was the first time I had heard that about Burton."

"It was a week night, I think, and the two of us made it happen to get out of work early enough so we could have dinner and get to the United Center. We ate and had a couple of drinks at a place called Reilly's Pub, which is gone now. It was bought up by investors who have a hand full of bars in Chicago. A friend of mine works at one of them," Skylar rambled just a little.

"The concert was great. Burton played just about all his classic songs and all the popular ones, too. It was what I'd thought the show in '94 was going to be. He took down the house with his classics while playing some amazing shreds in between. It was incredible. Then for an encore, Burton did a swing version of 'Over the Rainbow.' Seriously, the song just about brought tears to my eyes. I was blown away," Skylar finished shyly. "I told you I can be a little obsessive!"

"Jeez, Skylar" Quinn said. "You really do know your stuff. I actually thought I knew a little bit about Mark Burton, but you blow me out of the water!"

"Well, when I'm interested in something, whether it's piano, the law, NCAA volleyball, or, well, Burton, I really like to know it," Skylar confessed. "Of course, I love Elvis, too, but that's a story for another time."

"You didn't see Elvis, did you?" Quinn asked skeptically.

"No. I was still in diapers when Elvis died, but Elvis is The King."

"Why don't I cut you a break so we can enjoy the food," Quinn suggested as a busboy set up the folding tray stand next to the table. The waiter followed with the entrees and sides, served them, and poured a splash more wine in their glasses.

CHAPTER 22

Skylar had a couple of bites of steak when she tugged back the conversation. "Look, I'd already decided before we met tonight, I'm going through with this. Frankly, unless you were a Neanderthal, I was in. What do I have to lose?"

"That's high praise," Quinn feigned offense.

"Cut it out. You know what I mean. I expect that we'll have plenty of time to talk when we, well, get started. There are a few questions and my curiosity is getting the best of me."

"Okay," Quinn said warily.

"Well, you have this thing you do and it's sort of well known. If you haven't already, you'll seep into the cultural subconscious. People will not know whether you're real or an urban legend. It's not really a bad thing for people to know, although I think some people won't understand. Frankly, I don't really understand."

Quinn finished the last of his wine and found the Cabernet bottle empty, which did not elude the waiter, who arrived at the table almost before Quinn replaced the wine bottle on the table.

"After dinner drink, Skylar?"

"No thanks. I'm fine," she answered.

"Aberlour rocks for me, please," Quinn requested. Then, aside, to Skylar "I never was one much for Port. Like I said before, there's nothing that you can't ask. I'll always be honest with you. That means something to me and I want it to mean something to you, too. The things you want for the rest of your life are important. Frankly, it needs to be more important to you than anything else is. No matter the question, I'll answer. Honestly."

"Okay," Skylar said cautiously.

"No, no. I don't want you to feel uncomfortable," Quinn assured. "It's just that I want you to know that this is not about anyone else. It's about you."

"I think I understand," Skylar said. "You don't want me to ask you about anyone of your other, uh, Dream Seekers?"

"Well, yes and no," Quinn qualified. "There is no subject off-limits. Our conversations can go anywhere you want to take them. I've always found communicating with a person on a deeper level is both satisfying and intimate. I'm a pretty good listener. I can be a pretty good talker, too. In spite of what you've been told, we can talk about religion and politics. We can talk about philosophy and the meaning of life. We don't even have to go that far. We can talk about fast food franchises or music or great bars in Chicago or whether the Cubs will ever win a World Series. Of course, if you want to know about Life Dreams, I'll tell. But, I don't want anything I've done or will do to change the fact that this is about you."

Quinn sipped the cocktail the server delivered.

Skylar wasn't uneasy. From a very practical side, she understood being honest, direct, and truthful almost had to be a prerequisite for Quinn. Right then, though, Skylar recognized two more very important things. First, she stumbled upon something. It may have been something with which Quinn wasn't fully comfortable discussing, but he would if she asked. Second, she was, in Quinn's mind, the most important person in the world while he was with her, and he wanted her to know that. Quinn wanted her to know he didn't really want her to bring up any of his other Dream Seekers because, much like in real life, three's a crowd.

At that moment, Skylar decided that it just really wasn't that important to her to know more about Quinn. "You know, Quinn, I'm worn out and that's not just a line like, 'Not tonight, honey, I have a headache.' I am just exhausted," Skylar said, smiling.

For Quinn's part, he was impressed by Skylar's poise. She'd made some difficult decisions about the rest of her life. She was tactful and perceptive. Of course, her smile was electric. A subconscious thought seeped into his mind. Quinn was slightly embarrassed when he found himself wishing that he could've earned that smile. Quinn grabbed the credit card receipt and signed it.

"So, what happens now, Mr. Powers?"

"So formal, Ms. Smart?" Quinn answered. "Well, give me two or three days to get everything together. I'll send a car on Sunday. Amelie will call with a few specifics, you know, what to pack and what time the car will come."

"Sunday? You haven't even asked what I want to do!" Skylar responded, surprised.

Wearing a mischievous smirk, Quinn stood up and said simply, "Yes, I have."

"Are you going to tell me?"

Still wearing an ironic smile, Quinn said, "If you really want to ask me that question, I will answer. Otherwise, you'll know on Sunday."

"Fine!" Skylar answered. "I can already tell. You're a handful."

"I'll get your coat. Can I give you a ride?" Quinn drained his drink.

"No, I'm fine, Quinn. Thanks. I'd actually prefer a cab tonight," Skylar replied.

"Sure," Quinn said as he walked out a little onto Ontario to flag a taxi. It only took a few seconds before Quinn got one after it dropped a fare at Excalibur. Quinn opened the door for Skylar and gave her a hug and a peck on the cheek.

"I look forward to Sunday," Quinn offered.

"Thanks for dinner," Skylar fought the urge to wince as she slid into the backseat of the taxi.

"Any time, Skylar," Quinn said finally as he closed the door and the driver pulled out into traffic.

The taxi wasn't a block away before Skylar opened her purse, took out the prescription bottle of Percocet, and swallowed two pills with some water from a bottle she kept with her.

CHAPTER 23

Quinn had parked the Mustang a couple blocks away. As he walked, he pulled the bluetooth from the breast jacket pocket, hung it on his ear, and speed dialed Amelie's private line. She picked up before the second ring. Dispensing with any formality, she answered "How did it go tonight?"

It wasn't every day that Quinn met a potential Dream Seeker—on average, just about one a year. Considering Life Dreams had only been known by word of mouth, it wasn't like the phone minutes from incoming calls were breaking the bank. As a consequence, Amelie made sure she was available when Quinn was with a Dream Seeker. Sometimes, Quinn just needed something simple, like a chartered plane, lodging in a place that would be completely impossible to obtain, or special services that could range from a personal valet to a mystic. Once in a while, Quinn asked for something a little more difficult. It helped that money was not an impediment. Often, the machine needed grease, and Amelie was a master mechanic.

"It went well," Quinn tried to sound objective. "She's lovely." Quinn recalled the image of Skylar standing at the top of the stairs.

"Good," Amelie responded.

"You ready?"

Amelie answered, "Of course."

"Okay. Charter a plane from Midway to Antigua on Sunday. If we have to stop, make sure it's someplace we can get in and out quickly. Find a beach house on Antigua away from the resorts. I'm not sure how long we'll stay, but book it for two months. Try to find one that has a good gym, a sauna, a hot tub, all that stuff. Make sure we can extend if we need to. I'll need a caretaker who knows how to get things done. I'll also need a chef. I really don't care whether he or she is local, just has to be really good. Have a supply of dry-aged beef and a stock of the basics typical of the Midwest. You know, comfort foods. Also, set me up a contact where we can get fresh sushi-quality fish. Stock the liquor cabinet and wine rack. Make sure there is plenty of Absolut." Quinn didn't have to say there should be a few bottles of Aberlour, too.

"Got all that. Is there anything else, Quinn?" Amelie asked. She already knew that there would be.

"Yeah, a piano. I think a baby grand. Also, flowers. Have fresh flowers delivered daily, roses, lilies, mix in wild flowers from time to time. And one more thing, can you text me Embee's number. He should be down there with Jolisa and the kids this time of year and it would be nice if we could go over and say, 'Hello.' If you don't have it, I know Embee is still Kelly's client. Send Embee a sixteen-gauge Winchester Model 1100 and a case of number six shells. For the girls, get the Harry Potter collection, inscribed firsts."

"Jeez, Quinn. Is that it? I thought you would make it hard for me!"

"You'd better watch it or I'll have you deliver a time machine or a couple of tickets to the Extraterrestrial Zoo in Roswell," Quinn joked.

Amelie noticed the frequency of calls, even the frequency of hang ups, had steadily increased over the years. Like a growing sapling, an observer may not recognize day-to-day changes. But, if a person compares how a tree now looks to an old photograph of the tree, the change is more apparent. The increase in call volume would have been noticeable even if Amelie had not recently pulled out older phone records for comparison.

"Hey, Quinn, I want you to know, I have been getting a few more calls recently. Mostly curiosity and hang ups, but I thought you should know."

Quinn wanted Life Dreams to remain discrete. He knew if the thing became too well known, he might find it more difficult to continue.

"Okay, Amie. Thanks for letting me know," Quinn answered pensively.

"All right. I'll text Embee's contact numbers and update you late morning. Have a safe trip back."

"Thanks. I don't know what I'd do without you," Quinn said finally.

Quinn unlocked the Mustang with the remote, opened the door, and climbed in. He took a deep breath before he turned the ignition and pushed down the clutch. He slid the car into first gear, felt the surge of the engine as he increased the RPMs. He eased off his left and pulled the car into the Chicago night.

CHAPTER 24

Gina's primary care physician, Asim Singh, expedited the results. Asim would learn two days later that the counts were essentially normal except for elevated white blood cells. Although the screen suggested infection, the symptoms did not fit neatly into any viral or bacterial diagnosis. A couple of days later, Gina met an infectious disease specialist who asked questions about chemical exposure and contact with animals. Specifically, he wanted to know whether Gina had been scratched by a cat or had been in contact with feces from a short list of exotic animals. The exam yielded more blood tests but still no answers.

Quinn had previously planned a meeting with a prospective client and wanted to reschedule, but Gina insisted that he go. "I know how much you wanted to meet this guy," Gina said. "Besides, Lina said she'd take me to see the pulmonologist. I'll let you make it up to me in Bermuda."

"Please, call me Embee. That's what my family called me when I was a boy. Some of my mates still do. This is Jolisa," said Quinn's prospective new client, nodding to the attractive young woman.

Considering Embee's pop-culture notoriety, Quinn was surprised that his first impression of Embee was not only unpretentious but also quite unassuming. From divas to dictators, Quinn never knew what he'd encounter. Among his many celebrity clients, not all resided anywhere close to a state called Reality.

"Thanks, Embee. I will," Quinn answered appreciatively. Quinn offered a quid pro quo, "If you'd like, you can call me 'QuickPick,' which is what my wife calls me sometimes. I got the name when I played baseball. Some of my old buddies still use it."

During lunch, Quinn and Embee exchanged stories. Quinn shared sports anecdotes and Embee countered with stories about touring and abridged tales of excess. By early afternoon Quinn, Embee, and Jolisa finished lunch at the pub where, for the right client, Quinn arranged to rent the entire place. High-profile people appreciated Quinn's sensitivity to one of the more difficult disadvantages of fame. The pub owner not only liked Quinn's fee, but she also liked the innuendo and gossip that followed Quinn's meetings. Of course, the proprietor did nothing to suppress the flames of the rumors that surrounded the events; she often fanned the fire and sometimes added accelerant.

Quinn never needed to be anything more than a soft seller. His friendliness, confidence, and results spoke loud enough. By the time the coffee arrived, Quinn had earned Embee's trust, and his business.

"This might sound odd for a man my age, but I have only just recently taken responsibility for my own affairs," Embee explained. "Until just the past few years, managers and agents and other people have done everything for me: paid my bills, provided stipends, and even invested my money. I imagine that it was high time I do those things myself. That's due in no small part to this lady here."

Jolisa gave Embee's hand a tender squeeze and smiled at him.

"Better late than never, eh?" Embee finished.

Noticing that Embee was just a little self-conscious about the information he'd just shared, Quinn was supportive.

"Look, each of us takes a different path. I'll give you an example—what you naturally and instinctively know, your ability to connect to people through your music in ways that most other people will never understand," Quinn explained. "In many ways, I envy the life you have led. At the same time, my strengths are different than yours, so I made my own way. If I'd have changed a thing, I may not be who I am today. What's magic, whether you talk about meeting the woman of your dreams or whether you talk about two people like you and me, is that we realize that the abilities, the experiences, and the knowledge we have as individuals are complementary. Then, a healthy relationship grows, and both people benefit in ways we couldn't have expected. That's an example of one and one being something greater than two."

Quinn liked only coffee in his coffee. As both Embee and Jolisa added and stirred just the right amount of sugar and cream, Quinn's phone vibrated. Before the meeting, Quinn turned off his business phone. He believed that there should be no one any more important than the person with whom he was meeting. Quinn knew it was a policy his clients appreciated, and it helped him to win more than one piece of business. This phone, however, was his personal phone, and he knew Gina wouldn't call unless it was important.

"Excuse me for a moment, will you? I apologize; this is my personal phone and I need to take this." Quinn walked toward the bar so he wouldn't disturb his new clients.

"Quinn, it's Lina. Gina asked me to call. I hope it's all right."

"Of course it is, Lina. What wrong? Is Gina okay?"

"Uh, not really," Lina said, "Listen. The doctor found a clot in an artery in Gina's neck. She's fine, but as a precaution the doctor admitted her."

Quinn's head began to spin, "What did he say caused it?"

"Dr. Singh wasn't sure, but Gina just spoke with him while she was being admitted," Lina concluded.

After finishing his conversation with Lina, Quinn once again joined his guests. Quinn's client said in a way that suggested both education and sincerity of heart, "I hope all is all right, Quinn."

Quinn explained his wife's circumstances to Embee and Jolisa. "You have to go to her then," Embee insisted. "We'll speak again soon, I hope."

CHAPTER 25

In spite of his optimism for a prodigious financial windfall and for the fantasy of a life as restaurant mogul, a playboy, and a man of leisure, the recent days had not been good for Taylor Kerr.

As promised, Skylar stopped direct deposit of her paychecks and restaurant distributions. Even though Taylor knew it had been probably more than a little overdue, he'd also been relieved of his duties as a pharmaceuticals representative. It seemed the majority of the doctors, hospital administrators, or their surrogates weren't any more interested in spending time with him than they were buying the pill he peddled. During the week between Christmas and New Year's when business volume is not exactly cresting, Taylor's boss called him to meet for lunch. Taylor thought they'd talk about new products and maybe even about his level of commitment. However, Taylor was summarily terminated with only a few weeks' severance.

Taylor managed to pay the mortgage and most of the other bills for December, but his credit cards were at their limit. He wondered how he would make it through the month of January without a job and without Skylar's money.

The first time the doorbell rang, Taylor thought he was dreaming. He stirred, moaned from nausea that churned in his stomach. His head throbbed mercilessly. He rolled toward the middle of the mattress. When he heard the doorbell a second time, he opened his eyes and found himself face-to-face with a freakish creature that resembled Stan Laurel both in feature and stature. The overapplied, orangey makeup and smeared eyeliner were his first clues of gender. Her face resembled more a carved, oblong Halloween pumpkin than a human female. Taylor desperately wanted to rationalize that she looked better through the transformative power of beer goggles. He also prayed that he used a condom, although he was pretty sure that he didn't.

THE DREAM SEEKER

The third time the doorbell rang, Taylor realized the caller might not go away unsatisfied. He carefully rolled back so he would not wake his bedmate, but he knew that time would inevitably come. He stumbled up, pulled on a pair of jeans and a T-shirt on the floor near the bedroom door, and staggered down the stairs. His revulsion persisted as he looked at Charlie and a crater-faced Oliver Hardy passed out on the couch. Apparently, Hardy had been more enthusiastic than her partner had been. Charlie still had his shirt and socks on while his the girl was completely and unflatteringly exposed. Taylor looked away and tried frantically to put the image out of his mind.

Just as he reached the front door, the bell rang for a fourth time. Taylor was certain the nuisance would not have stopped, so he felt vindicated in his decision to get up. At least he escaped Laurel.

Taylor opened the door and found an attractive, young woman who held her hands behind her back. In contrast to the thing that waited for him in his bed, the woman at his door wore makeup sparingly. Taylor believed he was sophisticated when he said in his best charming voice, "Hi there, cutie. What can I do for you?"

Even if the young woman had not already heard about the guy she'd been dispatched to find, Taylor Kerr wouldn't have been someone she would have wanted to find herself. The odor of liquor on his breath and clothing was reason enough.

"Taylor?" she asked as if she recognized him.

"I sure am," Taylor regained some confidence.

"Taylor Kerr?" the young woman confirmed.

"Uh huh. That's me," Taylor assured.

The woman then pulled one of her hands from behind her back and offered Taylor an envelope, which he didn't hesitate to accept.

"See my friend in that car there? She's my witness." The woman in the car smiled and waved. "You've been served with divorce. Have a nice day."

Taylor could not have been more embarrassed if he'd been stripped naked on the fifty-yard line at Soldier Field. He closed the door and turned around when he heard a voice from the top of the stairs.

"Who was that, Taylor Bear?"

Taylor looked up and saw the same thing he'd found a couple minutes earlier slumbering in his bed. He thought to himself as his head pounded harder, "Jesus Christ! Taylor Bear?" His stomach churned as he turned his head away. He didn't want look at her, but the direction to which he was instinctively drawn gave no respite. Taylor was confronted with Charlie's bare red ass parted horribly as one leg was flopped onto his partner's rolls of blubber.

Taylor darted past the couch and the two hanging authentic World War II Japanese officer swords Skylar had given him for a birthday, but could not reach the bathroom soon enough. He vomited on the carpet and on the ceramic tile just inside the door. In his haste to reach the toilet, Taylor slipped and hit his head on the floor.

When she heard the commotion, Laurel descended the stairs and trotted toward the bathroom. The odor hit her. Before she fully realized what happened, she vomited a few inches from where Taylor groped and slithered. Adding more insult to the incalculable injury to his dignity, Taylor looked up to see two heads wearing puzzled and indulgent expressions peering over the back at the couch.

CHAPTER 26

Kelly's parents already knew Quinn was leaving again. Kelly mentioned it, so Bob was ready for Quinn's call. Bob had always been willing to do this favor for Kelly's best friend. After all, Bob drove past Quinn's house at the corner of Grand and Cherry at least eight times a day during his school bus route. Like just about everyone, Bob appreciated the opportunity to contribute. He included it as a part of his plans every morning to walk after dropping his student-passengers. On Saturday mornings, Bob woke early and walked an extended route. On Sundays, because he attended nine o'clock mass with Lina at St. Stephen the Martyr church before breakfasting at a place in Edenville, Bob shortened his walk, but still included the house.

"I'm not sure how long I'll be away," Quinn said to Bob as he handed him a check for $2,000. "This should keep the driveway plowed and, if I'm not back, it'll be a good start for the landscaper."

The most difficult part of his checklist for Quinn was leaving Dierdorf. He knew that Dierdorf had already lived a full life and worried how much longer he'd have the company of man's best friend. At least Quinn knew the animal was safe and had plenty of attention from Kelly's boys.

Quinn thought about his list and wondered if he had not become a little compulsive during his life as an emotional hermit, as he sometimes thought of himself. Considering he'd spoken about it with Kelly, at least, implied that his depiction was only partially accurate. Quinn quickly learned there was no wrong way to grieve as long as the grieving did not harm others. Routine was one of the ways Quinn found solace, so he rarely obsessed about it.

The benefits of his conventions continued to offset the disadvantages. Dirt or germs did not bother him, so he reasoned that his modest compulsions didn't reach the standard for a mental disorder. Those routines that included maintenance of a neat and well-maintained home, an organized financial plan, and a consistent fitness program had not only kept him healthy, but also seemed to have heightened his powers of observation, which he found particularly helpful in his chosen profession.

Quinn said good-bye to Dierdorf and thanked the Hill clan for their help. He drove the Triumph back to Grand Street to meet the car that would take him to his chartered plane. The past, the present, and the future pervaded his thoughts. Even after a decade, foremost on his mind was an old standard. Sometimes, it was simply a gentle mist in his subconscious. Sometimes, it was a full-blown tempest. Quinn made the short drive from the foothills that surrounded the Warwick Valley to the village. He glanced at the empty passenger seat of his roadster. He remembered the weekends Gina sat in that seat. Her ponytail fluttered in the wind as she rode shotgun in the open-top convertible. She looked like a dream, talking and laughing as they drove the two-lane roads connecting one charming New England village to the next.

A second thought rolling about between Quinn's ears was much more self-directed. He was entirely at ease with his rules and codes, even if those rules and codes approached the fine line between mental health and compulsion. Because he lived the way he did, he sensed things about people that had always made him successful in business and with his personal relationships. Because he made the decisions he did, Quinn continued to find meaning in the world and an ability to live a productive life. "If there is a heaven and a person's stay there is determined by the attitude a person has when he or she departs this world," Quinn thought again to himself, "then I know there are almost a dozen people who will enjoy eternity more than they otherwise would have."

Quinn believed the routines to which he clung so tightly would help him to make one more person's life just a little better. At least, he hoped so. He thought about Skylar. Since that night at dinner, Quinn could not get her out of his mind. In an attempt to keep himself objective, he told himself his thoughts were only his mind focusing on a single purpose. Didn't this sort of thing happen every time he started with a new Dream Seeker? Quinn didn't want to allow himself to believe something else happened when Skylar walked into that restaurant.

As he pulled the car past the waiting black Lincoln and into the garage, Quinn's mind drifted toward the reality and he checked himself. "Jeez, Quinn. What future can there be? She's terminal."

CHAPTER 27

Like a lot of people her age, Katie never had to face any of life's more unpleasant realities. Katie grew up in a family that provided all the love and support a person could imagine. Although she worked for it, Katie had a great job as an elementary school teacher and a barmaid gig that was more like play than work. She had a fiancé who she loved and who loved her back. Other than a few distant relatives who died after living full lives and a few people Katie was distantly acquainted who'd experienced misfortune or illness, none were close enough to Katie to have a meaningful effect.

After Skylar met Quinn the previous week, the truth hit like a tornado in a trailer park. Skylar had become a close friend. When Skylar left that night, Katie suddenly understood that very soon her friend would probably die. That realization was a lot for Katie to absorb. The reality became starkly evident as Katie drove to the airport.

Skylar and Katie walked to the back of the car, removed the luggage, and set it on the pavement. The moisture in their breath condensed and dispersed into the cold morning air. Skylar had an agenda as she arranged the bags on the curb. Not only did she want to make it easy to move through the terminal, she also wanted to give Katie a moment to compose herself. Skylar recognized her scheme was hopeless as a tear rolled down Katie's cheek. She opened her arms, hugged Katie, cried, and hugged some more. Finally, Katie said, "Be careful, Skylar. Have fun. And, I want you to know I love you." Channels of tears widened on their cheeks.

"Thank you, Katie. Thank you for everything. I'll call you in a couple days to let you know how things are going."

A muffled laugh escaped through Katie's tears. "I hoped you would. I expect you at my wedding in June. I want you to be a bridesmaid."

"I wouldn't miss it for the world."

Skylar turned, grabbed her luggage, and walked confidently away from Katie toward the terminal. Katie stood motionless. She watched her friend disappear through the glass doors. Then, Skylar was swallowed by the throng of travelers inside. Katie stood a moment longer. She warmed her hands in her pockets. Finally, she opened the car door and pulled herself back behind the wheel. She put the car in gear and maneuvered from the two-deep line into the flow of traffic. As soon as she could, Katie pulled into gas station, parked the car away from the pumps, and began to cry all over again.

CHAPTER 28

Compared to major airports in the United States and the rest of the civilized world, V.C. Bird International seemed downright primitive. Quinn and Skylar walked down the stairs from the charter onto the tarmac. A tropical breeze welcomed them and contrasted the piercing cold from which they had come. Quinn tipped the copilot while an airport worker unloaded about the half dozen bags from the hold.

Skylar carried only a purse. Quinn carried nothing, so he reached down and took Skylar's hand. She consented unconsciously and continued toward the building with the sun warm on her face.

On the first leg just after liftoff, Skylar had gone to the lavatory and exchanged her sweater for a white pullover with an embroidered navy pony. She kept the jeans, but changed her boots for sandals, exposing her delightfully manicured blue toenails.

"What a beautiful day," Skylar smiled and surveyed the surroundings. Palm trees, low-growing brush, and stone outcrops enveloped the tiny airport runway. The size of the terminal was not as remarkable as was the openness of the structure or the customs agents' seeming disinterest. The doors and windows in the airport were open. More than that, there was no glass in the windows, doors, or screens. Considering essentially every flight that arrived at V.C. Bird International Airport was an international flight, this was the only terminal in the small airport. Only two customs stations were occupied, and neither was busy. The agents chatted cheerfully with one another in an unintelligible English dialect.

The customs agent's eyes were wide and welcoming as Quinn and Skylar approached her station. She smiled and asked in a tempered accent, "You must be Mr. Quinn and you Miss Skylar?" Both Quinn and Skylar looked curiously at the agent, then at each other, and then back to the agent.

With a hearty laugh, the agent answered the unasked question, "It's a small island. News travels fast about the man who rented the villa in Half Moon Bay. Besides, Miss Amelie hired my sister, Afeefah, to cook for you."

Quinn laughed along with the agent, "You caught us off guard a little." He looked at Skylar, whose expression was either curious or stunned.

As if it were the answer to a riddle, the agent offered her name, "Lucianne," and after a few routine questions, the responses to which Lucianne had clearly already known, she said finally, "Enjoy your stay on my island."

The luggage passed separately through on the other side of a partially partitioned lane. Skylar looked back with just a little anxiety.

"Don't worry," Quinn assured. "Amelie has taken care of everything."

Once the bags were through and the two newest visitors to Antigua were on their way to ground transportation, Skylar excused herself to the ladies' room. Once there, Skylar opened her purse and took out a bottle of water, which she thought to herself she wouldn't have been able to carry on a commercial flight. She swallowed two Percocets and rejoined Quinn, who stood midway between the restroom and the terminal exit.

Amelie hadn't told Quinn anything about the extra prescriptions. She didn't need to. Skylar had given no indication that her pain was mounting, but Quinn assumed it was. He'd walked this road more than a few times. So, when he saw Skylar's smiling face as she opened the door, Quinn asked, "Everything all right?"

"Sure is," Skylar replied as she slid her purse back onto her left shoulder, grabbed Quinn's hand with her right, and walked outside to a waiting car.

A middle-aged, dreadlocked man wearing khaki shorts and a light, white, short-sleeve button-down shirt closed the trunk after loading the luggage. The man smiled broadly, opened the door to the backseat of the Grand Vitara, and declared, "Welcome to Antigua, Miss Skylar and Mr. Quinn. I am Stephenson Gregory, and I am at your service. Please call me what my mother calls me, 'Sonny.'"

CHAPTER 29

Half Moon Bay is about twelve miles as the crow flies from V.C. Bird, but there isn't a direct route from origination to destination. Unlike many islands, Antigua has no road that spans the perimeter, so Sonny drove through little inland burghs. The architecture of the old homes in Pares, Betty's Hope, and Newfield were borrowed from a number of European and African styles and influences. Although Antigua is about five times the size of Manhattan, the sparse traffic enabled Sonny to navigate efficiently. The car arrived in Half Moon Bay after only twenty-five minutes. As Sonny pulled the SUV into the driveway, Quinn thought, "Amelie really outdid herself."

Skylar caught her breath. She'd been quiet during most of the trip, but she reasoned her behavior was well within tolerances for someone in her position.

"This is beautiful, Quinn."

Quinn opened the door and helped Skylar out. They headed for the front door as he called over to Sonny, "Do you mind if we explore a little?"

"Not at all a problem, Mr. Quinn," Sonny replied. "I'll grab your bags."

"Please, Sonny, call me Quinn."

"Me, too," added Skylar. "Just Skylar, please."

The villa consisted of a two-story main house. From the foyer, stairs ascended to the bedrooms. To the right facing an east-southeastern view of the Atlantic was a living room, which like all of the other first-floor rooms, had fourteen-foot ceilings trimmed with classic ornamental moldings. Fine hardwoods accented the walls in all of the rooms and the floors were ceramic tile. There was almost as much window as wall. Skylar imagined the sun rising across the sapphire water in the early morning.

Adjacent was an ocean-view dining room, where suppers could enjoy a candle-lit dinner outside on the patio while appreciating the warm ocean breeze. A Yamaha baby grand piano dominated the library. Skylar was giddy when she opened the door to the garage and discovered a beckoning 2009 gray metallic Jaguar XKR convertible.

"Driving that," Skylar started and paused for affect, "will be a lot of fun."

When they swung around toward the back of the house from the garage, Quinn and Skylar met Afeefah, who'd already started dinner.

"*Feef,*" she commanded. "We'll have the best of Antigua and the best of the States. Antiguan lobsters Sonny pulled from the traps just this morning and veal filets. Would you prefer dinner inside or out?"

"Mmm! Outside," Skylar smiled. "Definitely outside."

"Now, don't you worry your little selves about a thing. Feef knows how to take care of you," the sprite, matronly woman announced. "Feef knows everybody on this island. If you need anything, you talk to me. Got it?"

"I know I do, Feef," Quinn nodded.

"Me, too," added Skylar.

"You two run along while Feef finishes her masterpiece," she ordered. "You'll know when I'm ready!"

They emerged from the hall connecting the kitchen and looked in amazement into a large room with a vaulted ceiling. The rear wall was made entirely of tinted glass extending several feet from the house toward the pool. Considering the largest high-definition television either Quinn or Skylar had ever seen, the room was easily identifiable as a playroom. A contemporary entertainment center contained a Pioneer stereo, DVD player, a blue-tooth disc player, and Bose speakers recessed into the walls. Large, comfortable-looking furniture, a pool table, a foosball table, a classic *Playboy* and a *Simpson's* pinball machines, table tennis, a two-player *Fast 'N Furious* video game, and a fully stocked ten-foot mahogany bar ensured plenty of diversion.

A 1,500-square-foot pool deck and a large pool surrounded by waterfalls expanded beyond the playroom. It seemed a bit like overkill, considering it would be unlikely Skylar would want to entertain, but Quinn supposed one never knew. A finger-length, greenish-brown lizard scampered on the ground in front of Skylar and Quinn toward the landscaped flora accenting both the house and the pool.

The deck connected the villa both to the pool and to the bungalow, which seemed to be a little more than a bungalow. Although Skylar and Quinn didn't go in, they could see though the full-length windows a stair-stepper, a cross-trainer, a treadmill, and weight machines. Discretely constructed about fifty yards from the pool area was a cottage that included two separate bedrooms and bathrooms. It was here, Quinn assumed, where Sonny and Afeefah would stay.

As Quinn and Skylar walked the grounds and looked back toward the house against the backdrop of the Half Moon Bay and the Atlantic Ocean beyond, Skylar said, "My firm had a client who built homes like these."

"That's a narrow market niche."

"Yeah, but a profitable one," Skylar answered. "I was usually the first chair in the client's actions, so I learned a lot about these houses."

"Look at where this house was built," Skylar continued in a way that was as commanding as it was endearing. "The house is right in the middle of the hurricane belt, but I wouldn't give it a second thought. The water out there, the beach, and this house are sheltered from the weather by these bluffs and hills. I'd bet that boats would even be okay out there. The house is tucked in; the winds are first blunted by the crest where the house sits and then are deflected by the hills behind. You see? It's safe harbor."

Quinn smiled and wondered how this woman could be alone at this time in her life. "Yes, I see."

"The builder didn't take any shortcuts either. Did you notice the pool deck? Those are skid-proof tiles. The walls in the library, office, and living room are native stone. That was smart. It's durable and local, which means the price was right—no international shipping costs."

Skylar realized that she'd begun to ramble. She paused. "Quinn?"

"Yes, Skylar," Quinn answered.

Even though she'd begun to understand just a little bit about Quinn and even though she knew she didn't have to, Skylar said, "Thank you."

Quinn avoided any modesty. He knew Skylar understood the arrangement. She was a strong personality, but a vulnerable soul. He knew she had neither the time nor the inclination for anything less than genuineness. In the context of their relationship, one which could easily be interpreted to be artificial, Skylar recognized Quinn had done it right. Completely. Absolutely. Without question. Quinn went all in for her, and she wanted him to know that she knew.

"You're welcome, Skylar," was Quinn's straightforward reply. Then, he said, "Why don't we head back to the house and clean up for dinner?"

"Great idea, Quinn. Let's go."

To avoid concern about sleeping arrangements, Quinn subtly broached the subject, "You get first pick of bedrooms. I think there are two that have ocean view. So, don't feel guilty about your choice, all right?"

Up to now, Quinn had been something more than a perfect gentleman.

He had been a perfect partner. Skylar appreciated the gesture, but had not yet completely considered how to proceed when it came to beds. She thought that she should've known Quinn would handle the situation with tact.

    She laughed and looked at Quinn. Skylar thought, "Where did this guy come from?" She said, "I bet there isn't a bad view in this place."

CHAPTER 30

Skylar and Quinn went in through the back kitchen door and found Feef and Sonny laughing and teasing one another. Sonny had a bottle of Coca-Cola in his hand. Feef looked toward the couple as if she was on stage and two new players had entered. Keeping with the script's cadence, she looked over to Skylar, adjusted her diction, and passionately objected to an injustice, "Can you believe this man here trying to tell Feef how to do her job? Especially considering this man has never eaten anything better than horse meat, much less cooked it!"

Amused, Skylar giggled, but before she could respond, Sonny countered, "Ah! It should be a man to do the cooking! Good meat needs to be spiced, just like a good woman!"

Feef grabbed a damp dish towel, quickly rolled it, and threw it at Sonny across the butcher block island. Quinn realized these two would probably enjoy sharing the cottage house if they hadn't already done so.

"You'd better be cautious, Stephenson Gregory! Hell hath no fury and you may not get another morsel from Feef's kitchen!"

The show could have continued indefinitely, Quinn thought, but before he could intrude on the spontaneous theater, Skylar interjected, "I'll do you a favor, Sonny, and get you out of this kitchen before Feef turns you into a casserole. Are our bags upstairs?"

"No, Miss Skylar, uh, I mean Skylar," Sonny corrected himself. "I left the bags in the entry because I didn't know which room you wanted."

"Well, why don't we head upstairs and figure it out. And, remember that I saved your life here today," Skylar added.

"None too soon that man does some work around here," Feef scowled.

Skylar and Quinn each had three pieces of luggage. At the front door, Sonny grabbed two of Skylar's bags while Quinn took Skylar's other bag and one of his own. Leading the way, Sonny explained that all three bedrooms had a view of the water.

At the top of the stairs, the room on the left was situated so that the king-size bed headboard was against the wall that the bedroom shared with the hallway. Like the hallway, the bedroom floor was covered with new mushroom-colored carpet. A nightstand on both sides of the bed, an armoire, a dresser, a love seat, chair, end table, and coffee table gave the room the feel more of a comfortable long-stay hotel. The style was contemporary, but the furniture was black elm. A few pieces of hanging art were likely locally produced islandscapes and were apt complements. The walk-in closet and the spacious bathroom, complete with marble floor tiles and marble walls were located opposite the windows.

Like the rest of the house, the bathroom was impressive as much for the materials as for the conveniences it contained, including "his 'n' her" everything. The whirlpool bathtub was large enough for two and included a side-opening door for easy access. The three-sided glass shower doubled as a steam room. The bench helped to make longer stays there more comfortable. All of the fixtures were two-toned stainless and brass and at least as aesthetic as they were utilitarian.

When a person lay in the bed, he or she could only see the property grounds that spread toward the sunrise and the backdrop of hills and outcrops that encased the property. But, when enjoying either the love seat or chair or while standing at the foot of the bed, a person could see that same side of Half Moon Bay.

Skylar stood with arms comfortably crossed in front of the window wall opposite the door side of the bed. "Quinn, look at this. It's incredible," she said looking out toward the ocean.

Quinn smiled. He wanted Skylar to have beauty all around, and Quinn's instincts were usually good. Of course, he couldn't be sure if his vision for his Dream Seeker would achieve the standard of sheer perfection or whether it would merely be just fine. Quinn realized that his intuition was right. "It sure is," Quinn agreed. "Come on. Let's look at the other bedrooms."

The next room was similar in size and arrangement, although the style of the furniture was more classic. The king-size bed included both a headboard and a footboard which, like the rest of the furniture, were dark cherry. The closet and bathroom were nearly identical to those in the first bedroom. Like the first bedroom, oil paintings hung on the walls, but the subjects matched the furnishings. The subjects appeared to be examples of the early Victorian architecture that typifies the official buildings and residences on the island. Quinn and Skylar saw a few examples in the towns as they rode from the airport. While the Victorian-style construction can been observed in almost any city and town in the United States, islanders have their own interpretation. The angles seem just a little sharper, but the most obvious adaptation is the color: lavenders, yellows, greens, blues, oranges, and various shades of red are not uncommon. The preeminent feature of the room, though, was its spectacular panoramic view of the beach, the bay in the forefront against a backdrop of the "tip of the moon" and the ocean beyond.

The villa that Amelie found for Quinn and his Dream Seeker was one built for comfort and for recreation. Skylar didn't even have to see the last bedroom before she asked, "Sonny, would you mind bringing my bags in here?"

"Yes ma'am!" a broad-grinned Sonny affirmed. "You have very good taste, Miss Skylar. This is the best room in the house!"

Skylar good-naturedly reproved, "From now on, MIS-ter Gregory, if you insist on referring to me as Miss Skylar, you'll have to pay me a quarter!"

"Okay! Okay! Since I don't even have two quarters to rub together, I promise it will not happen again, Skylar."

Quinn already headed toward the end of the hall. Skylar joined him a moment later. With her hands playfully tucked into her front pockets, she asked, "Hey, figure out where you're sleeping?"

"I think so," Quinn answered.

The last of the bedrooms was similar to the other two, but, the furnishings were far more informal. The bed, stands, and sitting furniture were pine. The cushions were big and puffy. Again, the paintings were originals, but this time the subjects included local sportsmen playing soccer and rugby, reeling in a trophy marlin, or driving a sports car on a narrow island street.

Sonny had just come in with Quinn's bags. "I knew this would be your room, Quinn. You looked to me like the laid-back sort of guy. You're the sort of fellow who falls in love with the island. You'd better mind yourself. You'll never leave!"

"You're already too late," Quinn smiled. "I already don't want to leave."

"I knew that. I knew that," Sonny repeated. "And I also know that you both had better get ready for Feef's dinner. She'll be a fright if you're not down when her food is ready. She claims that unlike wine, but like her affections, her food is at the peak of flavor when she serves it."

Skylar smiled. "I need to freshen up a little. Do you think it will be okay if I am down in about a half an hour, Sonny?"

"I think that would be perfectly fine, Skylar," Sonny carefully answered as he reached into his pocket and checked for anything from the U.S. Mint.

"Are you all set in there, Skylar?" Quinn asked.

"Hey, now. That's my job," Sonny interrupted.

"Everything is just perfect," Skylar replied. "But you know what? I'd love an Absolut and tonic. Could you ask Feef to bring one up, Sonny?"

"It would be my pleasure."

CHAPTER 31

An ocean breeze teased Skylar's hair as she sipped her wine. Quinn imagined Skylar's hair, bleached a little blonder on her bronze shoulders after a few days on the beach. Her hair wouldn't lighten today. The table was already shaded. Although they couldn't see it from the veranda, the sun hovered above the hill behind the villa. Three orchids were delicately arranged in a vase that sat slightly off center on the table. Waves broke against the white-sand beach. Quinn struggled to take his eyes from Skylar as she looked at the ocean. It was not the first time Quinn thought a woman was a work of art.

It was a disjointed thought. As Quinn looked at Skylar, he couldn't help himself. Whether there existed an omnipotent being that created the Heavens and the Earth, Quinn considered the possibility that there were actually real life angels. After all, the early custodians of the planet like those people who wrote the books of the Torah and the Bible believed there was something greater happening around them. Those peoples were a part of it but could not fully describe it. So, they explained it with words and in art. Quinn recalled his Catholic school education when his sixth-grade religion teacher tried to explain angels to the class. With the innocence of a child, the old nun began, "The Bible tells us that angels are very much like human beings, except they don't have free will. Angels aren't capable of sin because they cannot choose who or what they are. They simply are."

"Maybe that old nun was onto something," Quinn thought. "Some people simply are. They can't alter their behavior at least as it pertains to specific aspects of their lives. If a person is born with the gift of a voice and if that person also has the desire to sing, he or she cannot do anything but to make people happy using that gift. Quinn briefly thought of Noelia. In Skylar's case, simply being full of beauty and warmth was her gift. It made her an angel. Regardless of the gift, those people, those angels, cannot help but make other people feel happiness."

Quinn broke the silence, "You've been quiet since we left Chicago this morning, Skylar. Is everything all right?"

"Yes. Yes, it is, Quinn," Skylar answered distantly. "Well, that's not completely true. I'm just a little anxious, I guess."

Quinn was troubled but not surprised. Quinn knew Skylar was processing a lot of information. Considering her illness and new surroundings, she'd done pretty well. Still, every person copes differently and at their own pace. There was nothing Quinn could do about that. He learned long ago the best thing he could do was to listen and support. There was a lot Quinn could do for Skylar, but solving her problems was not one of them. It was then that Quinn noticed Skylar really only picked at Feef's dinner. It could have just been a long day of traveling, but Quinn knew that a lack of appetite wasn't usually a positive development. "Do you want to talk about it?"

Skylar started cautiously, "It's nothing really." She reminded herself that if there had ever been a place or a time when she had nothing to lose, this was the one.

"Actually," she began again, "There are a few things. None of them have anything to do with you. You've been wonderful. In no particular order, though, I'm getting accustomed to my surroundings, which are amazing by the way. But, it's a little overpowering. After the times in my life when something overwhelmed me, I've become exhausted, but not in a physical way. It's hard to explain, but the exhaustion is more emotional. This, all of this, is right up there among the most overwhelming. Then, of course, there was the travel. Moving from one place to another is also tiring in the physical sense. We crossed a time zone or two, so my body clock is out of whack. I think there's something about a body moving so far so fast, from a cold climate to a temperate one, that just takes a lot of energy."

"I think you're onto something there, Skye." Quinn added. He realized he'd unintentionally referred to her in a familiar way and wasn't sure if that was a good thing or bad. Quinn thought nicknames were like the personal space around a person's body. You didn't go there unless you were supposed to be there, unless you'd been invited.

Skylar smirked playfully, "Skye, huh? I like it. Although you would have thought so, no one has ever called me that. Hearing you say it, it sounds right."

"Honestly, I really didn't mean to, but I'm glad it's okay," Quinn replied with genuine self-consciousness.

"No, really. It's all right. I like it," Skylar assured him before she shifted to a new topic. "Anyway, the other thing is, Quinn, I'm scared. I am not second guessing my decision, but I am afraid. I am afraid of the pain. I am afraid of what I don't know."

"Hmm," Quinn paused. "I can't begin to feel what you feel, but I think most people are anxious about the unknown."

"I know, but, for me the unknown is not years ahead or miles down the road. For me, the unknown is just down the block. It's around the corner. I can feel it, Quinn. I can literally feel it."

Quinn winced, "I thought so. I couldn't quite put my finger on it, but I thought you might be in pain."

"It's not the primary site at all. I don't hurt where I thought I would. As a matter of fact, if it were not for my lower back, I still might not actually know I'm sick, other than the doctor's diagnosis of this Little Bastard I mean," Skylar clarified.

Quinn knew what she meant.

"The pain in my lower back where the cancer metastasized came on suddenly. I've been eating Percocets like Pez," Skylar admitted. "Between the pain and the Pez, not to mention the emotional and physical exhaustion and of course the whole fear thing, I'm just not myself."

"I'm sorry. I wish there was more that I could do."

Skylar replied after taking another sip from her glass, "You're doing fine. You're doing more than fine. Actually, I even feel all right after I take a few Percocets. I took some before I came down for dinner."

Quinn understood that Skylar may be abusing the painkillers, although it would not really have mattered very much. Still, the word, "some," concerned him. It meant that Skylar needed more than one, maybe more than two, to get relief, and he worried she would soon not be able to manage it at all.

"I was about to suggest a walk on the beach or a drive," Quinn said as the silhouetted shade from the house crept further toward the shore.

"Either would be wonderful, but I want to get to bed early tonight. I know I'll feel better tomorrow," Skylar said.

"You'll let me know if there is anything I can do, right?" Quinn asked.

"I will. Actually, can I have a pitcher of water?" Skylar answered as she stood up.

"Sure," Quinn said.

"And, Quinn?"

"Yes, Skye," Quinn said.

"Thank you. Again," said Skylar as she gave him a peck on his cheek, more affectionate than passionate.

As Quinn watched Skylar walk across the patio, he felt something more than the familiar pang of his own helplessness. "It would have been very easy to fall in love with this woman," Quinn thought.

CHAPTER 32

"Is everything all right?" Sonny asked a moment later. Quinn hadn't even noticed Sonny had come out onto the patio. Sonny repeated, "Quinn, is everything all right?"

Snapping his attention back, Quinn finally answered, "Oh, yes. Yes, everything's fine. Skylar is just a little tired from the trip. She went up to get some sleep."

"Good. I was worried there was a problem, and when you have Mr. Stephenson Gregory, it's no problem."

Quinn was amused by the inclination of the locals, at least the few with whom he was familiar, to speak about themselves in the third person.

"I'm sure there will be none, Sonny," Quinn assured. "Would you mind asking Feef to bring a pitcher of ice water to Skylar's room?"

"Not at all, Quinn," Sonny agreed.

As soon as Sonny disappeared through the patio door, Quinn reached into his pocket. He pressed two buttons on his phone and sent his request through a series of satellites and relays. After a moment, Quinn heard the phone connect to another phone several latitude degrees to the north and a few longitude degrees to the west. Another moment later, Amelie answered, "Hi, Quinn. I hadn't expected to hear from you so soon. You must've decided that you wanted that time machine, eh?"

"First of all, Sunshine, you really made this thing work down here. The villa is phenomenal. It's perfect. Sonny's great and we just enjoyed Feef's version of steak and lobster. Nice job."

"I'm glad, Quinn. Thanks," Amelie already knew Quinn would like the arrangements, but it was still nice to hear him say so.

"And, no, I do not need anything quite so difficult," Quinn mocked. "I do need something very specific, and I need it before the sun rises."

"Skylar took the first room on the right, didn't she?"

Quinn wondered how Amelie could've known so much about the house, having only been asked to find it three days earlier. He knew better than to ask her to divulge any of her secrets, though.

"Of course, there's not a bad view in the place. Let's take a break from patting ourselves on the back," Quinn teased. "Let me tell you what I need."

On cue, Sonny reemerged and walked across the patio to Quinn, still looking past the creeping shadows toward the ocean.

"According to Feef, Miss Skylar has everything she needs," Sonny reported proudly.

Quinn answered, "Thank you, Sonny."

Then, although he already knew the answer to the question, Quinn asked, "Do you have plans for this evening?"

"No. Sonny Gregory is at your disposal any time of the day or night."

"That means a lot to me," Quinn said appreciatively. "I have an errand for you."

CHAPTER 33

Skylar's thoughts raced. She thought about the five steps she'd learned years earlier in some undergraduate psychology class. "What were they? Denial. Then, anger. Then what? Bargaining, maybe? Depression? She knew the last one was, acceptance." Skylar thought that she'd breezed through "denial" and "anger" the day Dr. Walter gave her the diagnosis. Actually, there was more anger than denial. Given the previous diagnosis and treatment, it wasn't a stretch for her to understand the gravity of the results. Regardless, the outburst in the oncologist's office did actually include a bit of denial.

Taylor helped her get some closure on the anger step. Maybe even on the bargaining part, too. She neither reasoned with God nor offered a deal to the Devil. She believed that she had nothing about which to apologize, so she hadn't promised to become a better person. "I am good enough the way I am," she thought.

She'd be damned if she'd enable Taylor Kerr or continue to subsidize his miserable existence. Some people are net contributors to the good of the world and others are net detractors. There was no question of Taylor's category. If she wouldn't be allowed to be a part of the world, at least Taylor wouldn't as easily be able to make it any worse. In a peculiar way, Taylor helped her to take another step toward accepting the reality fate created for her.

Skylar stood naked before the mirror. It was hard not to notice the weight-loss. Unlike the preference of the stereotypical thirty-something, being the incredible shrinking woman was not a good thing. Her ribs were more evident and the suppleness of her breasts and her backside had been replaced by a hint of androgyny. It was true the travel and stress affected her appetite, but the Percocets were the more likely culprit. The pharmacist told her about the side effects of opiates, including nausea and decreased appetite, among a few other equally unpleasant consequences. The pills she needed to get relief weren't helping with anything other than the pain, and that benefit had marginally decreased even as the number of pills increased.

After Feef brought up the pitcher of ice water and returned downstairs, Skylar settled into a hot bath and turned on the whirlpool. The swirling water coursed around her back and legs, relaxing her muscles and disguising the ache that had crested a few minutes earlier. After the bath, she stepped into the sauna and sat on the marble bench. As her stresses and anxieties emptied from her pores in the form of droplets of salty perspiration, Skylar doubled over, resting her elbows on her knees, placed both hands over her face, and allowed herself for the first time to purge her emotions, at least temporarily.

"The rest of my life," Skylar mouthed the words as the tears streamed down her face. Skylar remembered the not-too-distant past when those words connoted some hazy idea of time that seemed like an eternity. If the phrase wasn't the practical equivalent of forever, it certainly suggested ample time to travel, to write, to create music and art, to share love with someone who deserved it, to construct a life that yielded something greater than just herself and one other person, like children. She wanted to watch those children grow in that mysterious equation in which one plus one equaled something far greater than two. She wanted to grow old with that person and watch in humor and horror as their bodies aged and slowly became ridiculously useless.

Rinsing away the perspiration and tears, Skylar opened the shower door and released a plume of steam into the bathroom. The exhaust fan struggled to manage the moisture. It reminded Skylar of the fog on cool summer mornings on the Lake Michigan beach front. Droplets of water condensed on the walls, mirrors, and fixtures as the edges of the cloud interacted with the air-conditioned stone and porcelain.

Using her hand, Skylar rubbed away the condensation from the mirror and dropped her towel to the floor. She took stock. For possibly the first time since her diagnosis, certainly since the time she first made the decision to contact Quinn Powers, Skylar felt at peace. Her body and her mind downshifted. The tension in her head and face released. The pressure in her neck and shoulders slackened. The hostility and resentment she harbored toward Taylor, her parents, her brother, and the decisions she had always felt compelled to make, were abruptly liberated. Skylar experienced a catharsis as an indefinable sense of acceptance engulfed her. She stepped forward to wipe the mirror again after the humidity obscured her image. She reflected with some amazement what she achieved in such a short period of time. With his gentle, supportive, and perceptive way, Quinn led her to a path where she saw more clearly than ever where she could achieve a degree of fulfillment that had up to then eluded her. It hadn't been twelve hours since the chartered jet left Chicago, and she already understood the path she had to take. Of course, Skylar still needed to walk the path herself, but Quinn showed her the way. She'd become unbounded from the constraints that previously prevented her from doing those things she wanted, those things she needed to do. Finally, she understood that there were no constraints. There were no limits. Her mind was free to go anyplace it wished and her body could follow. There were no repercussions. There would be none. She could simply be.

"Quinn," Skylar mouthed to her image in the mirror. "How had he done this? This place? The way he looks at me?" As Skylar towel dried, brushed her damp hair, and slid into her cream-colored silk pajama shorts and top, her mind drifted. Sure, he was attractive, but there was something else. Her fantasy. Her dream. Liberation. No repercussions.

Skylar wasn't sure how much of it was the bath, the sauna, the cry, or Quinn, but even the pain in her back had seemed to have subsided a little. Not so much, she realized, to neglect her medication, but better.

As she took more Percocets with a swallow of water, Skylar settled into her bed, which she found comfortable and surprisingly familiar. She fell asleep almost immediately after she closed her eyes, dreaming of a freedom she'd never known and a man who seemed to have changed the rest of her life.

CHAPTER 34

The sun rose over a cerulean sea under a cloudless sky. He sat alone on the patio and quietly enjoyed a breakfast consisting of three soft-boiled eggs, whole-wheat toast, Colombian coffee, and a smoothie made with strawberries, plantain, and soy milk.

Dierdorf wasn't available to stick his wet nose in Quinn's face, but Quinn didn't easily break routine. He woke early and took advantage of the exercise room. After a brisk three-mile run on the treadmill and twenty minutes with the kettle bells, he practiced the Taekwondo *Tae Guek* forms. The *Pal Gues* would have to wait until tomorrow. Quinn was simultaneously relaxed and energized after he sweated in the sauna and showered.

After he ate, Quinn read the *Wall Street Journal* and warmed his coffee with the decanter on the table. Like he often did, he allowed his thoughts to go to the places they wanted to go. Ocean waves created almost a hypnotic rhythm while an assemblage of frigate birds cackled and blended into white noise. Quinn's breathing slowed to a comfortable even pace and his heart rate decreased to less than one beat per second. He never worried where his mind would take him. He always embraced the journey.

Even though Quinn had long ago left the world of finance and investing, he'd discovered the *Journal* provided comprehensive and detailed news and analysis. Considering a forty-fourth president of the United States would be inaugurated in just a few days, analysis of the economy, tax policy, social policy, and foreign relations dominated each section. "Of course," Quinn mused, "everything came back to money."

Quinn's mind circled back to his little table for two, where he sat alone on the patio of the multimillion-dollar villa facing Half Moon Bay on a paradise island. As he wondered whether the world financial crisis contributed to Amelie's ability to get this place, Quinn lowered the *Journal* to turn the page. His trance was broken when a vision appeared before him almost as if it had divinely transubstantiated.

THE DREAM SEEKER

"You must have been deep in thought," Skylar stood before him wearing khaki shorts, a blue pullover, light leather sandals, and a broad grin. "I'll bet I was here for a minute and I even heard you whispering to yourself. You're really cute, you know."

It didn't happen often, but Quinn flushed just a little.

Skylar sat down with an energy that her body had clearly lacked just hours earlier. She playfully asked, "So, what were you talking about and, more important, did you answer yourself?"

"Well, if you must know, nothing terribly interesting, I was just thinking about the dynamics of the geoeconomic environment," Quinn replied with equal parts honesty and impishness, "But, now you're here, I have a much more appealing subject to ponder."

"Aw, you're such a charmer," Skylar answered. "I didn't know you could get the *Wall Street Journal* down here. I mean, I know you can get it most places in the world, but here?"

Looking down toward her place setting, Skylar found in addition to the china plate, coffee cup and saucer, fine silverware, and linen napkin, a clear plastic bag containing something wrapped in acid-free paper. Picking it up, Skylar realized that whatever the bag contained, it was too small to be a newspaper and too light to be this month's edition of *Cosmopolitan*. "What's this?"

"It's nothing, really," Quinn answered innocently. "Just some light reading."

After gently parting the opening at the top of the bag, Skylar slipped her hand in and slid out the contents. She gasped as she pulled back the brown, protective paper.

"Quinn! You have got to be kidding!" She looked down upon a pristine copy of the first issue of *The Amazing Spider-Man*.

Quinn grinned casually as if he were the tomcat that ate the canary.

"Quinn! This is the very first issue, #1—March of 1963! Do you have any idea how hard this is to find?"

"Well, yes. Actually, I do have a little bit of an idea," Quinn replied.

Skylar was spellbound as she ran her hand down the cover of the comic. "Twelve cents," she whispered unconsciously as she read at the hand-lettered price against the backdrop of a web in the upper-left corner to next to black outlined red letters, "The Amazing Spider-Man."

Skylar had all but forgotten about the conversation she and Quinn had about Spider-Man. If nothing else, she'd written it off to small talk. Obviously, it was something more than idle chatter and Skylar was profoundly moved by the gesture

A small act can fill another person's heart, especially when it is as personal as this. Skylar was only mildly irritated that Quinn's gift caused her eyes to tear. Skylar leaned over the table and kissed Quinn on his cheek. "Thank you, Quinn," she said.

Instinctively, Quinn understood Skylar's emotion in her honest, simple response. "You're welcome." Then after a reasonable silence, Quinn added, "You'd better be careful or you'll stain the cover!"

Skylar managed, "Well, is it any good? The story, I mean."

"It's all right, I guess. Of course, I had to read it. The plot is a little thin; Stan Lee was still trying to feel his way, but Ditko's artwork is classic."

Skylar immediately recognized Stan Lee and Steve Ditko as the writer and artist, respectively, who created Spidey.

"Any time something's created that has as much of an influence on popular culture and the collective conscience, it's a classic," Quinn concluded.

Regaining her composure, Skylar said, "I can't wait to read it!"

"Well, we've got time," Quinn reported, then changed the subject. "By the way, how did you sleep last night?"

"Very well, thank you."

Skylar flipped through the pages of the comic. "I took my time getting to bed. I took a bath and then a sauna. By the time I finished, I was ready to sleep."

Skylar omitted the fact that she downed a bunch of Percocets before she went to bed. Of course, she also failed to mention that she'd awakened at about three o'clock with back pain and needed another bump.

"Sonny should be out in a minute or two with your breakfast, and we can just enjoy the morning here for a while if you want to," remarked Quinn.

"About breakfast, Quinn, I'm not really that hungry. Maybe I can have just a juice or a cup of coffee. Maybe a piece of toast." Nothing really sounded good, but she knew she needed to eat something.

"I hope you don't mind the intrusion, but I know you haven't been hungry," Quinn ventured.

"There's no question about that. I think it's just all the travel and the changes."

"I'm not sure if this will help, but I know some pain meds suppress appetite. That usually happens at a time when a person can least afford to forego nutrition."

"Okay," Skylar said suspiciously and wondered where Quinn would take this.

"Well, I hope you don't mind, but I got something that might help," Quinn reported as he absorbed Skylar's wary gaze. "There is this thing called Fentanyl, and it comes in a patch. It's sort of like a nicotine patch. The way it works is you put in on your skin in a place that's convenient but out of the way. You know, in a place you won't think about it. The patch dispenses pain medication through your skin. You just take the old one off after three days and put the new one on."

Quinn reached into his shirt pocket and handed Skylar a small box. She opened it and pulled out one of the patches. Examining it more closely, Skylar read the tiny black lettering that identified "Fentanyl TD 50 mcg."

As he watched Skylar examine the patch, Quinn continued, "It's Fentanyl *trans-dermal*. That's what the letters 'T' and 'D' mean. The dosage is 50 micrograms. There are a lot of benefits of Fentanyl compared to oral pain killers. In addition to the elimination of the peaks and valleys someone experiences when taking pills, it is unlikely that the Fentanyl will make you nauseous, affect your appetite, or cause other problems."

In spite of herself, Skylar smiled at Quinn's discretion. "It's not enough that I have the Little Bastard to begin with, but it's a pain in the ass, literally!"

Before he continued, Quinn paused, considering the possibility that Skylar's sense of humor would help her when things get more difficult, "On the flipside, the concentration of Fentanyl will not be high enough in your blood stream to have any effect on your pain for about twelve, maybe even fifteen hours. Tonight, you can expect to feel quite a bit better, I think. If the pain becomes more severe, we can use a higher dosage patch or combine patches. If you have breakthrough pain, you can still supplement with the oral prescription. There's really no disadvantage to using both if you need to. The long and the short of it, Skye, is that it will help you cope."

"Christ on a cracker, Quinn! Where did you get these?"

Thoroughly enjoying Skylar's reaction, Quinn knew that Skylar meant, "How did you get these without needing an appointment with a doctor."

"We got it at the American University of Antigua College of Medicine in St. Johns. They're really not uncommon. Not quite so explicitly, we got it the same way we got everything else."

Skylar wanted for a moment to ask more questions, but she realized that in the great scheme of things it really didn't matter. She felt proud that she'd allowed herself to surrender control and not sweat the small stuff. Skylar knew she wasn't alone, which didn't hurt. "I don't know what to say."

"You don't need to say anything, Skye. Really. I'm not sure that you know that you deserve all of this. You do."

Skylar smiled self-consciously.

"I'm not kidding," Quinn assured. "Look. You're beautiful inside and out. You're funny. You're bright. You don't let the ugly part of life prevent you from seeing the pretty part. I can't imagine the forces that conspired to bring you here. What I know, however, is that you've endured the disappointments and you've survived them. Frankly, I don't know how you did it and still remained the incredible person you are. I could tell you that you'll go straight to Heaven because you have already served your Purgatory, if you believe that sort of stuff. Frankly, I'm not sure I do. How about, you've paid your dues and now it's time to take a little out of the kitty? You deserve it and I'm just the one who is lucky enough to be with you when you realize it."

If Skylar was not already speechless, she was after Quinn finished. She never thought of herself that way, much less heard anyone express it quite that way. Seeing her image so clearly reflected back through Quinn's eyes wasn't easy to absorb so suddenly.

Skylar deflected as she unwrapped the first of the Fentanyl patches, "So, where do I stick this thing?"

"Are you playing the straight man, here, because you really set me up with that one," Quinn joked. "Actually, I think most people put it on their shoulder blade. For some reason, though, some people don't get enough of a dose from there. If you don't feel better, then you can put it on either side of your chest."

"Well, will you help me put it on?" Skylar asked hopefully.

"It would be my pleasure," Quinn responded with just the right amount of interest.

Quinn slid back his chair and walked around the table behind Skylar. Without hesitation or a hint of embarrassment, Skylar reached back and lifted her shirt, holding it up at the back of her neck as the fabric gathered under her breasts and exposed her flat tummy in the front and her bare back to Quinn. Quinn peeled the paper from the patch and placed it gently on the upper left part of Skylar's back.

"Thanks," Skylar said as she pulled her shirt back down. "It seems like I am constantly thanking you for something."

Quinn walked back to the other side of the table and took his seat again as Sonny came bounding out of the sliding glass door with a fresh pot of coffee in one hand and a glass of something in the other.

"Good morning, Skylar," Sonny submitted.

"Good morning to you, Sonny."

Quinn briefed Sonny in some very general terms about Skylar's situation, underscoring a reaction to medication rather than revealing her underlying condition. Sonny obviously needed some information, considering he made the trip to St. Johns. It hadn't taken Sonny long to solve the riddle, so he supportively soft sold the contents of the glass.

"Feef made this very special for you this morning, Skylar," Sonny said. "She starts with a just a little bit of soy milk, and adds half a fresh plantain she just bought this morning at the farm market, some chilled strawberries, and just a drop of Antiguan honey and whips it up smooth. Good for the soul."

"Thank you, Sonny," Skylar answered as Sonny placed the glass on the table.

"Would you like some coffee?"

"Yes, please," Skylar smiled. "You and Feef are taking very good care of me, Sonny. I appreciate it."

"'Tis nothing at all," Sonny responded as he poured the fresh, hot coffee into her cup. "You are a guest here on Sonny's island, and this is how Sonny's guests are treated."

Then, to Quinn, Sonny asked, "Will there be anything else right now, Quinn?"

"No thanks, Sonny. This is just perfect," Quinn answered.

"Very good, very good. I'll be back out in a little while to check on you," Sonny said, as he cleared dishes from Quinn's place before he walked back toward the door.

"I hope that wasn't too obvious," Quinn apologized. "First of all, I haven't told Sonny or Afeefah anything about you unless they've absolutely needed to know. As you can see, though, Sonny didn't just fall off the turnip truck.

"I asked Sonny to go to the university hospital last night to get the Fentanyl and when I asked Feef to make you just the smoothie this morning, well, I'm sure they put the pieces together."

"Quinn, I'm long past worrying about what other people think. If I worry about it now, when will I stop? Besides, Sonny and Feef seem like good people. I don't know how much of this I can get down, though." Skylar sighed as she looked at the pink concoction in the glass.

"I'm glad you're okay with the two of them," Quinn said. "As far as your breakfast, just do the best you can. The soy protein will be easy on your stomach and you'll need the other good stuff in there if you want to keep your strength."

"Okay. I'll try," Skylar guiltily reveled in the paternal attention and smiled as she sipped. Upon reflection, Skylar really didn't feel too guilty about how she felt.

CHAPTER 35

Skylar looked down at the shiny, twenty-inch alloy wheels before she slid into the charcoal leather seat of the Jaguar XKR convertible. She adjusted the seat, steering wheel, and mirrors. She hoped that the street department on the island maintained the roads. She looked around and appreciated the patience the craftsmen must have exercised to create the walnut veneer on the dashboard and gear shift.

After Quinn opened the garage door, he planted himself in the passenger seat and grinned widely. "Start her up!" he encouraged.

With her right hand, Skylar gently slid the electronically coded key into the ignition slot. She reached toward the dash and pressed the button that incited the first of millions of tiny explosions in the bellies of the 300 horses under the hood. Skylar felt a surge of exhilaration as the car whinnied to life in her hands.

"Oh my *god*, Quinn!" Skylar said.

"You think that's something? Wait until you get it out on the road!"

Skylar rolled her eyes and replied "Cut it out." Then, Skylar asked, "Where are we going?"

Quinn answered, "We have no place to be and all day to get there. Just drive."

Savoring the anticipation, Skylar hesitated for a moment before she eased the automobile into gear and depressed the accelerator. Like a predator peeking out from its lair, the car emerged from the garage. The pin on the tachometer rose eagerly from its idling peg as Skylar guided the car onto the lightly traveled, paved two-lane road. Quinn saw through tussling blonde hair a devious grin spread across Skylar's face.

CHAPTER

After a few minutes, Skylar broke the blissful silence, "The Spider-Man comic was awesome! The #1. I can hardly believe it."

Quinn smiled, "How'd you like the stories?"

"You were right," Skylar conceded. "The first one, when Spider-Man saves John Jameson's life in the rocket was better than 'The Chameleon.' The premise of Spidey joining the Fantastic Four for money and then letting the Chameleon sucker him was not quite as admirable. It really doesn't matter, though. It's The Amazing Spider-Man—#1! I know it's a silly little diversion, but you realized it was more than that to me. You understood that my silly little distraction is like a security blanket. It's what I'd do and where I'd go in my mind when I had no one and no place else."

Quinn listened. Skylar changed the course of the conversation and maneuvered the car onto a better road. "It's as if you know my soul, Quinn. I know we talked and I answered a bunch of questions for Amelie, but that doesn't completely explain how you seem to know me."

Quinn rationalized, "It's really not difficult to know someone if we really want to. I don't know. I think I listen with my heart as much as I listen with my ears. When I hear something with my heart, I usually act on it. I think some people listen with their hearts but that they either choose not to hear or choose not to act. Maybe some people think it's too dangerous to open up, which is almost a prerequisite for the action part. I can't speak for anyone else, but I think life is too short to mince words or hide ourselves or not share special things we feel."

Processing what she heard, Skylar was as appreciative as she was astonished. These feelings had begun to be commonplace as she thought once again she'd never known anyone in her life as confident without being arrogant, honest without being pretentious. She wanted to understand. "What happened to you, Quinn? I know we almost talked about it, but I think I really need to know."

Recalling their first meeting when Quinn said there was nothing off limits, Skylar already considered the implications of peeking behind the curtain that cloaked Quinn's past. She supposed she could risk her own feelings if Quinn's answer made her uncomfortable. Skylar understood that, in the throes of a schoolgirl crush or even a relatively new relationship, talking about the past can result in resentment, however irrational. Even if it weren't for her terminal situation and she'd met Quinn someplace else, Skylar believed she'd still have wanted to know the events that cast the mold of the man he'd become.

Skylar already established that her passenger was just a little complicated. She wondered whether asking him about his past would affect him in some negative way, but she quickly decided that it wouldn't. She assumed Quinn must have been through this sort of stuff before. More than what might have been, the Quinn Powers who was at that moment patiently enduring her driving that exquisite sports car just a little bit faster than the forty-five-kilometer-per-hour speed limit and dodging the occasional pothole, goat, or stray dog was the sort of guy who'd understand if someone crossed the line a little. Besides, she wasn't shy about how she felt or what she wanted. As Quinn said, this was all about her. If she wanted to talk about Quinn, she would talk about Quinn!

"I can't tell you, Skylar," Quinn answered as if resigned to his decision.

Skylar felt her heart sink. Afraid she'd pressed too personal a subject, Skylar swallowed and caught her breath. "Quinn, I'm sorry I asked if your past is something you don't want to discuss, but I thought you said there was nothing that we couldn't talk about. You said that there were no topics that were off limits."

Quinn sat silently and looked away distractedly.

Emboldening, Skylar continued, "Quinn, I've already said in so many words you're unique. What I am just as curious about, though, is how I feel right now. I want to know you so I can understand me. I've never been to those places in my heart. Frankly, I thought I could never go to those places, but you've unlocked them and held my hand as I walked in. Those places are scary. Those places can be sad. But, you've shown me the forgotten hopes as well as disappointments in a way I can come to terms with constructively. It's unbelievable. I don't understand it and I want to. It's as if I'm learning more about me as every moment passes. I understand more clearly who I am, but I think I need to know who you are so I can open that one more door."

Quinn listened passively.

Skylar caught her breath again and tried to control her disappointment. "Frankly, Quinn, everything you've said to me and done for me, well, everything you seem to be has been wonderful. I have to admit, this is the first time you have fallen short."

Quinn allowed Skylar to finish and said finally, "I'm sorry Skylar. I didn't mean I didn't want to tell you. I just mean that I can't talk about it now."

Skylar didn't understand the reasons Quinn could talk later but not now. They were alone and had nothing but time today. Tomorrow, she couldn't be sure, but today, they had time.

Skylar almost implored, "Why, Quinn? Why can't we talk about it now?"

"Well," Quinn said carefully as he glanced at the passenger side mirror, "You're about to be introduced to one of Antigua's finest. I think he caught you speeding."

CHAPTER 37

Skylar giggled as the policeman walked back to his car. "It's sort of funny, you know. I really don't have to pay this. One of the benefits of terminal illness is never having to say you're sorry or pay traffic tickets!"

"Truer words have not been spoken." Quinn enjoyed Skylar's perspective.

"It's not that I am style obsessed, but I think the Royal Police of Antigua and Barbuda could benefit from a fashion consultant. Why do second-and third-world countries insist on their police looking like second-or third-world hooligans?" Skylar watched the constable in the rearview mirror.

"You think those are bad? You should see the Rhode Island State Police," Quinn said.

Skylar laughed.

"Pumpkin-colored, leather knee-boots, matching assorted straps positioned strategically around the body, slacks, shirt, and cap in a blue that is just a little too distinctive, all trimmed in another orangey-brown, a silver badge above the left breast and on the cap, and a utility belt that would be the envy of any comic book hero," Quinn continued.

"Stop it! You're killing me!" Skylar screamed. "Stop! Please!"

"When one stops you, you're not sure if you're going to get a ticket or a proposition!"

"No, seriously," Skylar said in spasms of laughter as tears streamed down her face. The policeman pulled back onto the road and looked curiously at the Jaguar. The officer's expression was priceless, and it reignited Skylar's laughter all over again.

Skylar caught her breath, "I haven't laughed for a very long time. You're really funny!"

"It feels great to let it all go like that, doesn't it?"

"Yeah," Skylar said. "You really had me going there."

"Did you see the look on his face?"

"No. Not about that, you knucklehead. You really had me thinking that you wouldn't talk about it," Skylar said, slightly embarrassed. "And then, Christ on a cracker! You let me ramble on like I was a crazy old cat lady!"

"Well, I was enjoying the show. You know, you blathering on as the cop pulled out of his little hiding place back there. Of course, I was too polite to interrupt!" Quinn added.

"Cut it out, now," Skylar replied in a growly, playful voice. "Since you put me through all that, you have to tell me your story."

"Of course, I will, but let's get one thing straight, Danica Patrick," Quinn said. "It was you who put you through that, although admittedly, I was a willing accomplice."

"Let's not split hairs here. Get on with it."

CHAPTER 38

It hadn't seemed like an hour. Quinn said he was both a pretty good listener and a pretty good talker. She could understand his assessment as he recounted his life before Life Dreams. Skylar listened as Quinn told the wonderful, agonizing details of his marriage, baseball, Kelly, Gina's work, Quinn's work, Amelie, their home, Warwick, Gina's illness, the miscarriage, her treatments, and finally her last days. Absorbed by the heartbreaking story, Skylar began to more deeply connect with the man who patiently opened his life like a book simply because she'd asked.

"After I had dispositioned—you know, corporate-speak for sold—my book of business to Amelie and Kelly," Quinn continued, "I was utterly by myself. No Gina. No clients. It was my choice, but I'd never been alone like that. Of course, I leaned on Kelly. I can't imagine a better friend. He stood by me, both figuratively and literally, the whole time. At the wake and funeral, Kelly was there. When I needed to talk or fight, Kelly was the perfect conversationalist or sparring partner. Of course, I had my family. My parents and my sister were amazing, but they were a thousand miles away. They wanted to help more, and I love them for the things they tried to do. For Gina's parents and for Michael, I was their support, but I really didn't mind.

"The fact remained that I was alone in obvious and in subtle ways. Although I liked Warwick, I had a dilemma. I couldn't be there alone and I didn't want anyone else there with me. There were too many memories just then and too many things I needed to sort out. With my clients safely transferred, I asked Kelly's parents to keep an eye on my house. Then, less than three months after Gina died, I was on a plane to Europe with a backpack, a few essentials, a laptop, passport, three thousand dollars in cash, and my American Express card. I didn't leave home without it or without my dog, Dierdorf. Our first stop was the UK, where the animal quarantine laws are insufferable. Fortunately, a friend made some inquiries on my behalf, and expedited the process. What could have taken months became just a few days before Dierdorf and I could start our journey.

"Gina and I didn't really believe in traveling for its own sake. It's hard to explain, but we thought that living in a place was actually the best way to know the place. The only exception was going somewhere for recreation or relaxation, like a beach or a hidden cabin in the mountains. We'd always been able to find that sort of stuff pretty close to home, though. Anyway, my point is, we'd never traveled to Europe," Quinn concluded.

"I didn't actually break my rule. I went there to come to terms with my life and, even though I didn't live in one place, I lived in Europe. I went to a place where I'd be unlikely to see anyone who knew me and I wouldn't see a commercial, hear a radio program, or see a billboard, newspaper, or magazine that would remind me of Gina. South America. Asia. Mars. It really didn't matter." Quinn explained, "I started in the UK, because I knew the language. In high school and in college, I took French, but it had been a long time since I'd used it."

"My time in the UK was productive, for lack of a better word. It was a good place to start. I didn't exactly rough it. My typical day started early. Remember, I only had a few changes of clothes, so some days started with laundry. As soon as I was ready, I checked out and just went out into the world. Dierdorf came with me everywhere. He looked menacing, but he's really just a teddy bear. It usually didn't take long for people to realize that he was trained and very gentle. Then I had breakfast and I talked to people. I walked through towns and villages, and I talked to people. I stopped at a pub, and I talked to people. You get the picture. I talked to people. Actually, I listened. I've always been able to connect with people. I like to think it had more to do with my country charm than it did anything I actually had to say," Quinn joked.

"When people asked about me, I told the truth even though I controlled the information. I told them that I'd played professional baseball, and I then had to explain the farm system. Even though I was only a minor leaguer, a lot of Brits were impressed. You'd be surprised how many people in England follow the Yankees or at least heard of them. Most folks wanted to know whether I knew Derek Jeter or what I thought of Joe Torre, who a lot of Brits admired. Anyway, I explained that I transitioned to a financial adviser, did all right, and took some time away to see the world. It was a story that satisfied most people. Of course, if a person wasn't interested in baseball or investments, he or she was often intrigued by my travel companion, who sat on the floor contentedly obedient until I decided to move elsewhere.

As Quinn described his experiences or, more accurately, the way he grieved, Skylar listened. Occasionally, she pulled her eyes from the road and stole a glance.

"Once in a while, I'd really hit it off with a guy or a gal or a couple who'd invite me to meet for a drink. Occasionally, someone asked me to spend a night. In almost every case, I said yes. It was never about sex. It was strange, but I was sort of asexual then. On a couple occasions, once with a middle-aged divorcee who had a teenage son and one with a man in his mid-thirties, my expectations didn't coincide with those of my host and resulted in hard feelings," lamented Quinn. "Most of the time, I enjoyed great company, interesting conversation, and new perspectives I wouldn't have otherwise had."

"I stayed in the UK for a couple of months before I continued to Paris. Considering I didn't know French as well as my native language and in spite of my college French classes, I struggled. Unfortunately for me, I didn't connect as well as I did with the folks back in jolly ol' England. At the hotels where I stayed, the clerks and managers were wary. I guess it could've been Dierdorf. It was not as much wary as it was cold. I got the same reaction in a lot of public places, too. Some people warmed to me a little when I tried to speak in their language. At first, I know I must have sounded like Frankenstein's monster, all grunts. I was happy when some of the vocabulary came back. I remembered the sentence structure, you know, where the object pronouns go, where the adjectives go. I even remembered most of the conjugation rules, at least for the simple tenses. After a week or two, I was doing okay. As my French improved, so did my relations with native speakers," Quinn said with a tinge of pride.

"I didn't get as many invitations to experience French culture as I did in England. That disappointed me a little. Still, I felt good about what I was doing and was occupied with something other than that missing piece of my soul. When I was worried about learning an accent or concerned about the cool reaction to my smile and my *'Bonjour, monsieur. Comment ca va?'* I wasn't thinking about Gina. The times alone at night were difficult. I had no other place to put my thoughts. So, I decided I would learn the language before I started toward my next stop," said Quinn. "I believe the things that I experienced in Spain were as influential as anything else."

Skylar was rapt by the story as she drove at a more reasonable speed. Ironically, she drove past the Fork-In-The-Road Centre, the hospital Mark Burton endowed and named for one of his more successful albums. She recalled the conversation she had with Quinn over dinner about Burton, but hadn't remembered his hospital was on Antigua.

As Quinn recounted the events that led him to this day on this island in this sports car with her, he spoke in a way that made her feel that he was listening at the same time. He connected with her body language, acknowledged her gestures, and satisfied her curiosity.

Quinn reconfirmed, "You're sure you're all right with this, Skye? Nothing about this makes you uncomfortable?"

"No, Quinn, not at all. I asked and, besides, I like to hear you talk." Skylar didn't add she wanted to get closer to Quinn and that getting closer to him emotionally like this was a good start. "Not a thing you've told me makes me uncomfortable, but my back is starting to."

Skylar and Quinn had barely noticed that the sun had risen high in the sky. Because Quinn never missed his breakfast and he wasn't usually hungry for lunch, his stomach never told him the time. Skylar hadn't finished even half the breakfast Feef made for her because the Percocet discouraged her appetite. Unfortunately, Skylar would need more of those little white pills very soon.

"Hopefully, that won't be as much of an issue tomorrow when the Fentanyl kicks in," Quinn optimistically offered. "Did you bring your medicine with you?"

"In my purse," Skylar replied.

"Why don't you pull over when you have a chance? I asked Sonny to put a little cooler in the trunk. We have Perrier—and I'm afraid you'll think I'm a little ridiculous, but I also brought some Ensure," Quinn said.

"Ensure? You mean the stuff that old people drink?" Skylar wrinkled her nose.

"Here's the deal. I know you haven't felt much like eating. I'm afraid that your body is just not getting enough of the good stuff. Ensure is a little trick so you get what you need, even if you only take a couple of sips. It's a liquid, so it also helps you stay hydrated. Maybe you could just use it to wash down the pills?"

Skylar laughed. "You really do think of everything. Don't you? See. That's what I'm talking about."

CHAPTER 39

Twenty minutes later, the Jaguar was back on the road. This time, Quinn was behind the wheel. As much as Skylar enjoyed driving, the effort exhausted her. Quinn's mouth was dry from the talking and from the blowing wind over the windshield of the convertible. He opened a bottle of Perrier for himself and opened another for Skylar before she asked.

"I feel much better, Quinn," Skylar said.

"Well, like I said, by this time tomorrow, maybe even by tonight, you should feel a whole lot better," Quinn replied.

"So Quinn, you piqued my curiosity with that last comment," Skylar recalled. "I believe the things that I experienced in Spain were as influential as anything else . . ."

"Jeez, Skye. Photographic memory?"

Skylar answered casually, "Just a little lawyer trick."

"I'll try to remember that when I try to tell a little white lie," joked Quinn.

"Just don't lie, you moron." Skylar scolded.

"Anyway," Quinn rejoined, "I took a few weeks to work on my Spanish, using a great language thing I could run on my laptop. By the time I finally left, and I was ready to leave by the way, I knew Spanish at least well enough to get by."

"I started the same way I started in the UK and in France. I stayed in a hotel for a day or two before I moved on, but as my command of the language improved, I realized that the people in Spain were quite a bit more welcoming than their neighbors to the northeast. People were happy to talk with me and even to help me with learning the language. Most of my conversations at first, I know, must've been pretty remedial. I almost never met an adverse reaction when I asked, *'Como se dice?'* or 'How does one say?' before I picked up or pointed at something. I'd ask, *'Como se dice?'* and pick up the butter dish and my companion would say to me, *'mantequilla.'* If I still couldn't figure it out, then I'd ask, '*Como tu deletreas?*' or 'How do you spell?' I think many of the people I met thought I was a novelty."

Without the responsibility of driving, Skylar gave Quinn her entire attention. Sitting just a little sideways on her right hip, Skylar's elbow rested on the top of the seat wedged partially under the head rest. Her wrist was bent as the back of her hand supported her head, which was tilted gracefully when she asked, "How did you get around? How did you travel with Dierdorf, I mean?"

"I don't want to make it seem like I was some wandering wise man. Anything but," Quinn clarified. "When I was in the UK and France, I mostly rented a car. Car rentals were not necessarily the most economical way to go, but making my own schedule and my own rules made traveling with an animal much easier. I pretty much figured it out by the time I made it to Spain. I slowed my pace and mostly walked from village to village or town to town."

"Rather than trying to find pet-friendly hotels, I found pet-friendly rentals. Instead of staying in one place for a day or two, I extended my stays to a week or more. I still had meals at the Spanish equivalent to the hole-in-the wall bar, but the additional stability in my accommodations gave me the opportunity to cook, which I did with increasing frequency. It wasn't the case that the appeal of meeting and speaking with locals and immersion in the culture declined much. Or, maybe it did. I don't know. I think my inclination for more stability was an indication that something in me had changed. It was maybe a kind of signal that I'd achieved something. Whatever it was, that new stability was the foundation for another, rather profound episode in my life." Quinn adjusted his tone as if his story was a symphony ending one movement and beginning another.

"I'm not sure it's the same with everyone, but after a certain point, meaningful experiences have less to do with events than they do with people. Remember when you were twelve years old? You couldn't wait for your next birthday so you could be a teenager? When you were a senior in high school, you could not wait to graduate? When you were twenty, your twenty-first birthday was a big deal so you could go to a bar without a fake ID? Then, it was graduating college, finishing graduate school, getting a real job, buying a house. It was all about the achievement. Once a person has the financial wherewithal to meet his or her basic needs, though, it has much less to do with achievement as it does with relationships. Have you noticed that?" Quinn asked.

Skylar responded thoughtfully. "I have, Quinn, but it's only been very recently. For me it took the Little Bastard to make me realize it. I wish I'd have gotten it earlier. I suppose some people learn that lesson on their own, just by living life, seeing, understanding, some sooner, but I'd imagine, most later."

"I think you're right. For me, the event was the loss of Gina. I didn't take for granted what we had and I'm not talking about the house or investments or the cars or anything else we could touch. I'm talking about what we had between us. Without having much context or knowing what else was out there, I knew we had something special. It took losing her to really know," Quinn finished his idea.

"Well, we crossed the border into Spain. As Dierdorf and I drove, we couldn't have gone the wrong way. We could've headed south and paralleled the Mediterranean coastline or gone southwest to Madrid. As it turned out, though, we went almost due west along Spain's north coast. As soon as we could, we found a place to stay. We returned the car and we continued on foot. For a few weeks, it was more of the same. We walked. We met people. We experienced the culture and connected with places." Then Quinn said under his breath, "Listen to me, I'm talking about 'we,' Dierdorf and me, like Dierdorf was another person."

CHAPTER 40

"Within a few weeks, I arrived in Cantabria. Regions in Spain are a little like the states back home, but it seems like the populations aren't quite so precisely defined. Borders are defined on a map, but are more cultural than geographic.

"The capitol, Santander, is at about the same latitude line as Milwaukee, but the climate and the geography are a cross between South Carolina and Washington State. The summer is warm and humid, the spring and fall are temperate, and the winters are short.

"I felt a connection to Santander. The combination of the Renaissance architecture, the climate, and the tapestry of young and old that composed a vibrant community was compelling. Not too big and not too small. The beach and the four colleges there are reason enough the city seems ageless.

"I spent a couple nights in a nice-enough boarding house near the water. The two-story, white-brick mansion was managed by a colorful, unlikely couple. Rebekah had been an Orthodox Jew and Sal was a Roman Catholic. They'd become more or less agnostic, but both maintained the stereotypical behavior suggested by their respective heritages. It was fun to watch. Even when they were doing their everyday things, like having their morning coffee or putting away groceries or making up guest rooms, it was controlled combat. The banter was entertaining for observers and perhaps even for themselves. Rebekah complained that Sal had the sheets on upside down and Sal replied that her sister spoiled their nephew. They must have been sparring with one another forever. I don't think I would've wanted to be around when they really went at it. Like vinegar and oil, they didn't really mix, but they were a very nice seasoning sometimes.

"It didn't take long to get my fill of that, though. Coincidentally, I also realized that I wanted to stay in Santander. On my third day, Dierdorf and I set out to find longer-term accommodations, which we did without much trouble.

"We started early. Man and dog waited outside a nearby rental office, ready and willing at the posted opening time, nine o'clock. Twenty-two minutes later, a rotund middle-aged man in an inexpensive suit seemed surprised to find us waiting. He introduced himself as Aljandro and initially seemed apprehensive as much about Dierdorf as he was about an *Americano* waiting for him outside his office. But, like most people who spend just a few minutes with us, Aljandro realized neither I nor my companion posed a threat.

"While my Spanish was still far from fluent, I was fortunate to find that many of the Spanish people who I met spoke at least some English. Aljandro was no exception. He spoke better English than about half the people in the United States. I explained what I wanted, you know, a small, clean, animal-friendly, furnished, weekly rental. A few minutes later, we were on our way to visit the list of rentals he had created using his smoke-and dust-stained desktop and a dot-matrix printer.

"It was before noon when we arrived on foot to the third of six apartments in Aljandro's inventory. It was the basement of an owner-occupied, narrow, three-story, gray-stone building. It was old, but judging by landscaping and what appeared to be a relatively new roof and windows, had been fairly well maintained. The back door opened into a small courtyard that was just as wide as the building but only half as deep and was enclosed by a wooden fence over which was a view of the Cantabrian Sea in the distance.

"I stood in front of the fence and admired the view. I looked down at Dierdorf almost as if to get his opinion. Hearing no objection, I turned to tell Aljandro that we'd seen our last apartment. Before I could speak, though, my eyes were diverted by a woman leaning mischievously on the balcony of the first-floor flat. When she saw my eyes and knew I'd seen her, she spoke in what I can only describe as melodiously cute, *"Buenas tarde, Señor San Giacomo! Quienes son sus amigos?"* the woman asked Aljandro, wanting to know who I and Dierdorf were.

"*Pienso que ellos son sus nuevos vecinos, Señorita,*" Aljandro explained, smiling, that he thought that we'd be her new neighbors.

Then, Aljandro turned to me and said, "Quinn, please allow me to introduce Luz Esperanza Bonifario."

CHAPTER 41

"Up to then, there had been only one other time I'd experienced *It*, the first time I met Gina. You know, It, the rare and magical, love-or-whatever-at-first-sight chemistry," Quinn explained.

"Yes. I think that has happened to me once," Skylar answered, trying not to reveal too much.

"Luz Esperanza Bonifario. In Spanish, *luz* means light. *Esperanza* is hope. I couldn't imagine a more appropriate name. I have to admit, I was more than a little conflicted," Quinn confessed, failing to notice Skylar's insinuation. "Of course, as I wandered in a part of the world I'd never been and experienced things I'd never seen, I also explored places inside myself I never even knew existed. To an extent, I hovered in place, knowing that I was in some ways lost. In some ways, I mourned and I came to terms with my grief. It was the idea of Luz as much as Luz herself that helped me to come face to face with that grief and deal with it once and for all."

"She was only about five-feet tall and weighed not an ounce more than 100 pounds even if she had a pocket full of rocks. She had the face of a doll, rosy cheeks that angled downward to her dimpled chin, dark, almond-shaped eyes, a cute and slightly broadened nose, tiny and perfectly shaped pinkish lips, honey-colored skin, and black bobbed hair. She wore flatteringly tiny blue jeans that perfectly fit her tiny legs, a white T-shirt displaying large, blue letters that read, '*Zapatos Por Imelda*,' and no shoes. Energy, confidence, and attitude oozed from her every pore.

"As it turned out, Luz wasn't Spanish. She was Filipina. She and her family, father, mother, one older brother and two older sisters, had all lived in Manila. The youngest by far of four children, Luz was her daddy's little girl," commented Quinn.

"Luz's father, Esteban, was some sort of diplomat and had been assigned to Madrid when Luz was about fifteen years old. Her mother, Antonia, was well educated and a perfect complement to Esteban's career aspirations. She was a supportive wife, a nurturing mother, and a great hostess for foreign and domestic dignitaries.

"The Bonifarios had also fallen in love with Cantabria. Antonia's and Esteban's older children had either already married or had jobs back in the Philippines. So, it was only the three of them. Even though Señor Bonifario was expected to spend two or three days each week in Madrid, he moved his wife and daughter to Santander.

"Luz was far from home, but she apparently didn't have much trouble with school. I think her experience was sort of like a southern belle moving to a place like New Zealand. Not only did she have to navigate the differences in dialect, but she had to adjust to cultural differences too. Luz was mostly successful. Being cute didn't hurt. I never did figure out whether Luz was puckish because she was tested by her new environment or if she survived as a result of it. Regardless, Luz was one of a kind.

Skylar noticed her hair was blowing more wildly. Quinn had accelerated as he managed hazards and steered through curves. Quinn's driving didn't bother her. The car, company, and conversation were about as close to heaven as she'd been. Skylar was curious, though, about whether Quinn leaned on the gas as a result of the pleasure he derived from driving or from the exhilaration he felt as he spoke about Luz.

"Neither Luz nor her parents expected her to finish secondary school in Spain," Quinn continued. "She did, though, because Esteban's appointment was extended. Then, Luz continued at the Universidad de Cantabria, or Unican. Her parents insisted their baby stay close to home, but they conceded that Luz could live on her own. The little overachiever had three majors, roughly the equivalents of Spanish history, public policy, and economics, and she had her three degrees in only five years. By that time, Luz had lived in Spain for more than eight years. So, after her first year of law school at Unican when her father was called back to Manila for health reasons, she decided to stay.

"When I turned around to tell Aljandro I wanted the apartment and spotted Luz up there on the patio, she had already begun her second year studying public law."

"After Aljandro answered, I scrambled to say something interesting, if not completely remedial, '*Somos Americanos, Señorita, y necesitemos una maestra de Español. Conoces a alguien?*' It was the best I could do on short notice, 'We're Americans, Miss, and we need a Spanish teacher. Do you know anyone?'

"Her answer, I'd learn, was typical Luz, '*Una maestra? Pienso que conozco una maestra, pero no creo que puedas enfrentar su lenqua,*' which was at a minimum a double, possibly a triple-entendre that literally translated, means, 'A teacher? I think I know a teacher, but I am not sure you can handle her tongue.'

"I was smitten. Of course, I finally managed to tell Aljandro I'd take the apartment. He asked when I wanted to start. I think he was only a little surprised when I pulled out my wallet, counted out a full month's rent plus the deposit, and replied, '*Ahora mismo,*' or 'Right now.'

"And, I think Aljandro saw in me what Michael Corleone's bodyguards saw in him when he first laid eyes on Appolonia in The Godfather. Thunderbolt.

"As Aljandro and I walked back toward the door to the kitchen, Luz asked me if I wanted coffee. She explained that she believed it was important to maintain good relations with her neighbors. I agreed, of course."

CHAPTER 42

"I really hadn't planned on spending more than two or three weeks in Santander, but I quickly realized the value of flexibility.

"I was attracted to Luz and struggled with that. For as long as I could remember, I only had eyes for Gina. I didn't think about anyone else. I didn't have to. In my heart, I struggled with guilt, but I was unambiguously drawn to this woman.

"For a while, the extent of our relationship was coffee three days a week on the afternoons when Luz had only morning classes. Eventually, we'd sit at a sidewalk table and watch people. On rainy days, we'd move inside to a discrete corner table that still offered a street view. We talked, well, I mostly listened. Like many Europeans, she spoke English, but I asked her if she would speak Spanish slowly to me. She did, but Luz was so animated and full or energy that I regularly had to remind her to slow down, which drove her crazy.

"At our first meeting in the courtyard, Luz was playfully suggestive, but I quickly understood that she was traditional when it came to matters of the heart. She explained that Señor Bonifario tried to guide her toward a relationship with the son of a colleague, Roberto Marcolino. On more than one occasion, her father even accidentally-on-purpose schemed places and times where Luz and Roberto could meet. According to Luz, she thought Roberto was nice but didn't consider him a romantic interest and easily exposed her father's thinly veiled ruses.

"There remained a fine line between familial expectations for women and arranged marriage among some quarters of Filipino culture, even in the twenty-first century, Luz explained. I knew she struggled with the expectations from her father, who she loved, and her needs to make her own decisions.

"'I believe in love,' Luz told me once as she sipped her coffee one afternoon. 'And, only I can decide who I love.'

"Not long after the Bonifarios moved to Santander, Esteban and Antonia realized, I suppose, that their active little girl needed constructive distractions to absorb some of her energy. I don't think Luz ever directed that energy counterproductively, but, because she was a foreigner and just a little different from her peers, her parents were probably concerned things could go the wrong way.

"The Bonifarios encouraged their daughter to play soccer or tennis at school. Luz did not cotton to those things. She didn't seem self-conscious about her size, but those little legs probably did not serve her well in traditional sports. After those misses, the Bonifarios finally scored when they hired a martial arts instructor to come to the house three days a week for private sessions. Luz had found her distraction," Quinn added. "Before Luz finished secondary school, she'd earned a black belt in Taekwondo. By the time she started her undergraduate work at Unican, she stopped the private lessons and joined the university martial arts club.

"The more time I spent with Luz, the more time I wanted to spend with her. She hadn't only found the place in my heart, but she also found a place under my skin. If she was a disease, I did not mind suffering. I've heard my friends talk about the lengths to which they'd gone to get the attention or win the affections of a woman. Ballroom dancing. Poetry. Leaving the Church and converting to Judaism. Listening instead of talking all the time!" joked Quinn with tongue firmly planted in cheek. "Heck! My best friend, Kelly, even helped to find a job for his girlfriend's obnoxious brother!"

Skylar started to laugh again. "Oh, cut it out!" Skylar spoke in mock offense. "You guys love that stuff. Besides, we're worth it!"

"Sometimes," Quinn admitted. "As it was, my compromise was not nearly as tough as any of those. All I had to do was learn Taekwondo. Of course, I also needed to enroll at Unican so I could join the club. I took a couple of classes, Spanish and Spanish history, which I barely passed. And, yes, it was worth it. Although I didn't see Luz on campus, the martial arts classes we shared effectively tripled the time we spent together.

"After a while, I knew my infatuation was something more. I'd fallen in love," confessed Quinn. "Eventually, we started to have dinner together at her or at my apartment. Usually at her apartment, though, considering she actually lived there. She owned the things like a spice rack, a cutting board, a pot and baking pans, plates, and dinnerware needed to make a decent meal.

"I knew Luz loved me too, although for a while, our relationship remained platonic. After we ate and talked and laughed and watched a movie or television or took a walk, I always returned downstairs to my apartment while Luz slept alone in hers. Then one night, Luz and I walked back to her apartment after a workout. We stopped at the market for fresh fish and vegetables. While I carried the groceries in a bag in one arm, Luz reached out and held my hand. It was the first time she'd done that. She pressed herself into my arm. After we ate, we sat close on her couch and watched *Y Tu Maman Tambien*. I was barely able to concentrate on the movie. I could only think about crawling inside her, becoming the air in the room so she could breathe me or the wine in her glass so she could drink me. I literally wanted to be a part of her.

"When the movie ended, she didn't say a word. She looked at me, grabbed the remote, and switched off the television. Then, she swung one of her adorable legs across my lap and kissed me. She moved into me even closer, put her arms around my neck, and pressed her cheek next to mine. Then, softly, urgently, Luz whispered in my ear, '*Te amo, Quinn. Te amo mucho y te quiero. Ahora.*' What she whispered to me hardly needs translation. The words, as expressive as they were, were not nearly as meaningful as the way they were spoken, 'I love you, Quinn. I love you so much and I want you. Now.'

"My arms wrapped around her back and the other held her as I stood up from the couch and carried her into her bedroom. Her legs enveloped my waist, her arms held me, and her head still rested on my shoulder. I knelt down on the bed, bracing myself with my right hand, still holding her with my left, and crawled up across the comforter and gently placed her head on her pillows.

"I remember that it was a Friday, because we skipped the Saturday-morning martial arts class and spent the entire day in her bed. We made love, talked, slept, laughed, held each other, and made love again. We left only occasionally to eat, drink, or use the bathroom. I remember waking up again on Sunday morning, having coffee and a light breakfast at our little café and contentedly thinking my life wouldn't be the same.

"From that weekend, we were inseparable. For the sake of appearances, I kept my apartment, but we spent as much time together as we could. If she and I weren't in class, we were together. It was fun and it felt right. We fit and filled the parts of each other's worlds we hadn't even realized we missed. I was surprised to feel the way I did. A guy is pretty lucky to find one person in his life with whom he can share a love. What were the chances I'd found it twice?

"We planned our lives together. I already accomplished everything I wanted to in my professional life. All that was left for me was the personal stuff. I wanted to have a family. I wanted Luz and I told her it didn't matter where we lived. It didn't matter what I did. We agreed that once she finished her law degree, we'd get married. I'd follow her, happily, to any place she wanted to live. If she wanted to return to Manila, I'd live in Manila. If she wanted to work in Madrid, I'd live in Madrid. If she wanted to move to the Canada's Northern Territory, I'd buy a parka. Luz assured me that there was no danger of that. She wasn't partial to the cold. Wherever we went, I figured I'd start a little business that would give me flexibility to help with the babies.

"Through the first part of her final year, Luz and I continued in our blissful, perfect corner of the universe. Actually, it was the three of us, Luz, me, and Dierdorf. Luz went to school and most of the time I made the home. Luz wasn't impressed with my cooking, not that it was bad. She just preferred a little more attitude in her food, and American just did not do it for her. She was a good sport about it even though she cooked or ordered out as often as she could. I took a class or two at Unican, and I became increasingly more fluent in Spanish. People could still detect my Western accent, but I was regularly complemented that I had a good ear. During the week, we worked out together. At nights, Luz studied and I usually read or ran. We explored Spain, Portugal, Italy, and France. We enjoyed romantic weekends on the white beaches of the Riviera. In Italy, we traveled the countryside, usually finding a room at a *fattoria*, where we sampled the local fare and enjoyed the Amarones and Amontillados with some amusing results. We made our way to Cannes for the festival. Sometimes, we just drove south and climbed rocks. Predictably, I found France more welcoming during those subsequent visits with Luz. We were a perfect little family and we were happy.

"Near the end of that year, Luz received a call from her mother in Manila. I remember thinking it was strange for Antonia to call so early. When the phone rings early like that, you hate to answer. Luz reached over for the phone as I rolled toward her, held my breath, and reached out and placed my hand on her naked hip. 'Hello?' she answered. Then, 'What's wrong, Mami?' Then, I watched Luz as her face contorted in disbelief, dread, and worry as she rattled a series of questions over the phone.

"What Antonia and Esteban hadn't told Luz about their return to Manila was the extent of her father's health issues. I suppose Señor Bonifario didn't want Luz to worry. After complaining of shortness of breath, having trouble walking up stairs, and even just getting around in his office, Esteban was diagnosed with a COPD. You might have heard of it. It's lung disease, Chronic Obstructive Pulmonary Disease. Basically, his lungs weren't able to absorb enough oxygen, so the rest of his body suffered as a result.

"After returning home, the COPD worsened, but that wasn't the most pressing issue. Esteban had also been diagnosed with bladder cancer. According to Antonia, he had only weeks, perhaps even days to live. Luz obviously needed to return to Manila.

"What happened next," Quinn alluded, "I can only speculate. I know, however, after I held and kissed and told her that I loved her, Luz boarded the plane and I never saw her again. I did my best to piece it together with the letter, the single phone call, and subsequent conversations with Aljandro. Although I'd never met Esteban and Antonia, I was no secret to the Bonifarios. Luz confided in her mother, but she idolized her father, and Esteban wasn't amenable to the idea of her little girl and a *blanco Americano*. Luz never talked much about it, and she never really let on, but I sensed an undercurrent of worry when the subject of an introduction came up. She insisted it would all eventually work out. The time hadn't yet come, and Luz didn't think the circumstances of her father's illness were right to introduce me to the family.

"When Luz saw her father, he was at home and I believe his condition was worse than she expected. The doctors knew no treatment would extend his time. More likely, it would erode the quality of the life he did have. So, he was home with family and friends, among whom was Señor Marcolino, who made the trip to support Esteban during his final days. Marcolino's son, Roberto, also made the trip.

"Luz was understandably upset, and I believe one, two, or both things happened. Overwhelmed, Luz may have sought comfort from her grief with a familiar face. Young Marcolino was probably honorable and decent. As resilient as Luz was, she probably took comfort in his company. Just as likely, Luz's father may have made a deathbed request of his daughter she'd have been unable to refuse," Quinn said.

"The next school session started and Luz didn't enroll. Weeks passed. I tried to call, but someone always answered the phone and told me Luz was unavailable. I was that much from getting on a plane to Manila myself." Quinn held his thumb and forefinger apart by an inch to illustrate. "But finally Luz did answer. She cried when she heard my voice, but all she could say was she was sorry. She was engaged to Roberto and couldn't talk to me anymore. It was strange behavior and out of character, at least what I had thought I knew about her character.

"Days later, I received a letter that seemed to confirm my theory. She wrote again she was sorry. I believed it. She wrote she hadn't realized how much she had cared for Roberto and she believed they'd be happy together. Of course, I didn't agree. She asked me to understand, to be happy for her, and not to contact her again. I complied.

"My opinion didn't matter. Luz married Roberto in a small private ceremony in the Bonifarios' home even before her letter reached me." Quinn hesitated. "The newlyweds postponed their honeymoon so Luz could remain with her father and family. They didn't have to wait long. Two days after the wedding, Esteban died in his sleep."

CHAPTER 43

"I'm so sorry," Skylar said finally. "Christ on a cracker! That's just not right!"

"Skye, I look at it like this. When Gina died, it was like there was something really wrong about it, like it was a perversion of nature," Quinn explained. "She would've added so much to the world if she were still here. Luz is still here as far as I know. She's still alive and I am sure she's doing her part. Losing Luz, losing love is the sort of thing that happens every day. And losing love is nothing compared to what you are facing. Not even close."

"That may be true, but it still had an effect on you. You said it yourself."

"Yeah. I just don't want to feel sorry for myself or think about the few, however big, disappointments I've had," Quinn said. "I've had a lot of breaks. Life's been okay, actually pretty good for me."

"So, what happened then, Quinn?" asked Skylar, wanting resolution. "What happened after Luz married Roberto?"

"There's really not much more to tell. By the time the movers came to pack and carry away Luz's stuff, I had no reason to stay. I told Aljandro I was leaving. I asked him to forward my mail. I wrote a letter to Unican to let them know I wouldn't be back. That was pretty much it.

"I started my trip to find something, but ended up lost again. As much as I liked to meet and learn about people, even the thought of doing more of that exhausted me. What I did have, thanks to Luz, was a new and useful diversion. Taekwondo was practical not so much in the sense that I expected to need it. Heck, I hadn't been in a scrape since I was a kid. It was a productive place to channel the frustration and disappointment that I'm sure I held inside. After all, I am only human," Quinn said. "So there I was. I needed a complete change of environment. Like I said, I no longer had much interest in human interaction. There was nothing I wanted to share just then.

"By that time, I'd advanced pretty far with martial arts. I was a black belt apprentice. I'd learned everything I needed to learn to be a black belt, but I hadn't yet demonstrated proficiency. So, where would a restless, emotionally exhausted, martial arts student go? I made some calls and jumped a flight to South Korea, where I lived the life of an ascetic in a martial arts monastery. Crazy, huh? The place was like a fantasy camp not unlike the places retired major league baseball players go after the cheering stops, but it was no frills and fairly disciplined. It was just what I needed.

"I lived the life, which was a part of the price of admission. I had nothing to occupy my mind other than martial arts and my grief, which I only then was able to process. I worked through a few things about Gina, about Luz, and about the rest of my life. Some of my thoughts were entirely new, while others seemed to be the natural progression of beliefs I already had.

"Rested and ready for the world again, I left South Korea six months later. I returned to Warwick with a black belt, some peace of mind, and an idea of how I could make a difference in the world with my life, if only in a very small way. That idea, which, of course, was Life Dreams, would allow me to remember what Gina meant to me. In my heart, I released resentment I carried for Luz. I genuinely wished her love and happiness. I made the conscious decision to live my life on the wings of fate, which is not to say I don't plan for the future. Rather, if life opens a door for me, I walk through. If destiny offers me a crossroads, I pick a direction and go. I've never regretted my choices and have made the best of every decision I made.

"More than a half a dozen years later," Quinn declared as he abruptly turned to avoid a pothole and accelerated through a turn, "I still practice Taekwondo with a master near my home, and now I'm quite happily here with you, thank you very much."

Quinn stopped and looked over at Skylar, who seemed to be distracted.

"Are you all right, Skye?" Quinn asked.

Skylar answered, "Yes, I'm fine."

"You sure? That was some pretty heavy stuff," admitted Quinn. "Is there anything you want to talk about?"

"Well there are a few questions I have, Quinn, but I don't think I can discuss it with you right now," Skylar responded.

When he heard Skylar's response, Quinn felt a sinking in his stomach. He warned that some stones are better left unturned. Now, Quinn felt he'd gone too far. "Jeez, Quinn," he thought to himself. "You had to tell her the truth. Everything? Haven't you ever heard of keeping your god-damned mouth shut? Apparently not, you friggin' Neanderthal."

Quinn's stomach churned as he equivocated his choice to be completely honest. "She deserves honesty, doesn't she? She's different. Special, right? Why am I letting myself feel like this? Huh? What happened to living life on the wings of fate and if life opens a door, walk through, bonehead?" Some place deep inside, Quinn had the answer.

At last, Quinn composed himself, looked over again at Skylar, and mustered the courage, "Why don't you want to talk about it, Skye?"

"I'm fine, Quinn. Really. I just don't think we can talk about it right now," Skylar answered.

Again, Quinn asked, "But why, Skylar? Can you tell me?"

"Well," Skylar said carefully as she glanced at the passenger side mirror, "You are just about to be introduced to one of Antigua's finest. I think he caught you speeding." She could barely control her laughter.

CHAPTER 44

"I think we may have to get another car," Quinn admitted. The same patrolman, Johnson, whose name Quinn read on the name tag above his badge, had nabbed Skylar earlier. "This car's unlucky."

Skylar bantered. "You'll actually have to pay your ticket! How fast were you going, Jeff Gordon?"

"Cut it out!" Quinn said with an exasperated sigh. "Johnson!" He carefully pulled the car back into the road while he watched the patrol car turn back to reset the trap for another unsuspecting foreign visitor.

Quinn changed the subject, "How are you feeling, Skye? I assumed you weren't hungry, but are you okay?"

"I'm fine, a little tired, though. All this excitement and the sun have taken a little bit out of me," Skylar explained. "Although, you know what they say?"

"What's that?" Quinn asked.

"Laughter is the best medicine," Skylar responded as if the answer couldn't have been more obvious.

"I should open a pharmacy, huh?" Quinn jibed. Her genuine happiness was infectious. Skylar's delight created a familiar sense of contentment in Quinn. As much as the way she pursed her lips and looked up at Quinn over her sunglasses, Skylar's entire body beamed a new energy.

"Listen, why don't we head back to the house," Quinn suggested. "We can maybe get some rest and just relax for a while. I didn't mention it, but I found out last night that an old friend is on the island with his family. He invited us over to his place for drinks and dinner. Do you think you'd be up for that?"

"Sure, I think so," was Skylar's lively answer. "I think after maybe a little nap on the beach, I'll be pert as a tomcat."

"You don't need a nap for that," Quinn retorted.

"You really know a lot of people, don't you? What are the chances you'd

THE DREAM SEEKER

know someone vacationing here?" Skylar commented, failing to notice the barely perceptible smile on Quinn's lips.

"Remember, Amelie worked with me when I managed money. She knows a lot of people I know," Quinn answered before his subterfuge began. "Maybe Amelie heard from someone that Embee and Jolisa were here. She probably called Jolisa and told her we were here, too. Who knows? Anyway, they're staying a couple of miles from our place."

"Hmm. That's an unusual name, 'Embee,'" Skylar mused.

"Nickname, I think," Quinn answered

"Let's do that, Quinn. It would be nice to spend the evening with another couple. I'm sure if Embee and Jolisa are your friends, they're good people. What do they do?"

"Well, I haven't spent much time with them lately. As far as that goes, I haven't spent much time with too many of my old friends lately. I know Jolisa is a stay-at-home mom for their three girls. Embee was one of my clients and is Kelly's client now. When I met Embee, he worked in the music industry," answered Quinn with just a fraction of the truth. He pulled into the driveway and replaced the Jaguar in its place.

"We'll find at least a few things in common for conversation. They sound lovely, and I'm sure we'll have fun," Skylar said. "I still may not eat too much. Do you think that will be all right?"

"I'm sure it'll be fine, Skye," Quinn said as they sat together in the car for a moment. The only sound that could be heard above their words was the clicking and clinking sounds that the car made as its metal components cooled. Quinn was thankful for the relative silence of the garage.

"Good. Why don't you give me a few minutes and I'll meet you on the beach," Skylar said as she reached over to open her door. She turned back, "And, Quinn?"

"Yes," he answered.

Skylar began, "I know you told me not to thank you for anything else, but this is different. You shared a part of yourself with me today. That meant a lot."

Startled a little both by her candor and the intimate way she spoke, Quinn simply answered, "No sweat, Skye."

CHAPTER 45

Skylar came downstairs after showering the beach from all the places where the beach tends to accumulate on a woman's body. She thought to herself as the water washed the tiny grains of sediment onto the shower floor, "It's amazing all the places sand can go during a day at the beach, and a short day at that. It wasn't even like I played volleyball."

Quinn met Skylar by the water after they returned from the drive. He carried reclining chairs under both arms and a bag slung over his shoulder. Skylar had changed into a flattering peach-colored, two-piece bathing suit and matching sarong. He found her wading in the shallow water, kicking sand and letting waves roll over her feet. The sun cast an enchanting silhouette. Her wind-blown hair rustled over her shoulders. Skylar was startled when she heard Quinn set the chairs down a few feet away.

"Hey," Skylar said. "I didn't see you coming."

"Oh, I am very stealthy," Quinn said. "I don't think it was as much me as it was you. You looked like you were daydreaming."

"I was," Skylar said.

"Wanna tell me about it? I'm a master of dream interpretation," Quinn answered.

"I won't be much of a challenge, Quinn," Skylar replied. "No mysterious metaphors. I was just thinking about how nice this is. Not just the sun, beach and water. And not even just you."

Quinn mockingly raised one eye-brow, which elicited a response from Skylar.

"You know what I mean." With an ironic smile she continued, "No you don't. What I mean is that I'll miss all this. I'll really miss all this."

Quinn listened. Without saying a word, he reached out and took Skylar's hand.

"What I really mean, is, well, I hoped you would put some sun block on

THE DREAM SEEKER

me so I can sleep for a while. You brought some, didn't you?" Skylar asked as she reached down into the beach bag and grabbed the bottle.

Quinn could hardly say, "I'd be happy to," before Skylar peeled the sarong from her hips. She folded it efficiently and placed it in the bag. Then, Skylar reached back and unhooked the clasps of her top with as much ceremony as she might have used to pour a cup of coffee.

She glanced at Quinn through her sunglasses to gauge his reaction. A wry smile appeared on Skylar's face. She enjoyed Quinn's expression almost as much she did his hands as he massaged her vulnerable skin. Skylar returned the favor. Skylar was sure the experience was at the very least uncommon for Quinn. It probably wasn't every day a topless woman rubbed sunscreen on his back and shoulders, and she relished the opportunity. She wasn't excessively proud, at least in terms of the word's definition pertaining to the Seven Deadly Sins, but Skylar believed she was fortunate with her endowment. She found Quinn amusing as he tried to resist stealing a peek. In his efforts, Quinn failed miserably.

After she had her fun, Skylar did finally sleep contentedly as the cadenced breaks of the waves provided soothing background noise and the heat from the sun warmed her. Only once when her arms numbed from idleness and neck stiffened over the spooled beach towel did she turned her body onto her stomach.

An hour and a half later, Skylar opened her left eye. Her range of vision featured a one-dimensional view of Quinn's torso and head. In his hands, he held a paperback. Skylar couldn't have known he had only just recently picked it up from his chest. He'd been sleeping, too. In the periphery of her sideways monocular view, she could make out the top of Quinn's dark blue bathing suit below and the green of the grasses, bushes, and trees beyond. Beyond Quinn, she saw beach bounded by more green on top and the vibrant blue of the ocean at the bottom.

Meditatively absorbed in his pulpy literature, Quinn was startled when Skylar asked without pretext, "Do you miss her, Quinn?"

Readjusting his perception from the escapism toward the delightful, mostly naked woman lying next to him, Quinn hesitated for a moment before answering with a question, "Luz?"

"Uh huh," Skylar nodded.

Quinn reached down and replaced the book in the beach bag. He rolled over onto his left side to face Skylar, who'd turned and lifted her head so she could see Quinn with both eyes. Quinn propped his head up with his left hand, rested his elbow on the chaise, and thought to himself how naturally feminine, how lovely Skylar looked just then.

"I can only imagine what it's like for a woman, Skye, when she falls in love. But for a man, or I guess more to the point for me, it doesn't happen very often," Quinn sighed. "Since I was old enough to look, maybe only one or two times in a year I see a woman who I find genuinely attractive. I don't know if the attraction is chemical or related to the shape of a woman's face or how she walks or what, but that's what it is, real, visceral attraction. But among those thirty or forty, assuming I have seen one or two a year since my early teens, a very few have the same sort of attraction to me. Thirty or forty women may seem like a lot, or maybe it doesn't. I don't think it does considering the tens of thousands of people we encounter. Frankly, I think I'm sort of particular when it comes to matters of the heart. Anyway, there are perhaps only a few, maybe a half-dozen, who I actually know well enough to know whether I like her, whether I respect the person she is, and whether we're compatible. What are the chances that woman who I find appealing not only feels the same way about me, but is also compatible in all the ways two people need to be?"

"Pretty remote, I'd say," Skylar answered.

"Pretty remote. As far as I'm concerned, it's a damned miracle that two mutually attracted and mutually compatible people ever find each other! It never happens for some people. I've been pretty lucky. It's happened to me twice. Luz was one.

"Still, I am not sure I miss her. I miss Gina. Gina and I had all of those things and then we committed ourselves to one another. With Gina, I was able to understand what it means to actually become one with another person. After some time, I no longer knew where I ended and Gina began. She was the melody and I was the harmony. When she was gone, though, even though I was physically whole—I still had two arms, two legs, ten fingers and toes—there was a piece of me that was gone. My song just didn't sound right anymore. In some ways, losing that piece in my soul or in my heart or in my mind was almost as debilitating as losing a limb. Do you know what I mean?" Quinn asked.

"I can imagine."

"Regret is what I feel for Luz. And, yes, I still do feel it. In the perspective of the infinitesimally small chance that lightning struck twice, I regret that

Luz and I didn't have the chance to share those things. Selfishly, I regret it for me. Because I loved her, I regret it for her. I know how wonderful it is to have that kind of love. For her sake, I hope she found it with Roberto, but I'm sorry for both of us we weren't able to have it and to share it and grow old together with it."

Skylar frowned and Quinn asked, "Are you all right?"

Apprehensive, wanting to ask the other question on her mind, Skylar fibbed just a little, "Yes, I'm all right. Those are just some very powerful words, Quinn. I'm trying to get my head around them."

"Earlier when we were in the car, I thought I'd said too much." Quinn admitted. "I worried I told you too much and made you feel uncomfortable. You asked and I thought you deserved the truth. You want to know things, whatever they are, and I don't want to hold anything back. More than that, though, I considered the fact—and I've believed this since the first time I met you—that you're a person who has decided what she wants and can handle the consequences. I decided you'd get the genuine article when you wanted it."

Quinn's and Skylar's eyes affixed to one another's.

"Was I right?" Quinn asked. "Was I right to assume that?"

"Yes, Quinn. You were perfectly right."

"Good. I'm glad." Quinn smiled before he changed direction. "We'd better get back to the house and shower. I think Embee expects us in a little more than an hour."

"All right. If I have to," Skylar groaned playfully as she stretched, arching her back and pushing her breasts skyward.

Quinn rolled his eyes, "I'd suggest you put those things away before we go back up. Sonny might end up in a coma. As it is, you've already given me a seizure or two."

"Funny. I've never heard it called that," Skylar smirked, nodding downward.

CHAPTER 46

Skylar made her way to the kitchen past the big glass windows that opened to the patio and the pool. She glimpsed Quinn, Sonny, and Feef through the door from the hallway. The three of them spoke comfortably with one another while each nursed a Wadadli straight from the long-neck bottle. As she approached, Skylar heard Quinn more clearly as he chronicled their encounters with the Antiguan Royal Police.

"It hasn't always been like that," Feef explained as Skylar walked in. "A while back, a couple of tourists drove over a cliff and got themselves killed. Since then, it seems like the Royal Police have become a royal pain in the arse."

"Hello, Skylar," Sonny was first to say.

Skylar answered, smiling widely, "Hi, everyone."

"If no one minds me saying," Sonny began, looking first toward Feef before he glanced at Quinn, "but you look beautiful, Skylar. Your date this evening is a very lucky man."

Although prone to exaggeration, Sonny spoke the truth. Skylar wore a simple dress that not many ladies could make work. A snug, strapless, yellow tube dress, a woman would need just enough on top and only the right amount on the bottom to keep it in place. Too much real estate in either jurisdiction would imply that the woman wearing it failed to recognize certain truths about aging and obscenity standards. Neither was a problem for Skylar. Her sun-browned legs stopped where her feet elegantly held down her lace-up sandals. Quinn considered the benefits of such liberal access to sunshine.

"Well, thank you very much, Mr. Gregory," Skylar replied as she nodded in Sonny's direction.

Directing her focus toward Quinn, Skylar asked, "And you, Mr. Powers, I hope I am presentable for our evening with your friends."

Considering her display earlier on the beach, Quinn was anything but covert as he gave Skylar the once over. Raising his eyebrows in a display of ersatz disbelief, Quinn responded, "I believe Mr. Gregory is correct, Ms. Smart. Your date truly is a very lucky man."

Skylar smiled as Feef interrupted, "Okay, okay. Down boys. A lady'd think that neither one of you had a momma to teach you any manners."

Quinn and Sonny grimaced and slunk back like scolded dogs.

"And you, Skylar. What's this I hear about you going out for your dinner after only one day?" inquired Feef, feigning insult.

"Oh, it's not my fault, Feef. If it were up to me, I'd stay here for your cooking morning, noon, and night!" Skylar insisted. "It was all Quinn's idea. I promise."

"The view is great from down here under the bus," joked Quinn. "As fascinatingly entertaining as is all this high-brow conversation, we really have to get a move on. What do you think? Should we take the XKR or the SUV?"

"I like a little excitement in my life," Skylar responded. "Let's take the Jag."

CHAPTER

The ride to Embee's house was no more than ten minutes. Just west of Half Moon Bay along the southern shore, Quinn turned toward the coast on a road less traveled.

The access to the compound reminded Skylar of an ultraexclusive resort. Along both sides of the drive toward a large house at the terminus were a number of small but charming cottages. The road curled through a revitalized lush isthmus. The proprietor obviously embraced a strong desire for privacy and atmosphere. Skylar, who was more curious than anxious to meet Quinn's friends could almost imagine how the first settlers found the island before the tropical paradise gave way to cane plantations.

As the car approached the main house at the cape, Skylar noticed the terrain plunged precipitously to the water on both sides. The house was built on what a Midwesterner would call a bluff. The light stone resembled the bedrock protrusions she'd seen all over the island. As Quinn guided the car toward the front of the house, Skylar could see a view of the patio enclosed by a stainless rail with narrowly spaced, vertical bars. Like many other scenes on the island the eye could witness and the heart could appreciate, the patio was framed within an expansive ocean vista. Skylar thought, "I'll bet that view is fantastic."

Before the house, the car path yielded to an interlinked-stone circle driveway that bended left, looped near the entrance. The flora was flourishingly varied, but tempered by traditional landscaping. A fountain prominently featured a figure in the center of loop. Thanks to his Catholic school education, Quinn recognized St. Jude. The icon seemed to oversee not only the flowing water that pooled at his feet, but the entire compound as well. Carefully cultivated grass spread away in all directions interrupted only by the circle before continuing again toward the descents on both sides.

Quinn veered left and drove through the long shadow thrown by St.

THE DREAM SEEKER

Jude. He stopped at the walkway in front of the door. Skylar gathered her purse and checked her face in the illuminated visor mirror as Quinn stepped out and courtly opened Skylar's door. Skylar offered her hand. She held a black pocket book in her left hand and Quinn's with her right as she swung her tanned legs out of the open car door, found a foothold, and smiled. "How are you feeling?" Quinn asked as he calculated the hours since he applied the Fentanyl on Skylar's shoulder. Quinn hoped that the medicine had started to work.

Endearingly unpretentious, Skylar wrinkled her forehead and scrunched her nose as if she were deducing a complex proof. "I took some Percocets before I left, but hadn't even really noticed. The pills take off the edge, but still let me know that I still have pain, if that makes any sense," Skylar explained as she reached behind her and touched the lower part of her back. "But, I don't feel anything right now, Quinn. Nothing at all!" She seemed genuinely surprised by her discovery.

As they approached the door and Quinn knocked, Quinn was able to reply, "That's great, Skye," before the door opened in front of them.

In the doorway stood a man who offered in an oddly affable, if not officious British accent, "Hello! You must be Quinn," he said first. "Embee has told me a lot about you. And, of course, you're Skylar. Come in, please."

As Quinn and Skylar stepped across the threshold into a large, semicircular room, the greeter continued, "I'm Girard. Embee, Jolisa and the girls are in the back. I'll bring you around." Just then, a little girl perhaps four or five years old darted into the room through a doorway. She was followed by another, slightly older girl, and finally, by two women. Both the girls wore adorable little pajama tops with matching shorts sprinkled with designs of fairies and flowers. The women wore delightedly exasperated expressions.

"Quinn!" the second woman almost shouted with a familiar, flat Midwestern inflection. The woman closed the distance to the place near the door where Quinn, Skylar, and Girard stood. Opening her arms, the woman hugged Quinn earnestly around his neck, kissed him on the cheek, and said, "It's been too long, Quinn. Embee's been looking forward to seeing you! I have, too!"

"Thanks, Jolisa. It's great to see you too," Quinn said as Jolisa took one step back as if to assess the changes time had brought to her old friend.

"Thanks for the books," Jolisa continued. "They're still a little old for the girls, but not for long. Very thoughtful and I know Embee will enjoy his new toy when we visit my parents."

"You must be Skylar," Jolisa smiled and gave Skylar an equally affectionate embrace. "I'm Jolisa. I see you've already met Girard. This is Fran, my indispensable help with the girls and all other things important."

After Skylar and Quinn offered the proper greetings, Jolisa proudly said, "And these are my two youngest little ladies." Both girls stood very politely and were bright-eyed and smiling. The smaller one giggled as if she shared some private joke with her sister. "This is Belle," Jolisa said as she placed her hand gently on the back of the older girl, "And, this silly little one is Lizzie."

Skylar's heart melted as she admired the two little playful princesses, "Well, how do you do, ladies? My name is Skylar."

Giggles were all the two little girls could manage as Jolisa said, "I promised Belle and Lizzie they could stay up to see our guests, but it seems the cat has their tongues. Can you say good night to our friends, girls?"

"Good night!" The little girls giggled as they dashed back toward the door where they'd emerged a few moments earlier. Fran followed after them and called back to Skylar and Quinn before she disappeared again, "It's a pleasure to meet you."

"Let's go out on the patio and find Embee," Jolisa suggested and started toward another door in the room. Girard headed out through the front.

"They're wonderful, Jolisa," Skylar said as she stepped next to Jolisa and walked down a hallway toward the back of the house.

"Thank you," Jolisa agreed. "They really are. It's too bad that they couldn't stay up any later, but they are little grouchy bears in the morning if they aren't in bed before eight o'clock."

"No, it's fine," Skylar agreed. She complimented Jolisa on her choice of girls' sleepwear and then entered into a dimension of girl-speak that quickly evolved beyond Quinn's ability to comprehend. Quinn was encouraged as Jolisa and Skylar clicked that the night would be everything he'd hoped.

A moment later, the trio emerged into a large, and, by the looks of it, comfortable family room. The size of the room was eclipsed by its furnishings: a big couch, a loveseat, and chairs, a couple of coffee and end tables, a fifty-four-inch flat-screen television that hung on a wall above an entertainment center that included several intricate-looking electronic devices, recessed stereo speakers, a baby grand piano, and two guitar stands on which rested a sparkling red Stratocaster and a very nicely appointed acoustic. Collectible classic rock memorabilia hung on the walls. Skylar noticed that some of the stuff looked pretty rare, dating maybe to the early sixties: a framed Beatles concert poster, a grainy, black and white autographed photo of a very young Steve Winwood, a Mark Burton gold record, and what looked like a fairly recent photo of Buddy Guy with Mark Burton. Skylar thought to herself that, if nothing else, she'd be able to talk about music. To the right was a partial wall, or more accurately, a partition beyond which Skylar and Quinn could see a kitchen that was almost as big as the family room and equally well equipped for its purpose. At the back of the family room and the kitchen was one wall that consisted of a series of connected, full-length windows not unlike the bedrooms at the villa. A glass door in the family room opened onto the patio, which did in fact offer an extraordinary view of the Falmouth Bay and the ocean beyond.

In the forefront, Skylar, Quinn, and Jolisa could see Embee, whose back was turned away from the house as he maneuvered his way around a built-in grill. The stainless steel, vertical railing made more sense now that Skylar had met Jolisa's two girls. Sitting at a table just behind Embee was another girl who Skylar estimated to be about eight or nine-years old.

"There are Embee and Julia. I'm sure he didn't hear the door," Jolisa interrupted her talking with Skylar to say. "Let's go on out."

Jolisa grinned widely as she stepped out on the patio. Skylar followed and smelled the humid evening air flavored gently by surf and barbecue. As she neared, she perceived a vague familiarity with Jolisa's husband. After just a couple of more steps, the vague familiarity yielded to a puzzlement that occurs when a person experiences something completely out of context.

Turning around from her chair, the little girl called in her mother's accent to the preoccupied man at the grill, "Daddy! Your friends are here!"

With wooden-handled tongs in hand, the man turned around, stepped toward his guests, and addressed Quinn first and shaking his hand, "Quinn! Didn't hear you right off; having a spot of trouble with the grill. It's great to see you again!"

"It's good to see you, too, Embee," Quinn answered and added, "Thanks for the invite."

"Pleasure's mine. Besides, it the least I could do!" Embee insisted. "You and your friend up in New York are the reasons I am not in the poor house."

"I don't know about that," Quinn answered. "Something tells me you are doing just fine."

Embee then hugged Skylar warmly and said, "You're Skylar, then. Quinn and his friends have told me a lot about you. It's a pleasure." Wearing a warm smile and head tilted slightly to the left, he continued, "This young lady here at the table is my eldest daughter, Julia. Embee is the name my family and a few friends call me, but some people call me Mark. I answer to both."

Ever so momentarily, Skylar reconsidered her earlier thought that, if nothing else, she'd be able to talk about music. She could not have been more right. Skylar's sandals held her ground as she slowly grasped a reality in which everything was actually in its place. Quinn had managed to astonish her once again. The man who had just introduced himself was Mark Burton.

CHAPTER

The fix had been on. With Amelie's help, Jolisa and Embee had been conscripted by Quinn. "Nicely done, you guys," Skylar said as she recovered and glared reproachfully at Quinn. "Embee. M.B. Mark Burton. I get it, now, but I really had no idea. It is a pleasure to meet you. I know Quinn knows you as Embee, but if you don't mind I'd prefer Mark."

"Not at all," the chef replied as he turned back to the grill.

"And you," Skylar turned sternly to her escort, "You are just full of little surprises, aren't you."

In the back of her mind, Skylar considered the likelihood that Quinn, who obviously had a rapport with their hosts, had told them about her situation. She decided that he most likely had and it was fine, although she did not want Jolisa or Mark to patronize her.

"I hope you don't mind what had been our little secret, Skylar," Jolisa explained. "Actually, Embee and I haven't seen Quinn for years and were happy to hear he'd be on the island. When he told us you'd be coming with him, well we were just thrilled."

"No. I don't mind even a little. Since I've gotten to know Quinn, I've learned that he's equal parts thoughtful and playful. Considering we must have driven past the Fork-In-The-Road Centre four times today," Sklyar answered. "I should've thought Quinn might be up to something like this."

Mark motioned to Girard, who had returned from the errand that had taken him back through the front door, and asked, "Skylar, can we get you anything to drink?"

"Sure," Skylar answered as she looked over at the barbecue. "A glass of white wine?"

"Can you bring a bottle of Riesling for the ladies, Girard?" Mark asked before looking over to Quinn. "For you, Mr. Powers, I have arranged for a special reserve scotch aged forty years. Rocks?"

Quinn answered, "That sounds great, Embee. How did you manage that?"

"The same way we got that Alsatian of yours through customs. Celebrity has its advantages," Mark replied dryly, "Ginger ale for Julia and me, Girard. Thanks."

Girard turned back toward the house, and Mark turned his attention to the grill. He arranged pink fish filets before casually dropping small poultry halves on the grates. After he turned the meats, he rotated ears of corn, which had already been steaming in the husk, and checked a covered pot containing long-grain brown rice on the side burner.

"I chose the menu," Jolisa said. "The trout is fresh caught from Upstate New York and pheasant harvested directly from Ohio cornfields.

The little girl then turned to Skylar and explained proudly, "Daddy caught the fish and got the pheasants himself!"

"Well, this will be a real treat then, won't it?" Skylar answered. She and Jolisa joined Julia at the table as the men talked.

"Since I'm older, I get to stay up," Julia said proudly. "I'm almost nine!"

"And a terrific help with her little sisters," Jolisa said, equally proud.

"I'm sure she is," Skylar affirmed affectionately.

A few moments later, Girard returned with the bottle of chilled wine and four glasses, Quinn's scotch, and the two gingers. Mark interrupted his conversation with Quinn for a moment to ask Girard to let Fran know that dinner would be served in about fifteen minutes and to come out when she'd finished with Belle and Lizzie. Twenty minutes later, Jolisa served the corn and rice. Starting with his guests, Mark asked everyone their preference of entrée, "Trout, pheasant, or both." Mark warned, "I can promise that there are no flies in the trout, but I'm not as sure there's no shot in the bird."

Everyone chose "both," except for Jolisa, who had just the trout while Julia had only a small piece of the fish and a drumstick from one of the pheasant halves. All agreed that the food was terrific, and no one found anything but bones in the birds.

During dinner, Mark entertained with stories. Fran, Girard, and Jolisa must have heard them once or twice before, but were good sports about hearing them again. Skylar particularly enjoyed the one about the time that John Lennon called after Mark finished a tour.

It seemed John wanted Mark to join him with the Plastic Ono Band at a concert in Montreal. It was obvious to Skylar that Mark believed John and Yoko were about as flaky as a day-old croissant and just as crunchy. But Mark was pretty much up for anything, so he agreed. He packed his guitars and clothes for three or four days and drove to Heathrow. Waiting for him was a long-haired, full-bearded John Lennon wearing a white leisure suit, white shirt, white vest, white jacket, white bell-bottoms, and white leather shoes. The passengers on that trans-Atlantic flight would have their own story to tell when they landed, because Mark, Lennon, and the other members of the Plastic Ono Band who'd carried their guitars on board themselves rehearsed for the show during the flight. Mark remarked that Yoko didn't take part in the run-through. He thought that was peculiar considering the band was named for her. He also thought it was strange when, after landing in Montreal where it had been raining, a limousine pulled up at the arriving flights terminal and John and Yoko climbed in without a word. The car drove away, leaving Mark and the rest of the band waiting at the curb.

CHAPTER 49

After dinner, Jolisa and Julia returned with chocolate chip cookies for which Julia promptly took credit. Jolisa smiled and amended Julia's revised version of history to include Belle, Lizzie, and Fran.

"These cookies are great, Julia," Skylar said. Quinn agreed.

As good as they were, Julia could only eat about one and a half cookies before her mother said it was time for bed. After giving Jolisa and Mark a hug and a kiss, Julia said goodnight to Girard, Skylar, and Quinn. Then, Fran bid the rest of the group a good night and walked Julia into the house. A moment later, Girard asked Mark and Jolisa if there would be anything more either would need. Then, being cleared for the night, Girard politely begged off, citing a football match on the satellite that he wanted to see.

"That was perfect," Skylar said. "All of it. I can't tell you how much I enjoyed the food and company. The fish and fowl were terrific, Mark, and Julia and your girls are incredible. Thanks."

Jolisa looked over at her husband before she answered, "Skylar, we're glad to have you. Your man, here, isn't bad company either."

Skylar blushed a little at Jolisa's remark and glanced over at Quinn.

Just then, Mark asked, "You don't have anywhere to be, do you?"

Quinn looked at Skylar and answered, "No, we don't."

"Well, I had hoped we could go into the playroom for a little while, and well, play," Mark suggested.

"I'm game if you are," Quinn asked Skylar. "Are you feeling okay, Skye?"

"Absolutely," Skylar replied enthusiastically. "We won't disturb the girls, will we?"

Jolisa answered, "No. Even though Mark doesn't play loudly, the room is sound-proofed. It won't be a problem."

"All right," Mark said with a boyish enthusiasm. "We're not getting any younger!"

The four returned through the glass door into what Mark called the playroom. Jolisa asked if she could freshen drinks and crossed the partition into the kitchen. Mark grabbed the acoustic guitar from its stand and plucked the pick from the neck. With guitar slung over his shoulder, Mark pulled a black stool away from the other side of the piano. He sat and his fingers began to dance on the strings with a facility that comes only from reinforced habit. As she found a seat on the couch next to Quinn, Skylar had the sensation of sitting down at an extremely hard-ticket *Unplugged* concert.

In much the same way Quinn remembered her when they met for dinner, Skylar perched with anticipation on the edge of the couch. Her knees were together and the heels of her sandals touched. Skylar was turned slightly toward Quinn. She rested her left hand under his just above his knee and her right across her own. As Jolisa returned with her wine and a club soda for Quinn, Skylar's back was arrow-straight and her eyes were wide as she watched her host ear-tune his guitar.

"Don't get too comfortable, Skylar," Mark told her as he started to play a few distantly familiar chords. "I'll need you in a few minutes."

As Quinn's friend, "Embee," shut his eyes and played some distantly recognizable shreds on the his guitar, Skylar sat on the edge of her seat and wondered which among the hundreds of songs Mark had recorded would spring from his fingers and radiate from his familiar, comforting voice. Teasing, slowly approaching a familiar melody, Mark found his place on the instrument as Skylar thought to herself how much his style reminded her of an experienced lover who uses his fingers to build expectation for something extraordinary. Soon, Skylar recognized the great pop song, "What Love Can Be." Skylar sang along with the next country-influenced "Wedding Band." He finished the miniset, peaking with a spiritual Mark had written entitled "Take Me Now." Skylar listened with closed eyes. Without a hint of self-consciousness, she moved her head in rhythm.

Skylar discovered Mark's secret as he brought her down from her high and returned to a more bluesy, free-form instrumental that poured over her like satisfied waves of release. He was priming. Again, he wandered, slowly at first, playfully, and seemingly with just a hint purpose. Then, slowly, his intention formed and another familiar melody emerged. This time, the songs themselves would be a part of the prelude. Gradually, gently, tentatively, the guitar questioned. Then, Mark sung the lyrics for "Lonely Drifter." He followed with an indigo Bob Dylan cover and another heartrending gospel, "Let Me Carry On." Skylar could have imagined it being sung by a Mississippi chain gang on a summer day. Slowly increasing the intensity for the third time, Mark surprised Skylar by speaking, "Skylar, on the piano is music. I'd like you to play."

Startled, Skylar answered with a question, "What?"

"Quinn told me that you play," Mark said. "I'd really appreciate playing with you. You can read music, right?"

"Yes, but..." Skylar was interrupted before she could finish.

"Well, come on over then!" insisted Mark.

Skylar looked first at Jolisa in an attempt to see anything on her face that might indicate whether her husband was joking. Jolisa just raised eyebrows and nodded. Next to her on the couch, Quinn encouraged her, "Go ahead, Skye."

Skylar stood up, used her hands to flatten her dress over her stomach and hips before walking purposely toward the bench behind the piano. Mark smiled and continued to play while Skylar sat down. "Ready?" he asked.

Skylar took a breath, nodded and joined in with the longing, almost regretful introduction to "One More Bill To Pay."

There is a difference between playing music and feeling it. Most people, even people who know little about music, can sense it. Quinn, Jolisa, and Mark realized right away Skylar felt it. Tears formed in Quinn's eyes and in Jolisa's as, for a few minutes while Skylar played, they heard the music of her heart. When the song ended, Mark stopped playing for the first time in almost thirty minutes. He had to pause to process emotion Skylar had poured through the keys. "Wow, Skylar. That was remarkable," Mark accurately observed more as a statement of fact than a compliment. "Start this next one. Have fun with it," he added.

Skylar stood up and, Jerry Lee Lewis style, started banging the ivories as she improvised the lead-up of "Country Nights" into an overture. After a minute, Mark joined with his guitar and the rendering continued for two or three more before he finally settled into the vocals. Skylar decided not only to add the keyboard, but also a harmony. The result was wonderful.

After the singing was done, Mark and Skylar continued and wandered from one place to another based on some secret musical language in which both musicians were amply fluent. It was difficult to determine who enjoyed it more, Mark or Skylar, but Quinn certainly liked it.

THE DREAM SEEKER

When they finally finished, Mark released the profoundly genuine laugh of someone who didn't want to be anywhere else doing anything else. Skylar's smile could have electrified the entire island for weeks. A moment later, Mark started the familiar, bold introduction for the original, rather than the Swing version of "Jennifer." Although it was a little strange to hear those notes played without electric, the three verses and three refrains fit as snugly as Skylar's dress and were almost as appealing. After the guitar climaxed, the denouement of the music written for piano continued, alone at first before it was rejoined by the complementary guitar. If Mark and Skylar found their common language with "Country Nights," they shared dialect with "Jennifer." And, if music is played to extract emotion, then Mark and Skylar were eminently successful. Given her situation, Skylar played the end of the song, well, like it was the end. The others in the room knew it.

Skylar and Mark were spent. Like two musicians sharing a stage before thousands of people, each stood up, met the other half the distance, and hugged. Quinn and Jolisa stood up and gave a two-person standing ovation. "Encore! Encore!" Jolisa said as Quinn whistled approval.

Skylar was first to speak. "Thanks, Mark," she began. "That was incredible. It was a dream come true."

"Thanks, nothing! You are amazing. It was my pleasure," replied Mark who wasn't being polite. He truly enjoyed the chance to play with a musician who challenged him. It made him feel alive, like the way he felt when he had played with other, accomplished musicians during his career. He continued, "No kidding. I would love to have you do a show with me sometime."

Skylar wasn't sure if Mark was sincere or simply being generous, but she accepted gracefully and without expectation, "That would be great."

"Look guys, I know it's getting late, but there is another song—more of a serenade than an encore really—I'd like to play. Can you stay a little while longer?"

Skylar looked questioningly at Quinn who answered, "Absolutely."

"Definitely," Skylar said, as she returned to her place on the couch next to Quinn.

Mark checked, "You don't mind, do you Lisa?"

"Certainly not," answered his wife. "Go right ahead."

Looking over toward Skylar, who'd sat down again next to Quinn, Mark took his place again on the stool. "Quinn tells me you have a special place in your heart for Elvis. Presley, not Costello," said Mark as he checked the tune on the guitar strings.

Skylar had already learned enough that when it came to Quinn, she should never be surprised to be surprised. Skylar's eyes widened.

"Well, it seems that both Elvis and I were influenced by many of the same blues musicians. He liked to play some of the old standards like 'That's All Right,' 'Hound Dog,' and some great blues and gospel songs, too. He worked those styles into the records that became hits," Mark explained. "He also did a lot of songs recorded by other artists, too. When he recorded someone else's song, though, he had a way of making it his own. 'Unchained Melody,' that wonderful Righteous Brothers song and 'Always On My Mind,' later recorded by Willie Nelson come to mind. Unfortunate for me at least, Elvis's vocal range far exceeds mine, so I am sort of limited in my selection. I'll admit that if I tried to sing 'Unchained Melody,' I would end up sounding like that hound dog. The good news is that I found this great Neil Diamond song he recorded in Memphis in 1969 during the same sessions he recorded some of the great ones like 'In the Ghetto,' 'Suspicious Minds,' and 'Kentucky Rain.'"

Skylar was like a kid on Christmas morning, fraught with anticipation. "You sure have a way of building suspense," she said finally.

"It's called 'And the Grass Won't Pay No Mind.' You might have heard it," were his last words before he began to sing with the tender, gentle guitar chords. After he sang the three verses and the bridge and ended in a flourish on the strings, Skylar and Quinn stood and applauded. At last, they walked over to Mark as Jolisa moved around and took her husband's side. The scene was not unlike the end of a dinner party after the guests finished Trivial Pursuit or Pictionary, except no one had played any games. It was late and Quinn offered, "We'd love to stay all night, but I think you guys will need your sleep to keep up with those beautiful daughters of yours."

Jolisa beamed with pride while she appreciated Quinn's etiquette relative to knowing when to call it a night, a propriety, to her occasional consternation, that not all of Embee's friends had acquired. "I cannot tell you how much we enjoyed having you guys here tonight," Jolisa told her guests as she looked to Mark for affirmation.

"Absolutely," Mark confirmed. "I had as much fun as anyone! I'd love to do it again sometime. I'm not sure how long you plan to stay, Quinn, but maybe we can picnic on the beach and bring the girls along?"

"We'd love that," Skylar answered as the group moved toward the entryway.

Just like they had earlier, Skylar and Jolisa walked shoulder to shoulder down the corridor while Quinn and Mark trailed behind. When the four reached the door, Quinn guided Mark away from the women and said, "I cannot tell you how much this meant to Skylar. Frankly, I can't tell you how it meant to me. Thank you."

"Quinn, look. When Amelie told me what you were doing, I was sort of shocked at first. After I thought about it, I realized that you wanted to give your friend a gift. Now I've gotten to know Skylar a bit, I can see how much she deserves to be happy now. I wasn't joking when I said that I doubted anyone had as much fun as I did."

Quinn knew Amelie hadn't told Embee everything. Quinn wondered if Embee still would've felt the same had he known more. Quinn decided he probably would have.

"Well, that makes me happy," Quinn replied. "As for a beach picnic," speaking a little louder so Skylar and Jolisa could hear, "That would be terrific. We'll call you."

Skylar and Jolisa hugged. Quinn shook Mark's hand before he walked over to Jolisa.

"That sounds great," Jolisa answered finally. Then, everyone said good night, and Skylar and Quinn walked out of the air conditioned house and into the agreeably warm Antiguan night.

CHAPTER 50

Jolisa and Mark watched until they heard car doors close over the whisper of light laughter. The engine turned and the sound of tires grew distant. Jolisa took Mark's hand. After peeking into the girls' rooms to check each was dreaming contently, they continued toward their own bedroom. Jolisa quietly closed the door and turned to Mark. In the dark, he hadn't noticed Jolisa started to cry.

"Oh my god, Mark!" Jolisa whispered. "Skylar is such a beautiful person. To know that she only has a little time and what Quinn is doing is so amazing! My god! I can hardly believe it."

"I know, Lisa," Mark answered softly, comforting. "I know."

"I look at everything we have. Not the material stuff, but the girls and each other. These are all things Skylar will never have. It makes me so angry! And she's so strong. She's so strong and so beautiful. It's just not fair!" Jolisa emphasized with tempered rage.

Mark was only able to say, "You're right, Lisa," before she interrupted him with a full, passionate kiss.

"And, you did a wonderful thing tonight. You really did," Jolisa said as she led him to their bed where she wanted less to please or reward him as much as she wanted to affirm life. She wanted to feel life, her life, Mark's life, her children's lives. Skylar's life.

CHAPTER 51

"When Mark said you told him I liked Elvis, I wouldn't have been shocked to see The King himself appear from behind some wall and stride across the room in his white, sequined bodysuit and that pretentious grin on his sideburned face as his concert entrance music played. You've heard it, the 'The Theme from 2001: Space Odyssey' and 'That's All Right' medley!" Skylar said excitedly as she followed Quinn into the kitchen from the garage. "You've got me to expect the unexpected, if not the impossible."

Quinn answered contentedly like someone who had done a good day's work, "Well, I am glad you liked your surprise. I had a tough choice to make. Obviously, I chose Antigua to see Embee and Jolisa and for a few other reasons. If I believed you'd have really preferred Elvis, we'd have gone to Hispaniola instead and spent at least a little bit of time on the western side of the island."

Puzzled, Skylar narrowed her eyes as if she were working out some legal problem. It didn't connect at first, but then she burst with a laugh, "Voodoo. Zombies. Very funny."

As Quinn and Skylar reached the foot of the stairs, Sonny entered from the direction of the recreation room. "Good evening, Skylar," Sonny said. "I hope you had a terrific evening with Mr. Burton. From the sound of it, I think you did."

Skylar asked playfully as if she'd been terribly offended, "Did everyone but me know where we were going tonight?"

Sonny answered, "No, Skylar. It was only Feef and me. Then, of course there was Feef's sister and second cousin. My brother-in-law and his family." He could not continue without laughing himself. "No, it was just Feef and Sonny. I saw the car lights as you motored in and wanted to check that you needed anything."

Quinn answered, "Thanks, Sonny. Would you mind a pitcher of water, mostly ice, and a glass. Anything for you, Skye?"

"I'd love a chamomile tea, decaffeinated," Skylar said to Sonny. "I need something to bring me down easy from this surprising lovely day."

"I'll have Feef bring it right up," Sonny assured her. "And, I'll bring your water, Quinn."

"Thanks, Sonny," both Skylar and Quinn said as the two began the climb to the bedrooms.

The door of Skylar's bedroom was open and she started inside, but she turned and faced Quinn. "I never really did much of that when I was married. You know, having dinner with other couples, talking, having fun, being normal."

Quinn looked at Skylar understandingly and responded to something Skylar didn't say. "It's nothing, Skye."

"No, it was not nothing," Skylar insisted. "The last thing I want you to do is patronize me. You know it was not nothing. It was something, something special, and I want you to know how much it means to me. Our hosts were a wonderful surprise, but it meant at least as much to me to be with you and to have a couples date. Meeting Mark was pretty cool, though."

"Skylar, I meant that it's easy to be good to you. It is easy for a guy to want to be around you. It is easy for me to want your attention. I didn't mean to imply tonight, today, or anything else for that matter is nothing. I guess what I mean is that it just comes easy for me to do things for you because you are who you are." Quinn didn't add, "And, because I've fallen in love with you."

Skylar stepped just a little closer to Quinn, reached up on her toes, and kissed him on the cheek. She wrapped her arms around his neck and hugged him with as much passion as gratitude. Catching her breath, Skylar stepped back and said, "Good night, Quinn." She turned, walked into her room, and glanced back at him before closing the door behind her.

After the door clicked shut, Quinn had to catch his breath as he stood alone in the hall for a moment before he continued to his room.

CHAPTER 52

Because of the arid Caribbean climate, Quinn kept his room air conditioned. He slept in a pair of flannel pajama pants with a blue and white plaid design. Perhaps because he'd become used to sleeping in a cold room at home, he rarely wore the matching T-shirt or long-sleeve button down flannel top. If his room was too warm, he slept above the sheets; when it was cold, he added a blanket or comforter and warmed a pocket in the bed with body heat. Quinn thought about all of the idiosyncrasies people have. He wondered how Skylar slept just a few feet away from him behind the common wall their rooms shared.

Quinn heard a knock on his door.

"That you, Sonny?"

"It certainly is," Sonny answered. "Got your water."

"Great. Come on in. Thanks," Quinn answered as Sonny opened the door with is right hand and held a tray with his left. He walked across the room and placed the tray on the coffee-table, removed the pitcher and the glass, and then removed the tray.

"Feef was just a few steps behind me with Skylar's tea. Is there anything else you need tonight, Quinn?"

"No, Sonny. I think I'm good. We're all set for tomorrow?"

"Yes we are," Sonny answered.

"Great," said Quinn. "We'll see you in the morning, then. Have a great night."

"Thanks. You too, Quinn. Sleep well," Sonny said as he carefully closed the door.

Before Gina got sick, Quinn rarely had trouble sleeping. He'd been able to sleep while sitting or literally any place where he could manage to get horizontal. It struck Quinn as peculiar that the more time that separated him from his old life, the more difficult he found managing rest. He hadn't yet achieved a degree of insomnia that required medication, but Quinn often needed to find ways to relax, especially when he was with a Dream Seeker.

In spite of the travel and the anticipation of today, Quinn got to sleep the first night in Antigua fairly easily. He understood that tonight would be a different story. The long drive, the unplanned contacts with Johnson, and his emotional recounting of his time with Luz taxed him. At the beach, Skylar succeeded in making an otherwise restful nap quite a bit more stimulating. Finally, there was dinner with Embee and Jolisa. As a result of the demanding day, Quinn's mind filled with images and emotions that required some method of relief.

For occasions like this, Quinn brought books. He preferred reading fiction to watching television because reading was more meditative. Besides, Quinn believed he learned more when he read than he did when he watched television.

Immediately after Sonny had closed the door, Quinn poured himself a glass of water and opened the small case he'd put on the closet shelf. He'd almost finished the book he read earlier on the beach and reviewed his choices when he heard another knock at the door. Quinn answered the knock this time without glancing up from the two books to which he had narrowed his choice, "Come in, Sonny. What 'd'ja forget?"

The door opened and closed, but it was his unanswered question that caused Quinn to raise his eyes. As Quinn glanced toward the door he rephrased, "What's up, Sonny?" As soon as he spoke, his eyes bolted back into a double take. It was Skylar who'd come in, not Sonny. Skylar stood timidly for a moment as she awaited Quinn's reaction. She didn't have to wait long.

In a split second, Quinn no longer had to wonder what Skylar wore to bed as she dropped her short cream-colored silk robe to the floor. Quinn's eyes met hers. He tossed the books indiscriminately onto the floor and bounded toward her. Skylar met him. She leapt and wrapped her arms around Quinn's neck and her legs around his waist. She nearly knocked him off his feet.

Quinn felt Skylar's warm soft skin against his chest, on his arms, and in his hands as he held her. Standing in the middle of the room wearing only his pajama pants, Quinn braced Skylar's bottom with his left hand while his right hand held her between her shoulder blades, pulling her tightly against him. Heat intensified where their bare skin touched. Still clutching Quinn around his neck with her right arm, Skylar pulled back her left hand, seized Quinn's face and kissed him impatiently.

"Your back must be better," gasped Quinn.

"Uh huh."

THE DREAM SEEKER

Quinn carried her backward toward the bed. Skylar straddled Quinn's lap as he sat on the edge. Still kissing him, Skylar pushed him onto his back and whispered an order that was equal parts sultry and anxious, "Scoot." She motioned him to move up. Quinn shifted and repositioned on the pillows. Skylar stalked on all fours with him as he moved. As soon as they stopped, Skylar kissed Quinn again before focusing her attention on his neck and shoulders.

Skylar noticed for the first time the peppering of gray hair among the other darker hair on Quinn's chest. Like the silvering of the hair on his temples, the discovery underscored the parts of Quinn she had grown to admire and perhaps even love—his patience, honesty, and vulnerability. "Of course," Skylar thought, "it doesn't hurt that I'm attracted to this guy below the neck." She savored Quinn's chest, nuzzling and kissing before pausing for a moment. She closed her eyes and, resting her head on his stomach, reached up and caressed Quinn's arms, shoulders, and chest. Continuing her journey, she brought down her hands and with her left, loosened the draw string on his bottoms. She slid her fingers under the belt line and pulled the flannels down over his legs and feet and dropped them over the footboard.

"There. We're even," Skylar said as she glanced down and saw she had Quinn's undivided attention.

Quinn could hardly help, well, his state of mind. From the moment she walked through the door, he could see the passion in Skylar's determined, feral eyes. Those eyes alone would have been enough to flip any man's switch, but then there was the rest of her.

If the beach was the preview, this was the feature. Skylar's skin was soft and browned and tight over her pert largish breasts and lithe muscles. In a moment, her body was on his. As he held her tightly against him, Quinn felt the warm moistness of her anticipation. He had the sensation of a key releasing a long-since-forgotten lock. He closed his eyes and breathed deeply as Skylar nestled her head again on his stomach. With her left hand, she reached up and touched Quinn's face. Her right elbow was bent and close to her body as she gently, but firmly held Quinn's attention.

Neither wanted to move from that spot, but both had an irreconcilable desire to do so. Skylar reclaimed her other arm and used it as leverage to push herself further down, kissing Quinn's stomach before finding with her mouth the hypersensitive space on his thigh just below the waist. As Skylar kissed and touched him, Quinn squirmed as his desire intensified.

Quinn, whose head was thrown back against the pillow, didn't see Skylar as she gazed up with those eyes. Abruptly and without removing her hand, Skylar pushed herself up, lifted her leg over Quinn's hips, and guided him gently inside of her. As she did, Quinn produced an almost imperceptibly vocalized sigh. Finding her rhythm, Skylar moaned as she alternated between looking deliriously down at Quinn and closing her eyes and throwing her head back.

Time was suspended. Slowly, patiently, Skylar's pace quickened. She reached down and took Quinn's hand, which had been caressing her thigh and placed it on her breast, making sure to position his thumb on the most sensitive area. Skylar released a whimper when Quinn's hand found its place. In vain, Quinn tried to concentrate on caressing Skylar with his hand as she directed while his grip tightened on her hip. More rapidly, now, Skylar's hips plunged Quinn inside her. Quinn removed his hand, slammed it onto the bed and violently seized the comforter. He bit his lip. Skylar thrust more quickly before she stopped suddenly, pushed down hard, moved forward onto him, pressed her face against his as her hair fell over him and released a deep, protracted groan that seemed to originate from some faraway place. Slowly, carefully beginning to move again, Skylar nuzzled more closely as she relished the remnants of her release. All thoughts left Quinn's mind as the erotic tension drained from his body.

For a long time it seemed, Skylar did not move. Emotionally and physically exhausted, she cuddled, exhilarated, in a child's pose, lying face to face, nose to nose, mouth to mouth with Quinn under the canopy of her hair. Connected. Alive.

There is something about the scent of a woman, composed of everything from the soap, the perfume, and every little thing else, but it is also more. In a moment of genuine intimacy, every part of her, from her breasts to her breath, radiates comfort and connection. There was probably an evolutionary benefit to this olfactory aura. In practice, it was a real-life love potion.

Skylar remained still, and Quinn, like an inhabitant in the atmosphere of her world, breathed her in. Drifting between dream and consciousness, Quinn broke the silence finally after several minutes, "Wow. I'm sure glad it wasn't Sonny at the door."

"Me, too," Skylar agreed as she exhaled. "When he jumped, he would have probably knocked you over."

CHAPTER 53

As close as she felt to Quinn at that moment, she wasn't accustomed to the temperature. Goose bumps formed on the parts of her not in direct contact with Quinn's skin. Reluctantly, Skylar rolled off onto her back. Then, she lifted herself, pulled down the sheets, and slid in.

Still basking in the remnants of what he and Skylar shared, Quinn remained motionless for a few minutes before the cool air helped him toward the same conclusion. Once under the sheets, he pulled Skylar close to him. Sharing a pillow, Skylar's back snuggled up against his chest and stomach, Quinn's lips resting on Skylar's shoulder. His hand gently held Skylar's perfect narrow thigh.

A tear silently rolled over the bridge of Skylar's nose as Quinn held her. As protected as she felt, she also felt helpless. As much as she felt passion and release and yes, she admitted to herself, love, she also felt regret. Her regret hadn't resulted from connecting with Quinn. Rather, she regretted all the days she'd been distracted instead of living life. Only now, after having been shown her dreams had always been within reach, she mourned her loss.

Reaching down, Skylar held Quinn's hand and once again pulled it up and held it between her breasts. This time, Skylar's intent was not physical stimulation. Instead, she wanted intimacy. She wanted to feel friendship. She continued to hold his hand and pulled it up just under her neck. She took her left hand out from under the pillow and wrapped it around Quinn's forearm. With a firm grasp, Skylar whispered, "Good night, Quinn."

Quinn pulled his legs up and nearly enveloped Skylar. After gently kissing her bare shoulder, Quinn whispered back, "Good night, Skye." He didn't have another conscious thought before finding deep sleep.

CHAPTER

An orange sun baked the land. Against a red and yellow sky, trees managed enough moisture and nutrients to erupt from the bare, rufous rock. Jagged, scraggly branches reached out like arms from the trees that were naked except for pocket watches, dozens of them, which hung from the branches like wet sheets. The watches had literally begun to melt from the heat and fall from the branches to the ground.

In the distance, a line of elephants that had impossibly long legs meandered through the bare tree forest. A man wearing a dark, hooded robe cowered in the elephants' path. The elephants neared. The man held his arms crossed in front of his head in an effort to protect himself. At that moment, a naked woman who simultaneously was Skylar and wasn't Skylar ran over to the man and pulled him to safety. As she escaped the elephants' trampling, holding the man's hand in tow, the hood slid down to expose the man's identity. Quinn saw his own face.

He bolted awake.

CHAPTER 55

Quinn assumed he was like most people when it came to dreams; he only recalled them just before waking. Most of the time, dreams he had earlier in the night were too far out of reach. The dream he remembered from this night's sleep yielded feelings he struggled to reconcile. Slowly, deliberately, Quinn focused his eyes and his mind as the sunrise hinted at the day's first light. In an attempt to define reality from dream, he reached across the bed. During the night, one of the pillows had slid down and rested vertically, effectively partitioning the bed. Breaching the boundary the pillow created, Quinn's hand entered the other space and came to a rest on *nothing*. He lifted his head to visually confirm what his tactile reconnaissance suggested. In the dusky room, Quinn could see enough to understand that the bed was empty except for him. He looked toward the door where he had seen Skylar drop her robe, but saw nothing except for wall-to-wall carpet.

Even as he half-consciously attempted to square the information his senses offered, Quinn realized someone had indeed occupied the other side of the bed. Ruffled sheets had been pulled back as if a person had slept and had gotten up. Then, there was the scent. Quinn recognized the unmistakably feminine scent all around him.

Quinn's eyes swept the room. On his second pass, he saw her leaning pensively against a column that separated and supported the abundant windows. A silhouette against the suggestion of sunrise, Skylar stood silently, wearing only her silk robe. Her head tilted to the right, almost touching the post. Her arms were crossed in front. She supported her weight with her right leg, as her left, bent, crossed in front where only her toes and the ball of her foot touched the floor. Her beauty and the moment were overwhelming. Quinn wanted her thoughts as she looked across the dark ocean.

He quietly flipped back the sheets and pulled his legs out and onto the floor. Then he walked around the bed, found his bottoms, and put them on. Quietly, he walked to Skylar and stood behind her. He gently placed his right hand on her shoulder as he placed his left on Skylar's arm. Without turning, Skylar unfolded her arms and reached up with her left hand and put it on the hand that rested on her shoulder. "Good morning, Quinn." Skylar smiled as she spoke reminiscent of the stillness in the predawn light. "I heard you get up."

"For a minute I thought I dreamt you," Quinn answered. "When I woke up and you weren't next to me, I wasn't sure. Then, I saw you standing here. I thought you were an angel."

"I hope it was okay for me to come here last night," Skylar asked.

"It was absolutely okay, Skye. As much as I wanted to, I couldn't come to you."

Smiling more warmly, Skylar squeezed Quinn's hand, tilted her head, and rubbed it softly with her cheek.

Quinn took a deep breath and exhaled, "Skye, I have something to confess. For a lot of reasons, it's something I've been reluctant to admit even to myself."

Skylar turned around to face Quinn and looked up expectantly.

"Look, Skye, from the first time I saw you, I knew I was in love with you. I know that love is more than a physical attraction and even more than a chemical attraction, which is what I felt when you walked through that door last night. Actually, I had a strong feeling I would fall in love with you. I have," Quinn said with a hint of apprehension. "My head knows there are fifty reasons why I shouldn't have let myself do that, but that assumes I had a choice. I don't believe we choose the person we love. We just do. I don't know what happens tomorrow, next month, or next year, but I know I love you now, Skye."

Skylar affectionately wrapped her arms around his neck and held him in a way that made Quinn feel she embraced his soul as well as his body. At the same time, Skylar was surprised by her reaction. For the first time in her life, she was completely natural and unconstrained by expectations from other people. She was uninhibited by the man on whose strong, yielding shoulders she placed so many of her burdens and so many of her hopes. Skylar pulled herself up as she pulled Quinn down, held his face close to hers, and whispered finally in his ear, "Quinn, more than you could know, I love you, too." She punctuated with a passionately gentle kiss.

Skylar moved her hands down, held Quinn low around his back, held her head close to his chest, and turned slightly toward the awakening ocean. Quinn rested his face against Skylar's head. He inhaled through her hair and drew her deep into his lungs. Then, without another word, he reached his right hand behind his back and found hers. Slowly separating from each other, Quinn led Skylar back to bed. This time, it was Quinn who loosened the robe and let it fall to the floor. He reached down and started to slide off his pajamas, but then had help.

Skylar sat back on the bed, pushed herself back with her arms while Quinn, hovering above her, paralleled her movements. Once settled, Quinn held Skylar close and kissed her full on her lips, on her neck, and on her face. They didn't have all the time in the world, but neither had any place better to be just then. Quinn patiently explored every part of Skylar with wonder and awe.

CHAPTER 56

Quinn grabbed his clothes and shaving kit for the short trip with Skylar to her bedroom, where they showered playfully together. With the liquid soap, Skylar made a creamy lather by running her hands over Quinn's chest. Occasionally, she allowed her hands to wander. Quinn held a shower mirror in one hand and his razor in the other. "A man shaving is somehow one of the sexiest things to watch," Skylar told him.

Quinn dressed quickly in white shorts, a braided leather belt, a lime green pull-over, and loafers with no socks. His close-cropped hair didn't require a dryer. He sat on the sink counter and watched with some amusement as Skylar labored in front of the mirror next to him.

When she emerged from the shower, Skylar resembled a wet kitten, albeit a very cute and extremely sexy wet kitten. Before she began her work, Quinn watched her slip on a flattering, lacy pair of white panties and bra. She started by running a thick, wide-toothed comb through her hair to release the abundant tangles congregated mostly near the ends. After pulling out a brush that looked more like a boat oar than an instrument of hair care and a leaf blower-sized hair dryer, she deftly tamed and styled her wild mane. Ten minutes later, she pulled out a bag full of makeup, which she applied sparsely, carefully, but completely. There must have been two-dozen varieties of tubes, cylinders, discs, cubes, and ovals, each of which apparently contained some sort of beautifying product. Skylar seemed to use every one. Incredibly, when she'd finished, she looked like she had no makeup on at all, which, Quinn supposed, was sort of the point. She did look incredible, but then, he thought she looked incredible when she was a wet kitten half an hour earlier.

Quinn followed her into the bedroom, where he watched her put on a pair of olive-colored cargo shorts and a short-sleeved white blouse that she quickly buttoned down from the third button and tied it off at her midriff. At last Skylar grabbed her purse, flashed an honest, wholesome smile, and fasked without the least bit of irony, "Ready?"

"Absolutely," Quinn beamed as he reached for her hand. "Let's get some breakfast."

Quinn had already started down the stairs a step ahead when Skylar, with some alarm, remembered, "I forgot my sunglasses. Let me run back and grab them."

"I'll come back with you," Quinn offered.

Skylar replied, "No, go on. I'll be down in less than a minute."

Quinn obeyed. He continued down the stairs through the foyer and the library, and finally out onto the patio where Sonny anticipated his arrival. Quinn found his coffee cup turned up, a fresh and hot coffee carafe on the table, and a *Wall Street Journal* on the table. Quinn marveled at Sonny's predictive abilities as he looked at Skylar's side of the table. He saw the package, nearly identical to the one she found the previous morning. He sat with an unfamiliar sense of contentment, poured a cup of coffee, opened the paper, and smiled in spite of himself.

Meanwhile, Skylar found her sunglasses. Rather than putting them in her purse, Skylar had inadvertently laid them on the end table next to the couch last night after coming home from dinner with Embee and Jolisa. She smiled as she thought about her mistake, "Considering what was on my mind last night, I was just a little distracted!"

She darted into the bathroom for an instant to check herself again and placed the sunglasses on her head. "It's sort of silly," Skylar thought to herself, "Absence makes the heart grow fonder and I've only been away for a couple of minutes!"

As Skylar skipped down the stairs, she couldn't have known the pain she felt in her back, a pain that did not simply pierce the umbrella of protection the Fentanyl had provided but literally exploded through it, was a condition known as cord compression. Cancer cells which had traveled from the primary site through the blood and past the lymph nodes, finally colonized in the vertebrae in Skylar's spine. The cancer actually affected the way her body functioned, changing the shape, density, and strength of the bone in her lower back. Bad cells existed near the nerves that carry information, including pain, from other parts of the body to the brain. In the case of a cord compression, one or more bones in the spine fracture and collapse onto others. At best, the person who experiences the condition suffers an almost unimaginable pain. In severe cases, the result is a loss of motor function and paralysis.

Skylar's pain was so intense her legs weakened and she instantly lost consciousness. Unable to hold herself upright or steady herself on the banister, she crumbled like a building at the hands of a demolition crew before she fell forward. When her body came to rest on the hard tile in the entry way, blood trickled onto the floor from inside her hairline.

CHAPTER 57

Prudence McDermott was a contradiction in three dimensions, which her appearance only began to suggest. Her dark-gray $1,500 business suit was accessorized with a black, shoulder-strapped Louis Vuitton briefcase, from which she removed a matching leather legal-sized notebook. She opened it at her place on the long side of the conference table. Facing the window, she had a view of the Sears Tower and Lake Michigan in the distance. Whether ending a relationship with a sex partner or negotiating a divorce settlement with opposing counsel, Prudence always controlled the door. She made it as much a point of pride as personal and professional acumen to arrive early for appointments.

Thick dreadlocks hung impudently close to her shoulders but didn't obscure Prudence's blue eyes. Her tailored Armani jacket parceled broad and rugged shoulders. The matching skirt wrapped her thick, muscular hips and thighs. Prudence wore no makeup, so the large and ample freckles she inherited from her indolent father were plainly visible on her darkish face and on the wide nose she'd gotten from her drug-addicted mother. When she thought about her parents, an exercise she tried very hard to avoid, she mused with bitter irony that her father's Scottish heritage did not include frugality while her mother was the quintessence of an urban stereotype. In both cases, fate conspired to make her life's journey as difficult as it was distasteful.

As a child, Prudence couldn't comprehend the forces that brought together her parents in North Providence, Rhode Island. Her father was a journeyman tool and die maker at machine shops that supplied the military and aerospace industries in New England. Describing Sean McDermott as a journeyman was her own contemptuous way to describe his propensity to drink himself out of jobs. In Prudence's memory, if her father wasn't drunk at the nearest corner bar, he was drunk at home, and she very much preferred the former.

It certainly didn't help that the other bar flies had trouble with the idea he was a "nigger lover." So, with the stigma of joblessness and being "unable to find a white woman," Sean directed his anger and rage at his wife, at least for a while.

It hadn't started in that direction for the McDermotts, but it probably could have gone no other way. Neither Sean nor Veronica had education beyond high school. Sean was a tall and wiry redhead whose priorities were smoking cigarettes, drinking beer, and hanging out with friends in the Cumberland Farms parking lot. After barely making the minimum requirements to graduate high school, he found a job sweeping floors at a machine shop. He thought he was a wealthy man when he received his first paycheck for $287.76. Sean blew it all on smokes and beer for himself and his friends.

Veronica Puopolo was the fourth of six children, two boys and four girls. Veronica was the prettiest. Considering her father had been a second-generation fisherman whose family had settled in Fall River after the World War II and her mother was Bermudan, Veronica sometimes struggled to find her place in life. Her good looks helped to minimize the derision some of her siblings endured. Still, she heard her share of contempt from blacks and whites alike.

College was a financial impossibility for Prudence's mother even if education was a priority. Not long after she met Sean sitting on his black and silver Camaro drinking beer with his buddies in Notte Park, she imagined a modest but meaningful life with him. Six weeks after Veronica turned nineteen, she became Mrs. Sean McDermott. The groom was three months short of this twenty-fourth birthday.

Veronica soon realized she hadn't known Sean very well when he started to stay out late after work and came home drunk. During the week, Sean woke up hung over, and it was all Veronica could do to get him out of bed and off to work. It wasn't long before he lost his job for excessive tardiness and absence. A few days later, Veronica's doctor told her she was pregnant and had been for about two months.

Veronica gave birth to a healthy baby girl, Faith Marie, eight months later, but Sean already had been fired from another job and started to take out his frustration on his young bride. Veronica began to worry about the fiscal viability of their little enterprise and told him so. Poorly equipped for rigors and stresses of a young family, Sean responded in the only way he knew. Veronica blamed herself and told no one even as abuse worsened. The frequency and severity of the beatings increased while the events triggering the abuse became more trivial. If dinner wasn't on the table or hot enough or what he wanted, Sean beat Veronica. If he happened to be employed and his boss spoke to him about the quality of his work, Sean beat Veronica.

Then, when Faith was about a year old, Veronica learned that she was pregnant again. Before she celebrated her twenty-second birthday, Veronica welcomed second daughter, Prudence May. Prudence would be the McDermott's last child. Veronica had no more children not because she denied John conjugal relations when she could manage it. That only antagonized him. The actual method Veronica inadvertently used as a contraceptive was arguably no better than the unpleasant consequences of abstinence. She'd become an addict.

Even when he wasn't working, Sean rarely spent days at home, so Veronica had some reprieve. When she wasn't too bruised to have been embarrassed by her appearance, Veronica spent days with childhood friends who hadn't even fared as well as she had. One friend in particular, a part-time dealer, regular user, and occasional prostitute, introduced Veronica to marijuana, then to crack, and eventually to heroin. In short order, the combination of Caribbean and Mediterranean cultures that composed her beauty disappeared. By the time Veronica reached thirty, she was barely recognizable. But that didn't discourage the abuse. On the contrary, the beatings intensified as Veronica became less able to keep a house and more the target of barroom mockery. Unfortunately, Veronica's circumstances did little to dissuade Sean's sexual energy. And again unfortunately, the object of his appetite became his ten-year-old daughter, Faith.

All during her childhood, Prudence saw and experienced her father's abuse first directed at her mother, then toward her sister. The culmination of her ordeal occurred on Sunday afternoon when her mother was gone and her father had come home unexpectedly. Prudence heard her sister's muffled screams through the closed door. Suddenly, Veronica showed up, stoned and bold, interrupting John with the ten year old. Humiliated, Sean advanced on her with a frenzied rage, beating her with his fists before he kicked her mercilessly into unconsciousness. Sean realized the terrible mistake, but it was too late. He understood that he would need an ambulance and there would be police, arrest, trial, and conviction for more crimes than he could even imagine. He decided to eliminate the evidence, and of course, the witnesses. In his drunken rage, Sean proceeded to beat Faith into what would be a persistent vegetative state, but not before he finished the unnatural assault he had started. When he stumbled out of the room to find Prudence, however, he was terribly disappointed.

Prudence had run the eleven blocks to her cousins' house where Veronica's sister made the emergency call. Prudence never saw her father again. Sean saw Prudence once more on a video-taped deposition before he was sentenced to second-degree murder, attempted murder, and first-degree sexual assault.

It is impossible to know for sure the reasons some people wither under extreme circumstances just as it is impossible to know the reasons others flourish. As Prudence matured, however, she discovered an affinity for academics. She demonstrated to herself and to her elementary school teachers, for whom she felt an innate disdain for what she saw as their weakness working in a male-dominated administration, unusually gifted intellectual skills. In spite of being the target of jokes for her appearance and for her social preferences, Prudence excelled in high school and finished as the salutatorian in her graduating class of 385. Her class rank, coupled with the achievement of National Merit Scholar, yielded a full scholarship to Providence College.

If her college grade point average that was just a few hundredths of a point short of a perfect 4.0 and an LSAT score to match was not enough, her extraordinary essay in which she described her considerable personal challenges was exactly what every law school admissions committee wanted to see. Three years to the day after she began her freshman year at Providence College, Prudence began her pursuit of a Juris Doctorate at Notre Dame. Predictably, she loathed South Bend, but managed to pass the time in the law library and a couple of weekends each month in Chicago, where she satisfied her physical needs with a succession of one-night stands.

Likely a result of her traumatic childhood, Prudence also realized she did not simply dislike men, she hated them. Most of the time, she could barely tolerate them. She also discovered preference for strong, feminine women. As she entered her third year, she decided that she wanted to narrow her practice to divorce law and represent only women. In such a specialization, she could potentially realize two of her life's pursuits: the closest thing to legal castration that existed in the civilized world and the opportunity to meet attractive, resilient, and pissed-off women who were likely to be a little disenchanted with the half of the population who carried their genitals externally.

Skylar knew Prudence McDermott was renowned for her refusal to accept some clients. Skylar noticed, as did everyone at the firm, Prudence never represented men and her insolence ruffled feathers. However, Prudence consistently achieved unexpected results for her clients and the partners relented and allowed Prudence to do as she pleased. She eventually became a full partner.

Skylar and Prudence had something else in common. Both Skylar's brother and Prudence's sister required special, long-term care. Prudence moved her sister to the best facility in the region as soon as she started with the firm. She occasionally spoke with Skylar about John, shared experiences, and long-term care. Even if Skylar hadn't been an attorney at the same firm, Skylar couldn't have known Prudence would have taken her case simply because Skylar fit Prudence's type.

While she waited with arms folded for opposing counsel, Prudence allowed herself to think about Faith and the last time she and her sister spoke.

CHAPTER 58

As expected, January was not a month for the record books for Taylor Kerr. His income could never have sustained his lifestyle, but it certainly could have given him at least a chance to get back on his feet.

Without so much as a single question or contention, Taylor signed the nondisclosure and noncompete consent in consideration for payment of six-week's severance. Along with his final paycheck and compensation for accrued vacation, his final check amounted to less than $15,000 after the government had taken the juice. As for the rest of it, Taylor didn't want to admit he didn't know where most of it had gone. Much was spent on booze, he assumed. Taylor always seemed to have friends as long as he had money. Then, there was his brilliant plan to bet the Cardinals in the Super Bowl straight up against the Steelers. After all, Arizona was due, weren't they? He got five-to-two odds and the $5,000 bet would net him $12,500, enough to support his lifestyle for at least another couple of months.

Taylor could not catch a break. Sober, he understood the mortgage, insurance, utilities, satellite television, and mobile phone bills hadn't been paid. He was in a very bad way, and that was the reason he wanted to talk to Skylar. Perhaps he could reason with her and they could reconcile. He'd apologize, regain her trust, and she would reopen the spigot that poured money. In a worst-, or rather a best-case scenario, he could get an idea of just how sick she was. Perhaps, he could sweet talk just enough to delay the proceedings so they'd still be married when she croaked. In spite of the amendment Skylar must have already made to her will, he could contest the changes, citing some mental instability caused by knowledge of the terminal illness. He may get a big payday yet.

Having tried to convince a few divorce attorneys to take his case on contingency, Taylor failed to persuade. Some of the attorneys to whom Taylor had spoken were familiar with his antics and declined instantly. When others learned Prudence McDermott was opposing counsel, the common reaction was a shudder and a response that ranged from a polite, "Our calendar is full," to a dumbfounded, "Are you fucking joking?"

Even though Dean Kerr had been disbarred, the meeting with Prudence McDermott was simply a preliminary conference. From a legal perspective, Taylor could represent himself or even hire a Shetland pony. Of course, Dean Kerr couldn't appear as counsel in a court of law without special dispensation from the judge hearing the case, but there was no reason he couldn't advise his son in an initial meeting. Besides, Dean Kerr believed there was no way that some "nasty, third-rate, dyke bitch lawyer" would take advantage of him or his son. So, with all of the confidence that General George Custer had as he unfolded his strategy on Sitting Bull at Little Big Horn, Dean strode confidently into the conference room with his dull-eyed son a half step behind.

CHAPTER 59

"Where's Skylar?" Taylor asked as he followed his father to the window side of the table.

Taking her seat and maintaining eye contact with Dean, Prudence answered flatly, "I wouldn't be at liberty to say even if I knew. Frankly, it's not important. I have power of attorney for Ms. Smart."

Taylor sighed audibly as Prudence pushed an executed and notarized document across the table for verification. Prudence assessed the opposition. She was well acquainted with Dean Kerr's very public legal entanglements and immediately understood Taylor didn't have the money for an attorney. She could hardly believe Dean Kerr could make such a blatant mistake by all but taking a full-page advertisement in the *Tribune* to announce that his son was broke and desperate. Prudence also realized Dean Kerr, Esquire, made the critical error by underestimating her abilities and her motivations.

"That is bullshit," Taylor responded.

"That's enough, Taylor," Dean Kerr scolded. "Let me handle this."

Prudence wondered who was in charge of the negotiation. Frankly, Prudence realized it didn't matter. "That's three strikes. I've got the door, they've tipped their hand, and now they're rattled."

The elder Kerr continued, "This looks in order, although I concur with my son's assessment. This is bullshit."

"Is that a new legal term? I don't recall seeing that word in my law dictionary," Prudence mused. "Bullshit or not, you are dealing with me. Now, as you requested, Mr. Kerr, our meeting today is completely off the record."

Dean Kerr responded, "Good."

"Yes, it is," allowed Prudence as she methodically removed a laptop, a stack of manila folders, and a compact disc from her case. "I think you agree it will be in the best interest for both parties to resolve this case quickly and outside the realm of the public eye." Having experienced his share of negative publicity, Dean Kerr squirmed noticeably as he nodded agreement with opposing counsel's opinion.

"It's a catastrophe when a marriage ends," Dean Kerr said, mustering as much false sympathy as he could. "The hopes and dreams two young people had when they started come crashing down in the desolate reality that love is gone."

It was all Prudence could do not to grin as she powered-up her computer, which she'd purposely waited to do for effect. She maintained eye contact with the man she scarcely considered worth the space he occupied.

"What makes this situation even more difficult is Skylar's illness. It's tragic, just tragic. Please allow me to offer my prayers for a complete recovery. Given these circumstances, however, it is my contention that the removal of the burden of these proceedings will allow her to more effectively deal with her illness," Dean suggested as Taylor feebly attempted to stare Prudence down.

Prudence imagined this sort of gilded dog shit worked like magic on the ignorant housewives and laid-off construction workers who composed trial juries. Neither Dean nor his silver tongue held any fascination for her, although she enjoyed the novelty.

"Based on my research," Dean continued, "Including the businesses and the life-insurance benefits that Mrs. Kerr inherited during the time she was married to Taylor, your client is worth in excess of sixty million dollars. These investments consistently yield income of about five million dollars annually. Again, considering the best interest of your client, I believe that the most reasonable and expedient course of action would be to divide the marital assets equally between Taylor and Mrs. Kerr," Dean finished.

"Where did this guy learn his trade?" Prudence asked herself in wonder and amazement. After this last blunder, she was a little surprised Dean had done any research at all. He apparently had. He was fairly close to the value of Skylar's assets. If it could possibly be helped, though any decent negotiator never made the opening offer. Sure, Prudence knew she could possibly have forced it from him, considering the position of his client, but this guy gave in without so much as a bleating resistance. Prudence paused for a moment as she willed herself to avoid the error of overconfidence.

At last, Prudence started, "Mr. Kerr, I appreciate your position and the research you've done to support your request. However, I have something else in mind." Prudence slid two identical file folders from the materials she had carefully arranged on the table where she sat and gave the first to Taylor and the second to Dean. "These are identical sets of sworn affidavits from some of Taylor's associates," Prudence explained. "Included are twenty-one statements from women with whom your son has had intimate relations. In addition, I've taken affidavits from individuals who were self-described as Taylor's friends or former friends and from hospitality workers who served your son when he entertained his romantic trysts with women who were not his wife."

In the horror that sometimes accompanies a clear understanding of an untenable situation, both Dean and Taylor leafed through the folder.

"What you see is overwhelming evidence from individuals who have avowed Taylor has long and chronically engaged in extramarital sexual affairs with women dating back to the start of the marriage," Prudence confidently stated as she wondered again how and why Skylar had married Taylor Kerr. "I have taken the time to investigate each of the claims independently and have found supporting documentation, including restaurant receipts, hotel bills, and other proof to verify witnesses' statements. Frankly, I could have found more, but I had less than a month to conduct my inquiry. I'm certain I'll be able to obtain additional information prior to a hearing before a judge."

Prudence paused, looking first at Dean and then at Taylor to make sure the information was sinking in. Prudence wished she could play high-stakes poker with these guys. Consternation formed on Dean's face, while Taylor's face turned pale and he flipped to the last affidavit, which bore the name of Charlie Mazzola. Observing Taylor's recognition, Prudence offered advice, "You should choose your friends more carefully, Mr. Kerr."

Prudence reveled to see Dean Kerr act like a spoiled child who'd been denied a piece of candy. "You know as well as I do, Ms. McDermott, that these documents will only be marginally relevant if this goes before a judge. Not only can I refute these statements with investigative research of my own, but I'm certain I can also provide claims Skylar acted similarly during the union."

"Mmm," sounded Prudence doubtfully, "I might suggest that you check your facts. Start by interviewing your son. My client has been nothing short of a saint. You will find no evidence to support any infidelity during the relationship. If you suggest it, I will file a civil lawsuit against you for slander." Prudence removed a compact disc from its case and placed it in the computer's disc drive. The drive clicked and whirred for a moment before media software appeared on the screen and Prudence deftly repositioned the cursor with the touchpad. After a series of clicks on the left button, Prudence turned the monitor.

To his growing dismay, Taylor recognized what he was seeing. It was a video of him and of Charlie in a bar as Laurel and Hardy flopped and toddled, respectively, to their table. The music was loud and Taylor could see that he was loaded, but he didn't have to see the video to know that. He was so drunk he barely remembered any details. That was maybe not been a bad thing, but seeing the video was like recalling a nightmare in high definition.

"What is this, Taylor?" Dean demanded.

"It's nothing, Dad. It's just me and Charlie at a bar."

Dean glanced from the screen, then to his son, and then back to the screen. On the monitor, Taylor bought shots from a pert, skirted waitress as she moved through the crowd carrying a tray of tiny plastic cups.

"Jello shots," Taylor explained. "I think."

"What the fuck?" Dean blurted more as an exclamation than a question. "When was this, Taylor?"

"I don't know. About three weeks ago, I guess," Taylor said. "It was the night before I got the divorce papers."

Although Dean wished that the video had been taken after Taylor was served, he caught his breath. With a sense of short-lived relief, Dean redirected, "This video isn't relevant, Ms. McDermott. It depicts an event that occurred after Mrs. Kerr had declared her intention to file divorce. The judge will not give this information any credence."

It hadn't been Prudence's intention to use this video as evidence. She used it to put the Kerrs on their heels. The strategy had been a complete success.

Taylor was relieved when Prudence removed the images from the screen as she turned the laptop back toward her. She responded while she moved her finger over the touchpad. "I'm not completely certain that the video is irrelevant, Mr. Kerr. I think the images support a pattern of behavior. Of course, that will be up to a judge."

"You've got to be joking!" Dean nearly yelled as his façade began to show signs of erosion. Although his face had reddened with anger or fear, not a single hair on his head was out of place.

"Don't tell me all you have is a few bullshit affidavits from persons of questionable repute and a video of an upstanding young man who is trying to recover from the prospect of losing his beautiful wife by enjoying some consolation with friends at a local watering hole! That's what you've got?" Dean smugly asked.

"Well, no, actually. There is more," Prudence answered without a hint of emotion as she turned back the computer monitor toward the son and father. "It seems that Ms. Kerr had considered divorce for some time, perhaps for months before she learned about the recurrence of her illness. As a very successful attorney at our firm, Ms. Kerr had access to a number of very skilled, discrete, and effective private investigators."

As Prudence evenly offered these facts, a new video streamed. Based on the information to the right of the progress bar, Taylor discerned that the clip was just shy of nine minutes long. It began with him sitting at a table alone at a restaurant in Cicero. A moment later, a woman arrived and sat down across from him at the table.

"What you two are seeing here is the first of four video reports provided by the investigator Ms. Kerr hired early last year. I believe this one was made in April. In spite of the cool weather and the fogging windows, the quality and detail of the images are surprisingly vivid."

"All right, Ms. McDermott. That's quite enough," growled the older man. Unable to resist the temptation to further provoke the man who Prudence considered a disgraced ambulance chaser, she innocently responded, "Are you sure? This does get very entertaining. The third one is my favorite."

"Enough!" Dean Kerr shouted. "Turn it off!"

"Okay. Okay," Prudence answered dispassionately.

"All right, Ms. McDermott, you've made your point. Nicely done," Dean offered, But, none of this changes the fact that your client is terminally ill. Based on my professional consults, Mrs. Kerr only has months, perhaps even just weeks to live. That fact hasn't been lost on me as we've undertaken this little meeting in her absence. Now, your situation is precarious. If your client dies prior to the conclusion of these negotiations, whether we are able to reach an agreement or whether we have to bear the burden of what could likely be a protracted legal proceeding, counselor, Taylor will get everything."

Prudence knew Kerr was bluffing. Had he truly believed the line he was selling, he wouldn't have opened with the offer of an even split. Maybe Dean was more concerned about negative publicity than Prudence assumed. Given the convincing nature of the evidence she collected, he certainly had to give pause. In any case, Skylar gave Prudence specific guidelines within which she was required to work.

"That may be true, Mr. Kerr. That may be true," Prudence conceded with the full knowledge she could say anything without the apprehension that accompanies formal proceedings. "Let's cut to the bottom line, shall we? The fact is you have no idea how much video I have of your son or exactly what those videos show."

"First, and not that I would ever do anything so crass, but you know how things work. These videos are entered into evidence. Maybe the court clerk sees the chance to make a buck. For all I know, the investigator's protocol may not be as strict as it should be. The next thing you know, these videos are on Fox News and YouPorn. Your son is humiliated, and his reputation is destroyed, for what it's worth. More important, archived video of your little legal problems are pulled out of mothballs. Just as you're able to have a dinner without being harassed, you have to start all over again. Not a very attractive alternative, is it?" Prudence asked rhetorically.

"Go on," Dean responded without nodding.

"Second and more important still, no one can say how long my client has to live. It's true, she may only have weeks, perhaps months, and possibly even years. Who can say? Even though the prospect of your son, "emphasized Prudence in a way that suggested a distinct contempt, "inheriting her assets is as repulsive to my client as it is to me, Skylar knows she'll feel no pain. So, I have a counteroffer for you to consider."

"I'm listening," answered Dean in the first person, which suggested he had similarly low esteem for his progeny.

Although Prudence didn't hold all the cards, she knew she had a strong hand. "It helps," she thought, "when you get to stack the deck."

"While I could play the game of starting low, like making the suggestion that Taylor make alimony payments to Skylar as is common in most divorce cases, I will not waste your time. Frankly, Mssrs. Kerr, the settlement is more than I think Taylor deserves given his egregious conduct. Regardless, Skylar has authorized me to make a generous offer in exchange for an uncontested divorce. Skylar wants this to be over and, like a bad dream, she wants to put your son and her marriage out of her mind.

The Kerr's continued to listen. Dean sat expressionless while a fidgeting Taylor now looked broodingly down. From Prudence's perspective, Dean and Taylor obscured not only the view of the Chicago skyline but also the reflection of the seasonally rare crystal blue sky on the shiny mahogany table. "First, the mortgage balance on the Lincoln Park home is approximately $250,000, while the market value of the real estate even in this economy is at least three times that. In a normal market, the place is worth one-point-two easily. Skylar is willing to concede the entire equity in the real estate presupposing Taylor assumes the mortgage," Prudence paused. "Second, all additional real property in common, including automobiles, furniture, art, and other common assets will not be contested. Like I said, she wants to put this behind her and she doesn't want so much as a coffee mug from the cupboard. Finally, Skylar will make a one-time cash payment of $500,000 to Taylor."

At that, father rocked back in his chair as he shook his head discontentedly. Son's eyes widened. Taylor glanced quickly at his father, who started to vocalize. However, before he could respond, Prudence interrupted.

"Considering you had a significantly higher negotiating point, I sense you're disappointed. I understand. Before you answer, I want you to think carefully about your position," warned Prudence. "Your son is a young, educated, healthy, able-bodied man who has denied himself nothing during his marriage to my client. He contributed little to the assets of the marriage. Notably, he detracted in numerous, lascivious ways. I think any judge will concur with that appraisal."

"On the other hand, you have here a legitimate offer that in these difficult economic times is substantial and, dare I say, more than fair. Conservatively, it's north of $1.5 million. That's a nice little nest egg for Taylor as he gets himself back on his feet," Prudence added finally, referring to Taylor's recent situation as a member of the unemployed. "And, I also have to explain, this isn't only a last, best, and final offer, but it also expires when I walk out of this room today."

Understanding that he was, in fact, likely not in line for a big payday, Dean's face reddened. "This is a nuisance offer and you god-damned know it! There is no fucking way that I'll take this bullshit offer, especially from some carpet cleaner!"

Calmly, Prudence folded her computer, replaced it in her briefcase, gathered the other documents and files she'd had placed on the table, and stood up. Finally, she said, "I'll take your response to indicate that you decline."

Seeing his salvation literally walking out the door, Taylor pleaded finally, "Dad! What the hell are you doing?"

THE DREAM SEEKER

"Shut up, Taylor," growled Dean. "Shut the fuck up. If you hadn't been such a fucking irresponsible little prick to begin with, we wouldn't be in this situation."

As she watched the drama unfold between the son and father, Prudence pulled on her coat and smiled with sanctimonious pride knowing she had exceeded even her own expectations of the meeting.

"Wait!" Taylor screamed at Prudence before he moderated, "Please, wait." Taylor appealed to his father, "Dad, this is almost two million dollars!"

Dean answered angrily, "You don't have any perspective, Taylor. I've tried all my life to give you perspective and just a little bit of common sense, but I'll be damned, you have neither! This is not the time or the place to talk about this!"

Prudence stood at the door wondering how this supposed dream-team lawyer could be such a colossal idiot. The first rule of hiring an attorney is, do not hire yourself. The second rule follows, do not hire an attorney with whom a personal relationship exists. It clouds judgment. Of course, the fact that counsel had absolutely no experience in divorce law should somehow be a part of the third rule.

"It's a bullshit offer and we're not taking it," Dean reasserted more on emotion than on legal precedent. "We'll take our chances in court!"

Prudence reached for the doorknob as she asked again, this time directing her question toward the younger Kerr, "Are you sure you want to pass on this, Taylor?"

"No! I want it," Taylor answered. "Give me the papers now! I'll sign!"

"Shut up, Taylor," screamed Dean to his son. Then, he hissed, "We're going to pass, Ms. McDermott."

As she opened the door, Prudence smiled politely and said, "It was a pleasure to meet you gentlemen today. It looks like you have a few things to discuss. I look forward to seeing you in court."

Prudence closed the door behind her and heard Taylor shout, "Stop!" Then, she heard the Kerr's arguing loudly as she walked toward the stainless steel elevator doors at the end of the hall. Even as the doors closed after she pushed the "L" button on the control plate, Prudence could still hear the yelling.

If security monitored the camera affixed in a corner of the elevator, the observer would have seen a wide grin on the passenger's distinctive face. What the guard could not have known that the strangely masculine but shapely woman was thinking, "That went surprisingly well."

195

CHAPTER 60

"This cannot be fucking happening," Taylor Kerr said aloud to no one. "Seriously? Seriously? This cannot be fucking happening to me!"

As he drove away from the meeting and from that hideous woman and from his ignorant cock-sucking father, incongruous thoughts ran through his mind. "Jesus Fist-Fucking Christ! I am fucked!" "God damned it! If that bitch had been there herself, but she didn't have the guts as usual," Taylor ranted. "If she was there, I know I could have made her see things my way! Where the fuck is she?"

Taylor'd had it. He had it with his friends. *Charlie, that asshole!* He had it, obviously, with his wife. *Skylar! Jesus! I hate that bitch!* He had it with his father. *God-damned it, Dad. Are you fucking kidding, passing on a couple million bucks? I need that money!* He had it with his entire miserable life. *What the fuck am I going to do?*

For the first time in his life, Taylor understood he was in no way capable of functioning in the real world. From the time he was a child, his father financed him and bailed him out. Then, when he thought it served him, he married a hot, if not slightly self-conscious, rich bitch for her bankroll and for a warm place to put it from time to time. When she got sick, it turned out that she'd become more of a hassle than she was worth. Well, almost. Taylor really counted on a nice divorce settlement for his trouble. Now, his father had probably even fucked that up!

With condescending disgust of which only the indulged-privileged seem capable, Taylor looked over to the passenger seat where he'd dropped the affidavits. He looked at the documents and directed the lion's share of his malice to that lazy fucking ingrate, Charlie Mazzola. Eventually, he remembered some of the other names Prudence, or as his father had so aptly referred, that "carpet cleaner," had dredged up. Taylor grinned spitefully and thought, "At least the old man got that right."

While he drove on the busy Chicago streets, which bustled in spite of the stifling cold, Taylor turned the folder toward him, flipped it open, and glanced down at the name on the first document and then the next. Many names were unfamiliar. Taylor guessed many were restaurant workers. He may have also just forgotten the names of some women who he'd bedded, or backseated as the case may have been. Others gave Taylor the chance to stroll down memory lane. One was a little Southside trash bag who Taylor met a couple years after he got married. She was cute enough and would have literally done anything for him. He strung her along for a couple of months before she started to whine about wanting to go out once in a while rather than just spending weekday afternoons in a motel room. Was she joking? Another had been given by that thin, pretty little thing who had long, gently wavy dark brown hair. She was a doll. Taylor was banging her just before he got married to Skylar. Skylar almost caught him with her one day when she surprised him.

After glancing over more affidavits whose names Taylor didn't recognize, he almost turned over another before he turned it back to read the name again, "Katherine Novac. Katherine Novac?" repeated Taylor. "How do I know that name?" Taylor thought. He couldn't quite find the place in his memory that held the information about Katherine Novac. As Taylor turned down the document, he continued to repeat the name as if it were a meditative mantra, "Katherine Novac. Katherine Novac."

Then suddenly, Taylor experienced a moment of total recall, "Katie Novac. Katie Novac! That's Katie from Kirkwood's!"

Before that little row with Skylar, he'd spent enough time at Kirkwood's to know Katie. She was smoking hot, too. He wasn't sure how he knew her last name. Maybe, he'd heard someone say it. Regardless, he was sure it was Novac. She certainly made him feel like a piece of shit, but Taylor knew he'd have to put that aside for now.

As he had walked past the windows on North Sheffield that afternoon, Taylor glanced back and noticed Katie talking to Skylar. Katie couldn't have known that the bitch wasn't worth the effort, but Taylor knew Skylar didn't have much of a social life outside her job. He wondered more than once where Skylar went after that day at the bar. "If I can only talk to her," Taylor said again to the interior of the otherwise empty sedan. "If I can talk to her, I can make her see things my way."

Taylor decided that it might be a good idea to grab a beer at Kirkwood's and have a chat with that pretty barmaid. From where he was, Taylor thought Clark Street might be a better bet than driving all the way out to Lake Shore and coming back in.

CHAPTER 61

Dismissal was 3:25. On the days Katie worked at the bar, she organized her desk and packed her briefcase with her fourth-graders' papers she'd read and grade. As soon as the pickups migrated through the hallways to the lobby and the buses were loaded, Katie scrammed, usually accelerating out of the teacher's lot no later than a quarter to four. In spite of pouring draughts and mixing drinks on most Friday and Saturday nights, Katie still found time on Sunday to plow through her homework. Of course, she never gave her incredible nine and ten year olds work on weekends. Katie steadfastly believed weekends were for fun both for kids and adults.

Katie's boss wanted the evening shift to start at 4:00, but he'd long ago made an accommodation for Katie, who'd always been not just consistent, but also unusually good with customers and coworkers. Katie's start time had been changed to 4:30. Wave checked Katie's inventory and iced up for her. He was even allowed to sign out and count Katie's cash drawer, which was another violation of protocol conceded to Katie. There had never been a problem with the arrangement.

More than a month had passed since Katie said good-bye to Skylar, who'd said she'd call within a few days. When a couple of days passed, Katie assumed Skylar was enjoying herself too much. When a couple more days passed and then a week, Katie started worry. Even though Katie had known Skylar for a short time, the two had become close, and Katie didn't get the sense Skylar was irresponsible.

So, Katie decided to call the phone number she'd given Skylar. She spoke to the woman who picked up, but got no answers. It wasn't that the woman was rude. On the contrary, it almost seemed she was sympathetic. In the end, though, the woman skillfully avoided answering and failed even to confirm that she knew anything about Skylar.

By the time Wave returned to the back bar, Katie had already found her rhythm with the happy hour crowd. She was still looking down the bar, smiling at a group of girls who'd started their pub-crawl bachelorette party, when she turned and saw Taylor Kerr standing in front of her. Katie's cheerful expression vanished. She learned a great deal about Taylor during the couple weeks Skylar stayed with her, as if she needed to know any more after the scene she witnessed.

Katie finished the drink order for the five guys who sat down on the short side of the bar, skillfully bunching the assortment of glasses and bottles in her hands. As she moved toward the group and correctly assigned each drink to its corresponding imbiber, Katie crossed in front of her bar partner for the night and said with a wincing whisper, "Let me get that one." The other barmaid worked with Katie long enough to know her communication codes and interpreted the request to mean either "he came here to talk to me," or "this guy's a prick." In this case, it meant both.

Katie didn't so much as try to conceal her disgust, "What do you want, Taylor?"

"Is that any way to greet a customer, Ms. Novac?" Taylor self-assuredly replied. "But since you asked, I'll have a Miller Lite."

Although she hadn't known Taylor before she met Skylar, Katie had seen him in the bar often enough to know he preferred bottles to the tap. With a single continuous motion, Katie reached down, slid open the cover to the cooler, removed a bottle, opened it, and set it on the bar on a cardboard coaster she'd deftly picked up and dropped with the same hand.

"What else?"

Feigning innocence, Taylor responded, "What do you mean what else? I just came here to my favorite watering hole to have a couple of beers and enjoy the atmosphere."

"Cut the shit," Katie ordered. "Tell me what you want, or I'll have Wave throw your ass out of here for the betterment of humanity and on general principle."

"All right! All right. Here's the thing. You know Skylar's divorcing me, right?"

"Uh huh," Katie replied.

"Look. That's my fault. It really is. In truth, I've been a bad husband and I deserve what I get," Taylor said simulating sincerity. "It's just that I'm worried about her. I know she's sick and I know that all of this has got to be unbelievably hard for her. And, well, I just haven't spoken to her for a while and I'm worried."

With an unchanged expression, Katie asked flatly, "So, what do you think I can do about it?"

"You and Skylar are friends, right?" Taylor cast his line.

"Yeah, so?"

"And, didn't you help her out for a while after she and I separated?"

"Okay, yes."

Aha, Taylor thought. *A bit!* "Well, I hoped you could maybe get in touch with her, you know, just to check that she's okay. If she'd be willing to talk with me, I sort of hoped I could talk with her, too. In spite of everything I've done, she is, or was or whatever, my wife, and there were some good times. I just want to let her know, well, I just want to let her know that I'm sorry."

Katie needed to think. She believed everything Skylar told her about Taylor and the terrible things he did. At the same time, she balanced the benefit and peace of mind of knowing Skylar was okay against doing something to help that conniving bastard. Conveniently, a stockbroker-looking guy walked up to the bar near the waitress' station and waved a $50 bill at her. The other bartender was occupied with the bride-to-be and her court, who had just finished a round of Blowjobs and ordered a round of Sex-On-The-Beach. *Half of the them will be puking their guts out before nine o'clock,* Katie thought as she stood back and said to Taylor, "Hang on a minute."

Taylor turned his body in the direction of the new patron so Katie could see his face if she looked. He swallowed another drink from the bottle and did his best impression of the forlorn lover. *Be cool, Taylor. Don't over-do it. Just set the hook and then reel her in.*

"All right, Taylor, look," Katie said in an abrupt whisper, "I don't like you very much and I certainly don't trust you, but I am worried about Skylar."

Taylor looked concerned as he wrinkled his forehead and nodded solemnly.

"Jeez, I don't know if I should do this. That day you were here with your friends and she came after she'd seen her doctor? I heard pretty much everything she said to you and everything you said to her," Katie explained as she wore an expression that suggested equal parts nausea and disgust. "Well, as it turned out, I gave her a phone number for this service, or this guy, who did some kind of a 'make-dreams-come-true' thing for terminal women. I didn't know if it was the real thing, but would you believe it, it is."

"Are you messing with me?" Taylor asked suspiciously.

"No. It's the truth," assured Katie. "She called and told me a woman answered and asked her a ton of questions. When she finished, the woman arranged for Skylar to meet this guy, which she did right here in Chicago. Skylar said he was pretty amazing and figured she had nothing to lose. A few days later, she met him at O'Hare and left."

"That's crazy."

"Maybe. Maybe not, but that's what happened."

"Where did they go?"

"Well, that's the thing. That's the only reason I'm even talking to you," Katie clarified, still unsure. "Skylar promised to call after she got to where she was going. I haven't heard from her, and it's been more than a month. I've tried to call the number, but haven't gotten any answers. Apparently, the things this guy does are very exclusive. That's fine and Skylar assured me I shouldn't worry, but frankly, I am worried."

Taylor did his best troubled impression, "Do you still have the number?"

"I do," Katie had already decided to give Taylor the number when she started the story. "Here it is."

"Thanks," said Taylor as he took the number from Katie's hand.

"Look, Taylor, two things. First, if you find her, you tell me. I need to know she's okay. Second, and this is important, do not make me sorry I told you, all right?"

"Come on, Katie," Taylor implored. He removed a ten-dollar bill and triumphantly tucked the trophy safely in its place and lied. "I'm as worried about Skylar as you are." At that, Taylor Kerr drained the rest of his beer, left the bottle on the bill, and turned to walk out. He hardly even minded leaving the big tip.

As Katie watched Taylor make his way to the door, she couldn't help but think that she'd made a mistake.

CHAPTER 62

"How are things?" Amelie asked the same question she'd asked each day for almost a month.

"Same," Quinn answered as he stood in the hallway in the patient wing of the American University of Antigua College of Medicine. "Skylar has more or less completely recovered from the surgery and just had passive range-of-motion physical therapy. She'll have chemo this afternoon."

"Hmm."

Quinn continued, trying to wring hope from an otherwise desperate situation, "Maybe it's better she's sleeping. The meds are supposed to be hard to take, at least that's what Reinsdorf said."

She hadn't screamed, but it would've been difficult for anyone in the house to not have heard her as she crashed down the stairs. Quinn was first to find her. Her body was twisted and her head bled and matted her blonde hair inside an expanding puddle of blood on the hard tile floor. Quinn resisted the urge to move her in spite of the unlikely position of her limbs. Feef arrived a moment later just ahead of Sonny and asked, "What was that?" She didn't need Quinn to answer when she looked down. "Lord have mercy! I'll call an ambulance," Feef shouted as she retraced her steps.

Although it would've been the romantic gesture to ride with Skylar in the back of the emergency transport, it was more practical to let the technicians have the room they'd need. It was only after Skylar was stable that Quinn reached for his phone and selected the entry for William Reinsdorf from the programmed memory.

"Hi, William. It's Quinn Powers. It's a really long story, William, and I'll be more than happy to tell it, but right now I could really use your help."

CHAPTER 63

Reinsdorf told Quinn, who up to then had been at the hospital with Gina for two and a half straight days, "We know what it is. Pneumocystic pneumonia. It's treated with antibiotics. She should be much better tomorrow. Why don't you get some rest tonight and come back in the morning?"

A Howard Hughes fellow, Reinsdorf was considered one of the leading oncologists in the country. He'd begun research with a perinatal specialist in an attempt to isolate a cancer-fighting protein he suspected pregnant women or their fetuses produced. Reinsdorf's keen intellect, sharp wit, and genuine compassion afforded him an ability to tell great stories and to effectively and empathetically communicate difficult news.

"Seriously, Quinn, sleep at home tonight," William repeated. "You're no good to her if you get sick."

Quinn realized William was right. Reluctantly, Quinn packed up his few belongings, including the three paperback hospital gift shop novels, the tooth brush, and toothpaste, and well-worn change of clothes into his green canvas, monogrammed gym bag. Quinn leaned over the bed where his wife sat. Gina's eyes were wide open, but she couldn't speak. "I love you, Gina," whispered Quinn. "I'll be back tomorrow. William told me that he knows what's wrong now and he knows how to fix it. You'll be fine, Baby. I love you."

There was something in Gina's eyes that made Quinn hesitate. Quinn didn't know how much she understood, but that look in Gina's eyes haunted. She couldn't speak. She couldn't shake her head or move her hands. Still, Gina almost seemed to say with her beautiful, brown eyes, "Quinn. Don't leave me. Not tonight."

CHAPTER 64

After reviewing Skylar's medical file that Quinn had faxed and speaking with the chief teaching doctor and the emergency room physicians, William Reinsdorf booked a flight from Reagan National that would depart that afternoon.

At a few minutes before ten o'clock that evening, Reinsdorf was greeted by Stephenson Gregory, who explained as he opened the door to the Grand Vitara, "Welcome to Antigua, Dr. Reinsdorf. I am Stephenson Gregory and I am at your service. Please call me what my mother calls me, 'Sonny.'"

CHAPTER 65

"Thanks for coming, William," Quinn said and embraced the man with whom he'd endured a very difficult time in his life.

"It's not a problem, Quinn," William responded in kind. "Besides, it's not like you've gone to the well too often."

Before and after William had met the Powers, William had treated or consulted with thousands of patients. He understood many patients came to him having difficult diagnoses for which prognoses were grave. He learned quickly he'd have to effectively cope with failure. Even for the patients who eventually submitted to their fate, William rationalized his input prolonged lives. Maybe he could provide his patients one more holiday, one more birthday or anniversary or graduation, or one more day simply to be.

The Powers were different, though. William continued to speak with Quinn and, over time, developed a friendship of mutual respect with him. However, it was more something about the two of them together, Gina and Quinn, which the loss of Gina struck William as unjust.

"You can fill me in later with what you're up to, Quinn. I probably won't even have time tonight," William explained. "I'm on a chartered flight out of here in just a few hours. I have consults in the morning."

"Wow, William. I always wondered whether you slept. Now, I know you don't."

"I'll sleep on the plane and when I'm dead," William answered dryly. "In the meantime, let's take a look at Skylar. Can you get the attending, the surgeon, the neurologist, and the oncologist, and anyone else so we can talk about a treatment plan?"

"I'll do it," Quinn said, knowing well that the personal honorariums he'd provide the doctors would facilitate a lot of cooperation. It wouldn't hurt that these island doctors who taught at the college to cloak a permanent vacation would meet the medical equivalent of Babe Ruth. "Absolutely, William."

CHAPTER 66

Through the narrow slits of her eyelids, Skylar watched a tiny nurse in a white, heavily starched one-piece dress that perfectly contrasted the skin it covered. The nurse busily worked around the bed as Skylar acclimated to the surroundings. The room was mostly dark, lit only by a small night lamp and ambient light supplied by either dawn or dusk.

Methodically, as if reviewing a complex legal case, she one-by-one evaluated each fact she could confirm. She adjusted her eyes downward and observed her chest rise and fall. She was, in fact, breathing. *Well, I guess I'm alive.* Skylar couldn't have imagined her covered feet were held upright by special braces and compression stockings that prevented muscle from atrophying and something called "foot drop." Skylar swallowed or, rather, tried to swallow. It seemed like she had ingested a golf ball and her esophagus couldn't quite finish the otherwise instinctive reflex. She focused just beyond the tip of her nose and discerned a tube, which actually had a diameter significantly smaller than a golf ball, inserted through her nose. *A feeding tube?* The evidence, coupled with that industrious little nurse, seemed to indicate she was a hospital patient. *I didn't see that coming.*

Using just her eyes, perhaps frightened by the prospect of discovering she may be unable to move, Skylar continued to collect data as she glanced around her room. The nurse bent down by the side of the bed to empty the collection bag attached to her Foley before she glanced up at her patient. She was startled to discover an active, confused pair of eyes looking back at her.

"Hi, honey," the nurse said with an adorably mousey island dialect. "Skylar? Are you with me?"

Trying her motor skills, Skylar gently nodded.

"Have you been awake long?" the nurse asked softly as she grabbed the control and inclined the bed slightly.

Buoyed by her recent achievement, Skylar shook her head this time.

"Well, good. That's good," the nurse answered gently. "Let me go out and find the doctor, okay?"

The nurse looked down and smiled before she started toward the door, but Skylar frowned and shook her head again.

The nurse was genuinely concerned. She leaned down and asked, "What's the matter, honey?"

Skylar struggled as she tested the unused muscles in her vocal cords. She felt the tickle of the tube in her throat as she rasped, "What's your name?"

"My name is Patricia, but everyone calls me Gerbil. Can you guess why?"

Skylar giggled and coughed. She sputtered, "I can think of two reasons, actually."

"Ooh, honey! Be careful! I'd be in big trouble if I put you right back into that coma," Gerbil warned with concern before she realized she had spoken out of turn.

"Coma? Why?" Skylar croaked disbelievingly. "How long?"

"More than a month. Frankly, some folks worried we might not see you again. I never had any doubt, though."

A coma? A month? Just like she'd systematically gathered and processed the information she could see, Skylar did the same with the new auditory stimulus. "I'm still on Antigua?" Skylar asked. She thought she knew she was on Antigua, but other than her caregiver's manner of enunciation, she couldn't quite reach the reasons she knew.

"You are," Gerbil proudly replied. "You're at the American University, and I have to tell you, you are quite a special patient."

Resting her voice, Skylar answered only with a curiously doubtful expression.

"That's right. In addition to having a couple of very special visitors, a certain part-time Antiguan and full-time music legend and his wife," Gerbil nodded toward the private room's ocean view window. "You have also been the beneficiary of daily long-distance consults from North America's leading oncologist"

On the sill, a copy of Mark Burton's *Backbone* LP stood partially open like a greeting card. Suddenly it seemed that Skylar's tired mind was overloading with sensory data. Then all at once, the fog that obscured her memories suddenly cleared as if dried up by a warm, midday sun. *Antigua. Jolisa and Mark. Quinn. The stairs! Oncologist? Quinn!*

Skylar immediately realized it was a mistake to try to sit up. When she pulled her head up for that moment, she called a whisper, "Quinn! Where's Quinn!"

"Please, Skylar," Gerbil scolded. "Please don't do that. I'm not kidding. You'll hurt yourself!"

Distressed and exhausted, Skylar asked again, "Please tell me, Gerbil. Where's Quinn Powers?"

"Aw, honey. Quinn hasn't left here for so much as a Guinness since you got here, but the Lord knows he's earned it. He's been right over there pretty much the whole time," Gerbil explained pointing at Quinn who slept on a hospital cot between the hallway and the bathroom doors. "He showers in the bathroom. Once a day, Stephenson Gregory brings him fresh clothes and a few other things, including a new batch of these crazy comic books he reads to you."

As if he'd dreamt the two women talking about him, Quinn awoke to caregiver and patient looking curiously down at him. Through the haze of a restless sleep, Quinn simply asked, "What?"

CHAPTER 67

Quinn unrolled himself from the sheets on the cot and stood up. "Hi there," Quinn said affectionately as he approached. "How are you feeling?"

Even had Gerbil not left to find a doctor, Skylar wouldn't have been reluctant to observe, "Those aren't what I remember you wearing to bed." She playfully looked Quinn up and down admiring Quinn's conservative, navy-blue pajamas.

"Well, I'm glad to see you haven't lost that sense of humor. How are you feeling?"

"It feels like someone is pounding my head with a mallet. My arms and legs feel like lead. I'm connected to tubes through just about every orifice in my body. Other than that, I feel great," Skylar reported. "What happened?"

"After, well, that night, when you came down the stairs, you had something called a cord compression. Where the cancer metastasized in your back, it literally weakened the bone in your spine. One of the bones collapsed. If that wasn't bad enough, you were near the top of the stairs. It might've been the pain or it might have been your legs simply could no longer support you, but you fell and fractured your skull. It was a pretty nasty concussion as concussions go and that's the reason you've been sleeping through your vacation."

Skylar asked, giggling a little, "I can't believe I've been out for a month! I must have missed a lot!"

"A few things have changed. Some things are the same," Quinn added. "I'm sorry I went downstairs without you. I should have stayed with you."

"Jeez, Quinn. I wasn't an invalid. I am now, but I wasn't then. How could you have known?"

"Well, there are a few things you need to know," Quinn changed the subject. He bit his lip and paused, wondering whether he should talk now considering she'd only just opened her eyes. He wondered whether she'd understand.

Looking at Quinn curiously and waiting as eagerly as only a recently awakened, trauma-induced coma patient could, Skylar said expectantly, "Well?"

Quinn breathed deeply and began, "Okay. After you fell, I had you brought here to try to get you stable. You were unconscious. Within a day or so later, two more things became clear. First, we knew you were comatose, although it was well within the realm of possibility you'd eventually recover. Second, you were otherwise okay, which meant you could breathe on your own and your heart worked by itself and all that other stuff. I spoke with the doctors, and we decided to operate on the cord compression."

Skylar listened, but Quinn wasn't sure how much of the information Skylar understood. Other than being a little tired, which she thought ironic, Skylar felt fine.

"The surgeon installed what's called a support cage around the compressed bone. The surgery went well, and you've pretty much fully recovered."

"Well, I guess that would be one of the things that changed." Skylar said dryly.

"Uh, yeah," Quinn hesitated. Quinn knew that this next part might be a problem. "And, Skye. Well, the thing is, it really did not make any sense to open you up for the cage without doing surgery on the cancer, too."

Skylar remained expressionless.

"Almost as soon after your fall I could think, I called an old friend, William Reinsdorf, a doctor at Johns Hopkins. William is not just a doctor. He is an oncologist and a really, really good one. I sent him your medical file and he was here that night. Before William left the next morning, he created a comprehensive treatment plan and met with the other doctors who'd actually be here to administer care. Frankly, Skye," Quinn said as tears formed in his eyes, "It's been a beautiful thing. Everyone has worked together without the slightest bit of egotism or pride to make you better. The only thing missing has been you."

"You've already started and finished radiation, five times a week for three weeks. You slept right through it!

With more curiosity than vanity, Skylar reached up to feel her hair.

"No, the radiation was just on your back," Quinn answered Skylar's implied question. "The chemotherapy doesn't cause hair loss either, but it makes up for it with other stuff. You'll have another course, Cisplatin and Topotecan, next week. Cisplatin is a little more malicious than the Topotecan, but both cause a decrease in your blood counts. You've been getting Neulasta to boost white cells and Procrit for the reds. Also, both chemos make you nauseous, but you probably haven't noticed. You will now. I think Atavan is on the list for that. Here's the amazing thing. William and the hospital oncologist were surprised that the cancer showed no indication of metastasizing again past the spine. That's uncommon. Once a cancer escapes the lymph nodes, it's usually a free-for-all. That wasn't the case with you. William also ordered labs every day. He gets copies of the results. This is what's really crazy. After the second course of chemo, your CEAs, which is short for carcinoembryonic antigen test, which measures the cancer proteins in the blood, suggest that the cancer is not detected."

"Not detected? What does that mean, Quinn?"

"I'm not sure, Skye. It doesn't mean that you're cured or for sure that your cancer is in remission," qualified Quinn. "But, William is guardedly optimistic. Frankly, I think he's curious and even a little excited. What seems to have happened is more than a little atypical. He wants to come back and do some tests to understand the reasons you've gotten ahead of this thing."

Quinn's enthusiasm faded as he looked down uncomfortably and avoided Skylar's gaze. Every day he'd sat at her bedside reading aloud. He'd showered in the hospital room lavatory and slept on the tiny cot only to be awakened at regular intervals by either Gerbil or the weekend third-shift nurse who checked Skylar's vital signs, administered meds, and did the other less-glamorous things that nurses were sometimes required to do. As he waited, Quinn hoped with every part of himself that Skylar would open her eyes. At the same time, he dreaded having to tell her he'd thought only of himself when he abused the health-care proxy and, against Skylar's wishes, authorized treatment.

Skylar watched Quinn intently. Although the muscles in her body had atrophied and her cheeks had grown ironically chubby, Skylar's eyes hadn't lost any of their inclusiveness or warmth in all the time they'd been closed. On the contrary, her eyes seemed to implore him to tell her everything.

"Skylar," Quinn said still eluding Skylar's gaze. "I know you didn't want to be treated, but I was selfish and just couldn't follow through. This was supposed to be about you, and I made it about me. I'm sorry. I just didn't think things were supposed to happen that way. Maybe, I didn't want things to happen that way."

"Look at me, Quinn," said Skylar firmly after her long silence. "You're right. I told you I didn't want to be treated. I think I was clear I didn't want to be revived when the Little Bastard had finished with me."

Quinn accepted the reprimand.

Skylar continued. "If this thing had gone the wrong way, and I'd suffered for your selfishness, Quinn, well, it would have been all right."

"Huh?" Quinn asked.

"Look. When I met you, something inside me changed, the way I look at the world, I think. I bet you're a psychologist's wet dream considering the things you've chosen to do in your life. Frankly, I didn't know there was anyone in the world like you. Then, I fell in love. It was before we were together. It was before we had dinner with your friends. All of that was incredible, but when we spent yesterday, I mean, that day together in the car, you were open and honest and nervous and polite and funny and interesting and real. I couldn't help but thinking that we were supposed to be with each other. I wished I could have more time if only to be with you. If only to be with you, whoever you are or would become. Then, there was the rest of that day. There was the rest of that night. How could I help falling in love with you? So, I'll make you a deal, I'll let you off the hook this time. But from now on, you have to do everything I tell you," Skylar finished as she carefully opened her arms for him.

Neither said another word, but hugged each other and cried. As they held one another, Skylar thought to herself that the oncologist might not find anything when he returns to "do some tests to understand the reasons you gotten ahead of this thing," as Quinn put it. She wasn't sure the reason for her resiliency was inside of her. It might have sounded silly if she'd said it out loud, but in her heart she thought that maybe she held the reason in her arms.

CHAPTER 68

"Oh my gosh, Skylar! That is unbelievable!" Katie responded. "I am so happy for you!"

"You're right. I am a lucky girl." Skylar was suggesting a secret double-meaning.

After Quinn spoke with her, Skylar was exhausted and wanted to sleep again. She remained lucid long enough to answer a few questions and be probed and poked by the resident who arrived with Gerbil. She slept for a couple of hours before she was roused again by the first-shift nurse, who ushered in a series of visits from the specialists, the oncologist, the surgeon, the radiologist, the physical therapist, and the nutritionist. Ironically, when the neurologist walked in, Skylar remembered she'd promised to call Katie.

"Christ on a cracker!" Skylar surprised the neurologist.

"Excuse me, miss?" the doctor replied.

Skylar explained, "Oh, I just remembered that I owe somebody a phone call!"

The following evening, Skylar finally called her friend, using Quinn's phone. It was a school day for Katie, so she was home grading papers with Chase when the phone rang. Katie had almost screamed with surprise and relief when she heard Skylar's voice on the other end. After the initial shock, Katie listened first with wonder, then with alarm, and finally with compassion as Skylar retold the events of her adventure. Then, Katie collected her thoughts, "Skylar, I have something to tell you."

"What is it, Katie? What's the matter?"

Katie began, "I'm not sure how big a deal this was, Skylar, but Taylor came into the bar a few weeks ago. He told me he'd just come from a meeting with your attorney, and expected to see you. He said he was worried. I didn't buy it, but I hadn't heard from you either."

Skylar interrupted, "And you were worried, too. Right?"

"Of course."

"Thanks, Katie." Skylar said.

"You're my friend. I worry. Anyway, I didn't believe him, you know, that he was worried about you. I knew he had an angle. Slimebags like him always do. But, like I said, I hadn't heard from you, so I told him about Quinn and gave him the number."

"Oh," Skylar answered.

"I thought if he could find you, he would let me know you were safe. About a millisecond after I had told him, I regretted it."

"It's okay, Katie," Skylar assured. "I'll let Quinn know, but I'm sure it won't matter. I'm not afraid of that man. Even if he did happen to learn where I am or what I'm doing, I can't possibly care any less what Taylor Kerr thinks."

Skylar stopped and refocused, "Thanks for letting me know. I know you were worried and I can't tell you how much it means to me to know you're my friend."

"Cut it out."

Skylar added, "I'll make sure Quinn knows to call if anything happens. Okay?"

"Okay," Katie agreed. "Promise you'll take care of yourself. I'd really love to go with you to Wrigley for a game or to Excalibur so we can tease those hotshot *playubs*." For the first time since she'd known Skylar, Katie had hope she might actually see her friend again.

Skylar dared, "That would be great. I will."

CHAPTER 69

"I thought something like that might have happened," Quinn said after Skylar told him about her conversation with Katie. "Amelie told me that she'd gotten a couple of calls that were a little out of the ordinary."

"I'm really sorry, Quinn."

"Come on, Skylar. It's nothing," Quinn pledged hiding his apprehension. "Don't worry about it. I'm not."

Even as Quinn reassured Skylar, neither could have known the investigator Taylor hired was attempting to verify information about the telephone number that connected to Katie Novac's cell phone. Predictably, Taylor hired an attractive female PI, who wouldn't have drawn unwanted attention to herself as she sat at Kirkwood's bar or waited in her car where she intercepted the cellular signal from Katie's phone. Actually, Katie noticed the woman during her shifts. Katie felt admiration rather than trepidation as the woman squashed juvenile punks who tried to gain her favor with lame pickup lines.

In reality, the woman had watched Katie and eavesdropped on her telephone conversations for almost three weeks. Because the flight plan she tried to find was a dead end, the investigator began to think she wouldn't get the bonus she negotiated. However, her patience paid off. She had great information for her client: a recording of the subject, specific information about the subject's condition, some very strong leads relating to location. As soon as the tracking service processed her request, she'd also have the name of the owner of the phone number and location where the call was made.

"There it is," the P.I. intoned as she read the information on the screen of her wireless laptop on the seat in her SUV. She read the name, "Amelie Dawud," and the Manhattan post office box to which the bills and correspondence were delivered.

The investigator wondered whether she could track the origin of the call as she thought about the $5,000 check Taylor Kerr promised in addition to her regular hourly billing. "Not a bad gig," she told herself.

The possibility hadn't even crossed her mind that she'd have to write off the entire invoice, less a token $1,000 deposit, at the end of the fiscal year. After attempting in vain to obtain payment, the investigator couldn't have predicted the improbable forces that conspired to lead her to enlist the collections arm of Skylar Smart's former law firm to prosecute Taylor Kerr's bad debt.

CHAPTER

Days passed. Skylar slept less and participated in her treatment more. She talked with Quinn and interacted with the staff members, who found Skylar tolerant and appreciative. Skylar quickly became a favorite patient, and her room became the locus of the hospital social web. Quinn spent every day in Skylar's room, just like Gerbil said. Although Skylar slept through most of his visit the first day she had come out of her coma, she saw Sonny deliver Quinn's sundries. A day later, Feef came along and made an effusive production about Skylar's recovery, which was as emotionally draining as anything else she encountered up to then. Feef promised to bring covered dishes with some of her "good food." Skylar had been able to eat solid foods for a couple of days after her feeding tube was removed, but she quickly tired of the commissary room service.

Like a woman who hadn't eaten real food for weeks, Skylar savored Feef's cooking. Every time, it was comfort food, which Feef insisted would "put some meat back on them skinny bones, girl!" Quinn sat on a chair next to the bed and shared the table that reached over Skylar's lap as she sat up. After digesting only nutritionally balanced slurry through a plastic tube, Skylar's stomach had shrunk to the size of a walnut. As good as the food was, she could only eat so much. Still, Skylar relished the gourmet meals. One day it was chicken lasagna for which, Feef proudly declared, she butchered the bird, marinated the breast meat, used a local cheese, and made her own red sauce. Another, Feef made an Antiguan version of shepherd's pie, using goat, local vegetables, and blue potatoes sweetened with cane juice.

Quinn hadn't exaggerated about the chemotherapy. Skylar's appetite had just started to improve when she was smacked with the Cisplatin and the Topotecan. Quinn suggested she moderate her enthusiasm for Feef's spinach and four-cheese macaroni and suggested instead a little Ensure or an electrolyte drink for breakfast. Skylar complied, but it didn't much matter. In spite of swallowing an Atavan before the nurse started "pushing chemo,"

Skylar vomited the contents of her stomach, a pinkish liquid that had earlier been diluted cherry Gatorade.

As her system, specifically, her ability to digest food, normalized, Skylar's physical therapy continued. The therapist insisted on more involvement. Almost immediately, the splint-like supports were removed from Skylar's ankles. When the circulation-supporting stockings were removed, Skylar had the sensation of gasping air after being held under water.

At first, exercises were mostly passive. As the therapist moved her arms and legs back and forth, up and down, and side to side within the constraints provided her sockets, Skylar felt dull, shooting pain in each corresponding joint. The simple range-of-motion exercises were followed by isometrics, which Skylar called Pilates for Invalids. The therapist provided resistance against each of the muscle groups and asked Skylar to push against it. She began with the neck and instructed Skylar to resist upward, downward, and side-to-side. Working counterclockwise around Skylar's body, she moved to the right shoulder, bicep and tricep, and then forearm, wrist, and hand. She repeated the process on the right leg, then the left, and finally the left arm. Skylar finished the session with the torso, first opposing the therapist's downward force with her abdominal muscles, and then against a pull to strengthen the back.

Skylar was agreeably surprised to discover that, with the exception of an almost indiscernible pinch, the exercises didn't cause the surgery area much discomfort. She was more than a little disappointed the next morning, though, when her muscles, her entire body in fact, felt like she had just run a marathon in stilettos. After the prolonged inactivity, even mild resistance resulted in a buildup of lactic acid that she was in no way capable of reducing by walking it off. The team already reintroduced the Fentanyl patch. Even though Ibuprofen barely blunted her discomfort, however, Skylar refused the oral opiate the doctor offered because she didn't want it to affect her appetite.

"I'm not sure I'm ready for this," Skylar told Quinn as she looked from her wheelchair at the parallel walking bars' eight-foot span. "I don't think my legs or my arms are strong enough."

"You've got to walk before you can run and you have to walk sometime. Besides, we'll spot you on both sides," Quinn assured Skylar and nodded to the therapist.

Even though Quinn tried to push the chair, Skylar insisted she wheel it herself. She stopped at one end of the apparatus and locked the wheels. "All right," she growled only half playfully.

Quinn came around one side while the therapist came around the other, but Skylar resisted the overture. "If I'm going to do it, I'll do it myself!"

She slid herself forward on the chair, paused, and, in one fluid motion, pulled herself up with her arms as she pushed with her legs. Standing was unfamiliar and only possible with support from her arms.

"You okay, Skye?"

"Uh huh," was her preoccupied response. Skylar steadied herself. Then slowly, cautiously, she slid her left foot forward on the floor as her left hand slid forward on the bar. Again, she paused to secure herself as Quinn and the therapist stood anxiously on opposite sides of the wooden banisters.

"You okay, Skye?" Quinn nervously repeated.

"I'm fine, but you won't be if you ask again!" Skylar shot Quinn an it's-really-okay grin and moved her right foot and hand. A step later, Skylar half finished the span.

After the fourth step, Skylar felt more accustomed to the otherwise-instinctive activity, but her arms were no more recovered than her legs were. By the time she reached the end, her muscles trembled.

"I think we should stop there," the therapist suggested. "Quinn, grab the chair and wheel it down?"

"No!" Skylar breathlessly insisted. "I'm going back!"

Skylar instantly picked up her left hand, moved it to the other bar with her right, and supported herself for a moment. She slid rather than picked up her right foot as she quickly moved her right hand toward the opposite bar. Her finger tips touched but her hand was not high enough. She missed her grip and, for a split second, felt herself falling. In that moment, she was angry at her own obstinacy, which may well set back therapy and recovery. Before she could finish her thought, Skylar felt resistance on her hand and she steadied herself again. She looked up and saw Quinn's hand around her wrist and a reproachful expression on his face.

"I'm not going to say anything," Quinn pledged.

A few moments later, the therapist held the chair steady as Skylar dropped into it. It seemed to Quinn that he hadn't exhaled in four minutes.

Only the chemotherapy stemmed Skylar's progress. She found a routine, including diet, that helped her to manage the effects of the drugs. Thirty-six hours after treatment, her appetite returned. In part due to Feef's cooking, she gained weight and eventually eclipsed 100-pounds. With help from the physical therapist, Skylar regained muscle tone, too. She even began to walk on campus outside with Quinn. The walks were at first short, but exhausting. They'd rest on a bench to enjoy the sunshine as students who'd met Skylar or heard about her recovery smiled and said, "Hello." Soon, the outings lengthened.

Considering her condition when she arrived, it was nothing short of a miracle when Skylar was discharged one sunny afternoon near the end of March. Nurses, doctors, students, and support staff stopped to wish Skylar luck with her continuing recovery. Tears flowed when Gerbil came in. Although Skylar had other friendships, none were closer than with Gerbil, who stayed on her own time to wheel Skylar into the lobby. As Quinn went for the car, Gerbil could be consoled only by Skylar's promise that she could visit anytime at Half Moon Bay.

Quinn packed the keepsakes and necessities from the room. The bag barely fit into the Jaguar's trunk. Quinn walked around to the passenger-side door to help Skylar from the chair, but Gerbil had the situation under control. Gerbil leaned down and put her arms around Skylar. After more than two months of constant oversight by doctors, treatment, observation, and therapy, Skylar was finally on her way home.

CHAPTER 71

Quinn broke his own rule about the Jaguar. He wanted Skylar to enjoy the sun and ocean air on the ride to the villa. In the excitement of having Skylar back and the exhilaration of driving the car on such a beautiful spring day, Quinn didn't notice he was driving ten kilometers above the speed limit. The obnoxious siren of a patrol car was Quinn's first indication of the traffic stop. A check in the rearview mirror confirmed it.

"Did he get you again, Quinn?"

"Yep," Quinn said as he pulled the car onto the shoulder and watched in the side mirror as the car slowed to a stop behind him. "I don't believe it. It's the same cop!"

The patrolman spoke first, "Good afternoon, Mr. Powers. It's a pleasure to see you again."

"Hello again, Officer Johnson," Quinn answered politely. "Is it already time again for me to make a contribution to the Antiguan Police Benevolent Association?"

"I'll let that slide today, Mr. Powers, because I didn't stop you for excessive speed," Johnson declared genially, before he cautioned, "Although you were driving about fifteen kilometers above the maximum."

Skylar shrugged as Quinn stole a glance, "Why did you pull us over then?"

The officer answered as if it couldn't have been more obvious, "I stopped you so I could wish Miss Smart success with her recovery." Then, looking at Skylar, Johnson continued, "Patricia Johnson is my niece, Miss Smart, and she's kept me apprised of your progress."

"Patricia Johnson?" Skylar asked.

"Gerbil," Johnson explained. "Gerbil is my niece."

Without trying to flatter, Skylar answered honestly, "Your niece? I know Gerbil is young, but you don't look old enough to have a grown-up niece, Officer Johnson."

"Well, she's my oldest brother's daughter," Johnson said proudly. "And she has told me all about you. You too, Mr. Powers."

Then, Johnson lowered his voice as to confess, "I and my brother lost a sister and Gerbil lost an aunt three years ago. She had woman's cancer."

"I'm very sorry," Skylar answered with uncommon perspective.

"Thank you. Anyway, I just want you to know that we're all praying for you, Miss Smart. We're all very happy to know how well you are doing."

Curious, Skylar inquired, "We?"

"Everyone at the headquarters," Johnson answered again as if the answer couldn't have been more obvious.

Then, abruptly, Johnson turned back to Quinn. "I haven't seen you driving this car around since you first arrived on my island. I've seen Sonny in that big Vitara, but not this little sports car. That wouldn't have anything to do with the fines, would it?"

Quinn raised his eyebrows and looked up, "Well, actually, yes it would. I figured that we'd eventually get so many tickets that you'd either have to impound the car or impound me. Neither alternative seemed very appealing."

Johnson offered, "As long as you keep it reasonable, Mr. Powers, you will not have to concern yourself with the Royal Police." Johnson smiled as he emphasized, "Reasonable."

After Quinn thanked Officer Johnson, he waited until the patrol car pulled back out onto the road around the XKR. As he turned the key in the ignition, Quinn looked over at Skylar who said only, "Small island, huh?"

CHAPTER 72

Skylar walked into the examination room a step ahead of Quinn. "There's our little miracle," William Reinsdorf cheerfully said.

"Hello, William," Skylar smiled and took the doctor's hand in hers. "It is great to finally put the face with the voice."

William took Skylar's hand and pulled her close for an embrace. "It's great to meet you, too," he answered with some understatement. "Hey, Quinn," William smiled expressively and repeated the ritual. "Sit down. Please, sit down."

Skylar lifted herself onto the table as Quinn scooted a chair along side. He lifted his arm and rested his hand on her lap. Skylar grimaced nervously and took his hand.

"Actually, I thought I'd have about as much chance of giving you this news as I would winning the lottery. It's not just improbable. Frankly, it's impossible."

"You're killing us here, William," Quinn said as Skylar, who was too anxious to breathe much less speak, sat on the edge of the examination table statue still.

"Generally, the chemotherapy regimen required for metastatic cervical cancer would continue every three weeks indefinitely. Forgive me, but to put a slightly sharper point on it, someone like you would continue Cisplatin and Topotecan until you, well, until you died. I would have expected the disease to have made that happen before now, especially given your condition after the fall. I'm sure it's no news to you that your disease was advanced," William explained with compassionate candor. "If I were to suggest you continue chemotherapy, however I would be forcing toxic and expensive medicine on a woman who appears by all measures to be in remission and otherwise completely healthy. It would be akin to performing a bypass on a vital heart or amputating a healthy limb. It wouldn't make any sense."

"No evidence of disease?" Skylar spoke and squeezed Quinn's hand on her lap.

William replied, "I can't explain it, Skylar. Like I said when you walked in, it's a miracle."

CHAPTER 73

"I've waited a long time for you," Skylar said as she gazed at Quinn through her dreamy, sexy eyes. His left arm was under her neck while his right hand was comfortable on her naked hip. Both of her hands stretched down below his waist gently touching what she found there. She needed to be cautious with her newest piece of jewelry on the ring finger of her left hand.

The bright morning sun beamed through the vertical blinds on the window across the room, lit the bits of dust and left louvered shadows on the floor, the dresser, the headboard, and the wall behind him where he lie. Quinn never thought he'd feel as much one with the universe.

She kissed him and whispered again, "I've waited a very long time for you."

"Now look." Skylar's smallish warm hands continued to touch him, "I need you to understand something. I'll be everything for you. I'll be anything for you. I'll be everyone for you. I will be anyone for you.

"If we're in bed in the middle of the night and I'm asleep and you wake up and have to have me, wake me and have me. I like to sleep nude, you may have noticed. After we come home at the end of the day and you are bruised and bloodied from the battles you'll fight and you want me to take you so you can let it all go, I will have you and I will take it all away.

"You can have me any way you want. You can do anything you want. If it feels good to you, I want you to do it. I'm serious. When I see you and feel you and I know I am satisfying you, Quinn, I get so turned on I can barely stand it. It pretty much doesn't matter what you're into. Let your mind wander. Use your imagination. I'll dress up. I'll dress down. I'll dye my hair. I'll shave myself bare. I'll be a porn star. I'll be a saint. Anyone. Anyway. Anything. Anytime.

"Now, I want you to know I'm not trashy or cheap. I am only for you, but I think you already know that. I'm not damaged goods. I respect myself and you'll respect me, too. Clearly, you already do. I am confident. I am strong.

I am educated. I am well read. For the people who earn it, I am a caring and loyal friend. None of that will change. I'll continue to be all of those things and I don't need a man or anyone for that matter to show me who I am. Since all of this, though, I know I'll never again be anything more important than your partner, your wife, and maybe if we have a little luck, the mother of your children. That's what I want.

"I don't want you to worry about me becoming something or someone for whom you lose desire. You know, I've heard men talking about this woman or that one, 'You know, if she were my wife, she'd never see the light of day.' Well, that will be me for you. I'll always take care of myself. I'll exercise and I'll eat right and I'll stay sexy for you. I know you already want me for who and what I am, so when I get older and my girlish charms begin to fade, I'll pay a doctor to replace them.

"As Uncle Ben said to Peter Parker, 'With great power comes great responsibility.' Well, I'm not sure it's that great a responsibility, but I do have three, tiny little rules about all this. First, you'll have to satisfy me, too. Believe me, it won't be very hard and I'll help you. Second, and I think you can understand where I'm coming from here, you can never abuse or take advantage of me. I just told you that I'll do anything for you and I will, but you will never, not even once, purposely hurt me either physically or emotionally. Finally, it's only always us, a united nation of me and you. There will not be anyone else involved. No groups. No extracurricular activities. I am yours and only yours and I guarantee that you will never ever want anyone else. Neither will I. I'll make sure of it. I'll be your fantasy. You'll be my superhero.

"I am not naïve. I know there'll be times when things don't go perfectly. Who knows? There may come a time when we argue about money or about how to raise the kids or about your parents or about the goddamned color to paint the living room or some other stupid thing. I'll be bitchy. You'll be obstinate. Because I love you as much as I do, I'll also be capable of almost hating you. That's a fact of life. That's just a fact of marriage. You'll feel the same way sometimes. After we argue and say terrible things to one another, I will fuck you and I mean fuck you. You will fuck me, too, until we exorcize every last trace of those demons. Then, we'll fall fitfully to sleep and start all over and all better the next day. Just because you have a problem with me or I have a problem with you, it does not mean you have a problem down *there*.

"You got it?" Skylar asked as Quinn snapped back as if he'd been under a spell.

"Uh huh," Quinn managed.

"Like I said, I've waited a long time for you," Skylar repeated.

She kissed him again and smiled. To make sure she'd been understood, she pushed him down, pulled back the sheets exposing his torso to rays of morning light, and emphasized her point.

CHAPTER 74

Quinn's question suggested and unexpected lightheartedness, "How's Dierdorf?"

Kelly answered, "He's good, Quinn. I have to admit, he's slowed down a little. I can tell mostly when the boys are playing with him. He gets tired. He sleeps more."

Quinn lamented the time he spent away from Dierdorf and answered, "Yeah. I know. But he's okay. That's good."

Quinn shifted, "Marisol's good?"

"Yes, she's good, Quinn. Mari's fine. I'm fine. Kelvin and Melvin are fine. We're fine! Would you stop beating around the bush and tell me what's going on?" Kelly asked finally.

Kelly remained sensitive to the difficult things Quinn may have done since the last time they'd spoken. Careful not to ask too many questions about the Dream Seeker, Kelly waited for his friend to offer. Quinn rarely did. Quinn set the table for him this time, though, when he started the conversation with, "I've got some news for you, but first tell me about my dog."

"Okay," Quinn relented. "First, I want to know if you guys want to meet us, Skylar and me, in Chicago. The Knicks are playing the Bulls and, well, I pulled some strings and have tickets."

"Wow! That's great, Quinn."

"And, well, there's more," Quinn confessed. "I thought the boys might like to meet Donnie David after the game. We may even be able to have dinner with him."

"You're kidding!" exclaimed Kelly who was clearly at least as excited as the boys would be when they heard the news. "That's incredible. Thanks!"

"That's worth a trip to the Windy City, isn't it?" Quinn asked.

"Absolutely!" Kelly answered decisively. "Did I ever tell you that I thought Donnie David will eventually be the *man* in the NBA? I can't wait to tell Kelvin and Melvin! They'll flip!"

Kelly couldn't see the grin on Quinn's face.

"I'll call Marisol as soon as I'm off the phone and ask her to make the reservations. Kelvin and Melvin will be so excited," Kelly repeated.

When he tried, he'd always been able to get Kelly worked up. Saving the best for last, Quinn smiled tenderly at Skylar, who sat next to him on the patio.

"Oh, by the way," Quinn asked with some effort to sound casual. "I wonder if there is something you can do for me."

"Here it comes," Kelly joked. "I knew there'd be a quid pro quo."

Quinn continued, "It's an easy one. Can you get my birth certificate from my bank safe deposit box?"

"Sure, that's no problem Quinn," Kelly replied. "Why do you need it?"

"For the marriage license," Quinn answered.

Stunned, Kelly stumbled, "Marriage license? Why do you need a marriage license?"

"Will you stand for me again, Kelly? Skylar and I are getting married in Chicago."

CHAPTER 75

Men and women who comprise the justice system are as prone to preconceptions as anyone else. The Supreme Court and traffic court consist of people who are capable of love, hate, and every emotion between. People elected or appointed to the bench had parents who were loving or abusive or who benefited from welfare and affirmative action programs or suffered from them.

In Skylar's absence, Prudence counted on this human nature as she guided the divorce case through the courts. Many of Prudence's fellow barristers knew the name Taylor Kerr, not necessarily in the context of the law, but rather for his notorious exploits relative to Chicago's constantly evolving social circles. As young successful lawyers are apt to do, many spent time in the bars and other places that catered to the young professionals and their disposable income. For the same reason, those people were also familiar with Skylar, who was an occasional topic of conversation not only because of her marriage to Taylor, but also because of her legal career and significant inheritance.

While Taylor's reputation preceded him, Prudence wasn't certain whether his social standing would necessarily benefit her client. However, she believed his arrogance and ignorance, evidenced by his father's participation in his case, would yield an advantage among the judges who were familiar with the elder Kerr's exploits. Prudence misjudged neither the Kerrs' conceit nor the court's low opinion of them.

No one knew Judge Floyd Sommers was at least as familiar as most people with Dean Kerr. As it happened, Judge Sommers's brother-in-law, the husband of the magistrate's only sister, had invested heavily in Dean Kerr's bogus mining company. Sommers's brother-in-law had been unwise for putting so many eggs in one basket, but the fact remained that he lost a significant sum of money in the transaction. Sommers's sister and her family, including his five-year-old niece and three-year-old nephew, lost their home as a result. When Sommers saw Dean Kerr's name on court documents, he was only too happy to expedite the case. Of course, Sommers granted the senior Kerr special permission to practice in his court. It didn't surprise the judge that Dean Kerr was too incompetent an advocate to discover the conflict himself.

Even had Prudence McDermott's representation not been so competent as she demonstrated Taylor's moral turpitude and emotional abandonment, the judge would likely have granted the divorce and awarded Taylor no remuneration. Judge Sommers considered Skylar's case for divorce air tight and beyond review. Although he would gladly have done so, Sommers didn't even have to compromise his ethics to exact retribution for his little sister's suffering.

So, as the perennials began to bloom in Lurie Park and Skylar Smart prepared for her return to Chicago, she was completely unencumbered if not yet completely unaffected, by her ex-husband. As far as Skylar was concerned, if she'd never see Taylor Kerr again, it would be too soon. She only wished she'd taken her personal documents from the wall safe at the house before she left for Antigua a season earlier. She couldn't have imagined she'd need them.

CHAPTER 76

The stop in Atlanta was more for the passengers to stretch and lunch than it was for fuel. As the plane ascended again into a cloudless sky, Skylar encircled Quinn's arm with hers and held his hand with her other. She pushed up the armrest between the Beechjet 400A's seats and would have gladly gotten closer if she possibly could. Exclusive of the physical attraction, Skylar possessed an unrelenting desire to occupy the same space Quinn did. Although she'd never before experienced anything like it, Skylar wasn't self-conscious for wanting nothing more than to literally be one with the man who occupied the seat next to her.

Like he always seemed to do, Quinn planned the week more thoroughly than an efficiency expert at a Japanese manufacturing company. Astoundingly, Quinn managed ten tickets four rows behind the Knickerbocker bench. Granted, it wasn't like LaBron or Kobe was in town, but *still*. The Hills would join them and so would Katie and Chase. Skylar could barely contain her excitement about seeing her friend again. Katie agreed to be Skylar's maid of honor, and Quinn said the night would almost be like a bachelor and bachelorette party rolled into one. Quinn insisted on inviting Prudence McDermott and a friend, too. He thought it was the least he could do for helping Skylar resolve her legal issues.

Skylar wanted to meet the incredibly empathetic person with whom she shared the most intimate details of her life, but she'd have to wait. Amelie declined the invitation to the game, but would arrive the following day in the afternoon. Quinn didn't speculate about the reasons, but it would probably be for the best. As it was, Skylar would meet Kelly and his family. She'd reconnect with Katie and Chase and see Prudence again, too. Perhaps it was easier to meet a few of Quinn's friends and family at a time.

Either that afternoon or the following morning, Quinn would take Skylar to the Cook County government building to apply for the marriage license. Then they'd be married in a small, private ceremony witnessed only by Quinn's family, Katie, Chase, the Hills, Bob and Lina, and Amelie. Quinn made reservations for a reception dinner at The Chicago Chop House, of course. He requested the two big tables in the back. The following weekend, she and Quinn would get back on a plane, make a quick stop in New York for Dierdorf and a few other things, and leave again for an extended Antiguan honeymoon, which Quinn said would truly never have to end. They'd split their time between the villa, which he planned to buy, and a house they would build maybe somewhere in Big Sky Country or in the Southwest. Considering they had the means and freedom to do just about anything, Quinn and Skylar decided to start looking for land in Wyoming or Montana.

The wind tousled the small jet in its final descent, but the turbulence was no more severe than it had been during the ascent from V.C. Bird hours earlier. Billowy clouds drifted westward across the blue sky canvas as Skylar and Quinn walked down onto the tarmac and grabbed their bags that the copilot had unloaded.

"Chief cook and bottle washer," Quinn smiled as he handed the officer two small pieces of greenish paper each displaying the portrait of Benjamin Franklin. Handing the copilot two more identical documents, Quinn said, "Thank you. Could you make sure the pilot gets these?"

Having already passed through customs in the Peach State, Skylar and Quinn glided through to the ground transportation Amelie had arranged. While the temperature was milder than expected, the climate was still a far cry from the tropical conditions to which they'd become accustomed. Comfortable in jeans, Quinn wore a thick blue and white, cotton, rugby shirt, and Skylar sported a spring sweater. Quinn checked his watch before he slipped the red BMW Z3 into gear.

"Kelly and Marisol's plane doesn't arrive for three hours. Do you think we could get your papers in the morning, Skye? I thought we might get settled at the hotel?"

"What would you like to do?"

"We've got time. Let's go to the hotel first. I'll make it worth your while," Quinn promised.

"I'll hold you to that."

CHAPTER 77

Skylar spoke several times with Prudence who, after the first time Skylar called, seemed very happy to finally talk with her client again. Prudence not only updated Skylar about the divorce decree, but also about what Prudence concluded about Taylor's personal situation. Prudence understood from the start that Kerr & Son had already begun to struggle financially. Rumor had it Taylor moved to Little Rock, where Dean had been able to keep a home, a luxury condominium actually, after the SEC lawsuits had been settled. Apparently Taylor couldn't afford anything else. Skylar also spoke several times to Katie, who circumstantially confirmed Prudence's report. Neither Katie nor anyone else had seen Taylor Kerr. She'd bumped into Taylor's lapdog, Charlie, a couple of times, but always without his handler. Skylar felt no compunction about enjoying his predicament.

A few days earlier, Skylar directed Prudence to contact a real estate agent to sell the house. Considering the market, she planned to price the house aggressively. Skylar wanted the chapter in her life to end. Knowing she needed to access the safe one more time, Skylar decided to list the house after she was out of town. Besides, she assumed some of Taylor's stuff was still inside. If she didn't have to, she didn't want to stoke his fire until she and Quinn were long gone.

Although the idea of revisiting her past already crept into her subconscious, Skylar hadn't allowed herself to consider the prospect of seeing the monuments of her old life until she stepped out of the shower and began to towel herself dry. She hadn't needed any help from the Beechjet to put her head in the clouds. Thankfully, during the past couple of hours, Quinn occupied her mind along with some parts of her body as well. Now, Skylar could almost feel the texture of the bare brick walls, the familiar smells, and the places in that house where she lived many of the consequential but seldom happy moments of her life. She believed she'd risen from the ashes of her old life and had begun to spread her wings and soar toward the new. The thought of returning to the city she had once loved almost convinced her that she could be burned again.

"Skye? Are you all right?" Quinn asked as he followed her out of the shower. He stepped toward her, surrounding her in his arms, as they both faced the steamed mirror.

"I'm fine, Quinn," Skylar answered half-lying. Then, she smiled, turned around and let the towel fall to the floor. The water had been toweled from her body, but her skin was still warm and supple. She reached up and put her arms around Quinn's neck and assured "I'm really fine, Quinn. I just can't believe we're here together."

"Believe it," Quinn reassured.

Skylar trained her thoughts on the moment rather than on ghosts of the past. "I can't wait to meet Kelly and Marisol," she said.

CHAPTER 78

Kelvin and Melvin saw Quinn before he saw them. He and Skylar stepped out of the elevator and spotted the two small human projectiles rocketing toward him. "Quinn! Quinn!" the boys shouted and stopped only when their four tiny arms wrapped around his torso.

Skylar giggled and said, "You must be Kelvin and Melvin, but I sure can't tell who's who!"

"I'm Kelvin," said the older brother by a few scant minutes. "That's Melvin."

Like a shell game, Skylar lost track of the boys' identities as they bounced around. Kelly and Marisol witnessed the melee and came to the rescue.

It was apparent to Skylar that Quinn and Kelly had already traveled the road of male bonding, because the men hugged without a trace of self-consciousness. Quinn repeated the gesture with Marisol, who Skylar noted was unexpectedly attractive. He stepped back, took his place at Skylar's side, and proudly said, "Kelly, Mari, this is Skylar."

The four adults and two boys shared a GMC Suburban limousine stretched with an extra door. They piled three to a seat. Kelvin and Melvin insisted on sitting with Quinn in the back. Skylar beamed understandingly as the boys took their places on either side of him before they pushed the button to roll down the Suburban's tinted windows.

Within minutes, they arrived in front of the United Center's Michael Jordan statue where Quinn suggested the rendezvous with the rest of the party. The hundreds of people who milled and waited for friends near the bronze figure could almost imagine Jordan launching from the top of the key toward the hoop, suspended perpetually above helpless defenders. The image could just as easily have been one from a television commercial.

Skylar described Prudence to Katie and told Prudence a little about her friends, Katie and Chase. When the entourage disembarked from the limousine, Skylar wasn't surprised when she discovered the rest of the group had already self-introduced. She was literally startled, however, by Prudence's partner, Johnna, who stood at least six feet tall in heels and possessed distinctly dark, handsome features, but who was at the same time conspicuously feminine. As only a child can, Kelvin condensed into words what the rest of the group thought when he said truthfully to Johnna, "You're tall and pretty."

Skylar stood hand in hand with her fiancé, took the lead, and made the remaining introductions. The group then reformed into two smaller groups, one consisting of Chase, Prudence, Quinn, and the boys, and the other of Skylar, Katie, Kelly, Marisol, and Johnna, before they migrated toward the turnstiles into the concourse and to their section. Quinn showed his ticket to an usher who, with surprising professional aplomb, glanced back at the assemblage and guided them to their seats. Even though Quinn already knew the seats were good, he hadn't anticipated the impression the towering leviathans made just a few feet away. Kelly nodded his approval as everyone filled the row.

Just before the public address announcer began to introduce the starting lineups, Donnie David glanced toward the seats, found Quinn flanked by the identical twins, and shot a wink on the sly.

"Did you see that, Kelvin?" Melvin nearly jumped out of his shoes. "Donnie David winked at me!"

Kelvin countered, "No, he didn't, Melvin. He winked at me!"

Before the fraternal dispute progressed, the lights in the United Center dimmed and "Sirius" by the Alan Parsons Project played behind the "Running of the Bulls" video on the Jumbotron. With pompons quavering, the Luvabulls lined up in front of the home team bench. Then, the voice of Bulls' public address announcer, Tommy Edwards, roared familiarly, "And now, the starting lineup for your CHICAGO BULLS!"

Given the atmosphere, the seats, and the circumstances, it would have been impossible for the game to have been a letdown. Neither the Bulls nor the Knickerbockers disappointed that night, though. The game was close to the last. The real excitement, however, took place after the game, when Donnie David came out of the locker room and Quinn introduced the Knicks' star to the boys.

"Donnie David," Quinn said ceremoniously. "I'd like to introduce you to your two biggest fans, Kelvin Hill and Melvin Hill." The little boys, who'd survived the entire game brilliantly in spite of the late hour and an eventful day of travel, were amusingly out of their little minds.

Neither was able to speak, so the humble giant took control. "Your friend, Quinn, told me all about you. Thanks for cheering for me and for the team. On behalf of the Knicks, I want to present you with official jerseys." Donnie pulled one white and one blue, tiny, autographed Donnie David jerseys from his shoulder bag and handed one each to the two boys.

The expressions on the boys' faces were priceless. "Thanks, Donnie!" both boys said as if they had known the man for their entire lives. In their minds, they had. Then, Kelvin and Melvin turned and ran to their mother to show her their treasures. None of the casual observers, including people who waited for other players nor a single one of the vested, did not at that moment wish to relive his or her childhood. Marisol looked over appreciatively first to the athlete and then to Quinn.

Quinn took the opportunity to introduce Donnie to the rest of the group, qualifying, "Now, you will not have to remember everyone's name." Then, Quinn looked up and said with heartfelt appreciation, "Thanks for the seats, Donnie. They were incredible. I owe you one."

"Anytime, Quinn, anything for a fellow Red Devil," Donnie said referring to the mascot of their alma mater. "Especially for such a big stick like you. You know, you're kind of a legend, at least you were when I was still in school," Donnie added.

"Well, thanks," Quinn responded modestly, "But, I get a funny feeling that someone's taken my place." The comment seemed to make Donnie a little uncomfortable. Shifting effortlessly into networking mode, Quinn said, "I hope to repay the favor sooner, rather than later. This is the guy I told you about, and I wanted to get you together," Quinn added, nodding toward Kelly.

CHAPTER 79

Skylar looked past Quinn's shoulder at the big red numbers on the digital clock. She and Quinn hadn't gotten home until almost one o'clock, but neither had bothered to set the alarm. Skylar knew they wouldn't have trouble getting up, and she wasn't the least bit tired at twenty-five minutes before seven.

Quinn continued to snore gently as he slept on his side. Skylar held her head up with her arm, mentally reviewing the days' schedule for a couple of minutes before she unconsciously leaned over and kissed Quinn thoughtfully. She rested her lips pensively on the side of Quinn's nose and cheek for a few moments as she continued to think. Slowly, Quinn became aware of Skylar's warm lips and breath on his face, opened his eyes, and adjusted just enough to kiss her back. "I can't think of too many other ways I'd rather be awakened," Quinn said, breaking Skylar's peaceful trance.

"Try," she teased.

Quinn looked again at Skylar in the scant light that escaped past the imperfectly fitting hotel curtains. He thought again that Skylar's beauty originated deep inside of her and could only radiate out for others to see. She was just as pretty in a breathtaking, vulnerable way after a night's sleep with sand in her eyes as she was made up like she was at the basketball game the night before.

"Listen," Skylar said, jarring Quinn from his own daydream. "I talked to Prudence last night about a few things I need to wrap up with her."

Slightly concerned, Quinn asked, "Is there a problem?"

"No," Skylar answered. "I just need to sign on a couple of things. I thought I could meet her at her office around eight and have her drop me at the brownstone at 9:30 or so. I'll only need five minutes there. Then, we can get the license. With any luck, we'll be done by lunch."

"Do you want me to come with you to see Prudence?"

"It's really not a big deal," Skylar answered. "It's mostly real estate stuff. Besides, I bet you wouldn't mind getting another hour of sleep."

"That's sweet," Quinn said sleepily as he pulled the sheets up over his shoulders.

It had been a late night with Katie and Chase. It turned out that Donnie David couldn't have dinner after the game, so Kelly and Marisol peeled off to get the twins to bed. Prudence and Johnna used that as an opportunity to excuse themselves, too. Later, Chase had the misguided idea of sampling some of Chicago's many flavors and suggested a place about a half mile southeast of Wrigley on Clark. The L & L Tavern featured Pabst Blue Ribbon longnecks for two bucks, a surprisingly wide selection of Irish whiskeys, and an equally surprising number of entertaining patrons. Katie was disappointed to have learned they'd missed the late Jeopardy game, when the affable, red-headed bartender poured free drinks for patrons who had the right question for Final Jeopardy. The four of them had a great time at L & L while it lasted, but Quinn hadn't been used to that sort of stuff anymore.

"I think I'll take you up on that," Quinn relented.

"I thought maybe we could do something to help you get back to sleep."

CHAPTER 80

Quinn waited outside the brownstone as Prudence maneuvered her phantom black pearl Audi A4 out of the flow of traffic and temporarily double parked.

Because he knew Skylar would only need a few minutes inside the house, Quinn had held his cab. After ten minutes, though, he had assumed that Prudence had been distracted with some other legal crisis or had gotten caught in traffic. He handed the hack $10 and asked him to circle back in twenty minutes.

"Everything all right, honey?" Quinn asked as Skylar squeezed out of the passenger side door.

"Absolutely," Skylar said to Quinn with a hug. Skylar leaned down and stuck her head in the window and said, "Thanks, Prudence."

"I'm not sure if you'll believe me when I say this, Skylar, but it was truly my pleasure," Prudence answered before she looked over at Quinn. "Take care of my friend, Quinn. Don't make Skylar hire me again! Take care of yourself, too."

Quinn grinned widely and promised to follow advice of counsel before he closed the car door. Prudence smiled and glanced peculiarly at the house before she crowded back into traffic and disappeared down the street. Quinn turned toward the walk up to the house.

As she opened her purse to find the house keys, Skylar offered, "Sorry I'm late, Quinn. A couple of things took a little longer than I expected. Of course, Prudence also couldn't stop talking about last night. It was the first time she has really opened up to me. I think she really had fun."

While Skylar turned the lock and pushed the door open, Quinn smiled a contented smile and said, "That makes me happy."

Skylar reached over to flip the switch, but neither the foyer light nor any lights in the larger room went on. "That's strange," Skylar said as she moved further into the house.

Quinn looked around the living room and up the stairs. The first-floor shades and curtains were drawn, and it appeared the upstairs doors were all closed. The absence of light, save a little from the open front door, transformed the furniture into shadows. Quinn followed Skylar, who found another switch plate and tried again. Still nothing.

"Huh? I asked Prudence to leave the electric and gas because we'd be showing soon," Skylar said more to herself than to Quinn. After trying the switch a couple of more times, Skylar suggested, "Why don't we head upstairs. The wall safe is on the landing. If we open a couple of doors up there, I'm pretty sure I can read the dial."

As he turned to follow Skylar toward the stairs, Quinn glimpsed a shadow closing distance behind him. With three or four spring-like steps, the shadow was on him. It leapt up on its left foot, turned slightly in the air, and unleashed its sweeping leg toward Quinn's head. Instinctively, Quinn ducked, but the kick grazed his crown. Quinn staggered, but caught himself on the wall before he fell to a knee and braced himself with his hands on the floor.

Skylar turned. Before she could produce a syllable, Skylar recognized in the muted light a frightening and familiar face, "Taylor!"

Through gritted teeth, Taylor spat, "You disgusting whore. You think I wouldn't find out what you've been up to? You cunt! You think I'd let you get away with this after what that dyke lawyer did to me? Think again, bitch!"

In that moment, Skylar realized how irrelevant Taylor had become to her. She started toward Quinn. Her movement instantly triggered two similar and rapidly sequential actions. Taylor darted forward to intercept Skylar. Quinn, who'd recovered enough to recognize a need for action launched across his body a punch that landed squarely below Taylor's ribs but above his left hip.

Something more than adrenaline coursed through his veins as Taylor staggered back against the couch and released a hollow, exhaling moan. In his mind, Skylar was the reason he'd lost his job. It was Skylar's fault he couldn't get a lawyer. Maybe if someone other than his asshole father represented him, he would've had settlement money. It was Skylar who'd embarrassed him by having divorce papers served that morning when the girls and Charlie were at the house. Charlie had a big, god-damned mouth and word traveled fast. Then, there was that nigger carpet cleaner who had prevented him from getting anything at all. The final straw, the last valuable nugget of information from the investigator that he had hired, was this guy,

Quinn Powers, who Skylar planned to marry? Seriously? Why couldn't that bitch just have died like she was supposed to?

Taylor was surprised at the precision of the blow to his kidney. "Lucky shot," he said under his breath, but the punch would still probably mean that he'd be pissing blood for a week. Taylor's rage compelled him to engage again. He regained his equilibrium, but he wouldn't have another chance for a sucker punch, or kick as it had turned out.

"Oh, God! Quinn!" Skylar shrieked as she could make out in murkiness the wound dripping blood down the right side of his face and neck.

Quinn stood up without taking his eyes from Taylor and assured Skylar, "I'm okay."

Skylar saw Taylor's wrathful eyes as he pulled himself back upright and demanded, "Stop it right now, Taylor!" When Taylor stepped intently toward them, Skylar repeated more firmly, "Right now!"

Even if he had heard her, Taylor would have ignored the command. His rage precluded the sensory processing that most people take for granted during normal, human interactions. This was far from normal.

Quinn's back was against the wall in front of the staircase. He had little room to operate. He'd always believed when a person is backed into a corner, he still has the choice to fight his way out or give up. Quinn could never have imagined he'd ever literally have to face that decision.

Quinn had only a split second to act as Taylor seemed to fly toward him. "Move!" Quinn shouted to Skylar as Taylor jumped straight up on his right foot, coiled his left, and whipped it down toward Quinn's head. Quinn tried to avoid the kick by backing up, but the wall stopped him. The heel of Taylor's foot came down indecisively, grazing Quinn's forehead and his nose. There was a muted but perceptible snap as his nose broke, which surprised more than hurt him.

Taylor sought to end the undercard so he could move on to the main event. Twice now, he used some of the most effective techniques. Considering the blood, Taylor believed he had Quinn on the ropes. All he needed to do was deliver the knockout. As soon as his left foot touched the floor, he pivoted, chambered his right foot, and snapped it around toward Quinn's head. He didn't yet realize it, but Taylor had already twice misjudged Quinn Powers.

In actuality, neither of Taylor's blows had much of an affect. Even though both had drawn blood, Taylor didn't fully connect. His surprise attack had failed because Quinn sensed him early enough to duck. The flying roundhouse kick had glanced off the hardest part of Quinn's skull. Because the head has so many blood vessels, even a small cut inside the scalp tends to bleed a lot. The axe kick only grazed Quinn's face. It had just the right force and location to break Quinn's nose, but Quinn looked worse than he felt. Taylor's second mistake was at least as significant.

Had Taylor even made one more payment to the investigator he'd enlisted to find Skylar, he would've discovered a level of competence uncommon in any profession much less the often dubious world of private investigation. The detective would have given him an unusually complete summary, including ostensibly disjointed information about Skylar's oncologist, Dierdorf's American Kennel Club registration number, and Quinn's association as an athlete/member of United States Taekwondo. She'd already told him everything he believed he needed to know, so, when he aimed the rapid fire roundhouse kick at Quinn's head, Taylor was more than a little surprised when his target ducked and his kick whizzed seemingly harmlessly over Quinn's head.

After he avoided the combination, Quinn slid down against the wall when he heard an extraneous thud. When Quinn reached the floor, he braced his body with both hands and sprung out his right foot toward Taylor's left knee which still supported his entire weight after the recoil of his kick. Snapping like a water-logged tree branch, the ligaments in Taylor knee popped separating the femur from the patella. Quinn saw Taylor's silhouette crumble and hit the floor. A split second later, Quinn heard a body fall with a grunt.

Sitting up, Quinn wiped away the blood and opened wide his eyes to absorb as much light as he could. He focused on the place where Skylar had been standing, but was only able to make out the wall where a door and a few pictures of indeterminate subject matter still hung. Finally, he looked down. "Oh, no!" Quinn said aloud. Skylar lay motionless on the floor.

Disregarding Taylor who writhed in pain in front of him, Quinn crawled on hands and knees to the place where Skylar's body rested. The kick Quinn ducked did find a mark, but not the one it intended.

Skylar's eyes were closed and Quinn saw something dark and oily trickle from her ear and puddle on the carpet. "Skylar! Skylar! Answer me!"

He couldn't be sure, but he thought Skylar opened her eyes just enough to see him through the narrow slits of her eyelids. He didn't see the wry smile cross her lips.

"Skylar!" repeated Quinn, relieved.

"Quinn."

"Yes, Skye. I'm here. Let me call an ambulance."

"Wait, Quinn," Skylar repeated softly but with conviction. "Will you kiss me?"

Quinn wiped his face again.

"I don't care about that. Kiss me. Please?"

Quinn bent closer and kissed Skylar gently on her lips.

With some effort, Skylar said, "Thank you, Quinn."

"You're welcome," Quinn answered. "Any time."

"No, not for the *kiss*, you *moron*," Skylar said. "Not for *that*."

Quinn wondered if Skylar might be confused. "For what then? Why are you thanking me?"

"Quinn," Skylar started innocently, "You made all of my dreams come true, just like you said you would."

Quinn was startled by Taylor, who stood behind him sneering facetiously, "Aw, now isn't that just sweet?"

Quinn snapped his head around. Taylor stood like some indestructible monster from some bad horror movie on his good leg, supporting his weight with his left arm on the couch while he held an ornate sword in the other. Quinn had only just then noticed the weapon a moment earlier hung on the wall with its facsimile.

"I really wanted to take care of the two of you with my own hands, but the ends will definitely be justified by whatever means necessary," Taylor began to speak. "Jesus, you dumbass bitch, did you really think that I'd let you get away with this? Did you really think I'd let you do this to me?"

Quinn remained silent, preferring to maintain his concentration on the long blade that glinted in the reflected light from the doorway. He only vaguely registered the approach of another figure from the direction of the front wall near the door.

Prudence had come in seconds earlier. It had taken a moment for her eyes to adjust. Once she processed the scene, she acted on impulse. Swiftly and stealthily, she crossed the room to the back side of the couch where Taylor stood with the weapon. She stopped to his side just out of range of his peripheral vision. Before Taylor could utter another vile word, Prudence released a powerfully compact punch reminiscent of Laila Ali. The punch landed squarely on the side of Taylor's head, in front of his ear and above the hinge of his jaw. Taylor was unconscious before he hit the floor, which he did only after dropping the sword and tumbling over the couch into the middle of the room.

"Thanks," Quinn said.

"My pleasure," Prudence honestly replied, rubbing her hand.

Quinn looked back at Skylar, but her eyes were no longer open.

CHAPTER 81

Lake Michigan's capricious western shore compensated for the world's intrigues. Conditions were unusually mild since the Beechjet landed earlier in the week. Quinn woke up, showered, and pulled open the curtains. Through the hotel window, he saw a bustling city in contrast to the calm lake beyond. As he donned a tailored black suit and checked his tie in the full-length mirror opposite the closet in the room, people walked, jogged, bicycled, and pushed three-wheel child carriers on the streets and park paths below. A moment later, Quinn stepped out of the elevator and found Kelly waiting in the lobby. Marisol and the kids had already gone ahead. Outside, Quinn gently placed custom sunglasses on his face more to conceal the bruises under his eyes than to defend against the stark rays of the sunlight. Inside the limousine, he didn't bother to replace the glasses in their case.

Kelly broke the silence, "You all right, Buddy?"

Quinn answered detachedly. "I'm doing the best I can."

Kelly flipped on the satellite radio on the center console in the backseat of the Town Car. The front seat window barrier had been up since he and Quinn got in, so the music would not compete with the driver's choice. Kelly found a channel he knew played new music recorded by mostly established classic rock artists. Green Day's new song, *Know Your Enemy* just ended when Quinn recognized a familiar melody. Quinn's head snapped away from the window. Wordlessly, he looked at the tuner display for the song and artist before turning back again.

When the song ended a few minutes later, the disc jockey explained, "What a great song! That was the first single from Mark Burton's new CD, which is scheduled for release later this year. That was, *The Grass Won't Pay No Mind*. And, here's another one from an artist you might not have expected to release this sort of thing. Talk about a crossover! This is the Latin band El Galipote whose lead singer Noelia Vega sadly passed away late last year."

Quinn shifted uncomfortably in his seat.

In a distinctly radio voice, the announcer continued, "She had time to record this one, though, and she's credited with both music and lyrics. This is *September Dream* from the CD entitled *Eternidad*, which, of course, is the Spanish word for eternity"

A brief Motown-inspired aria, as likely to be heard in a local blues club as it would in a swanky piano bar, introduced a voice that hovered like an apparition above the music:

Seeds were sowed,
But refused to flower.
Like a dream
In my darkest hour.
Opened the blossom
Under warmth you cast;
Found a destiny
Before Winter last.

You're everything you seem,
My September Dream.
You're my September Dream.

Kelly couldn't have been more amazed by the irony. "Do you want me to change the station?"

"No. Leave it." Quinn wanted to hear what else the ghost had to say.

CHAPTER 82

Scents from blooms on the variety of flowering trees swirled gently in the breeze. Perennials slumbering secretly below the surface just scant days earlier pushed upward their green stems. Most had already blossomed and created a festival of color for anyone one who had eyes to see it.

Quinn stepped out of the chapel onto the stonework platform above the stairs. He breathed deeply and looked insentiently at the gardens. He seemed startled when Jordan, who was the first to follow him through the oversized oak doors, stepped around and, hugging her brother, offered, "It was a beautiful ceremony, Quinn."

Quinn answered through a thin smile, "Thanks, Jo."

Only then, Jordan unreservedly released her emotions, "I am so sorry, Quinn. You don't deserve this. It's not fair."

Quinn looked back hesitantly at the rest of the group who'd assembled behind him. Each had come expecting a wedding, but got something quite different instead. Only Kelly and Amelie understood Quinn didn't really want sympathy. His two closest friends long ago learned Quinn would just want to be alone.

CHAPTER 83

After Prudence had delivered Skylar to the brownstone, an uncomfortable feeling not unlike those she experienced in her home as a child that something was not right settled in the pit of her stomach. Before she reached the next block, Prudence realized the blinds in the house were drawn. Earlier in the week, the real estate agent made a production of opening the blinds and curtains, she said, "To bring out the beautiful details inside the home." A moment after the gestalt, Prudence made a hard left onto the intersecting one-way street and circled back around.

Her timing was good, but not good enough. She returned to the house, double parked, and slid cautiously through the front door. She wanted to be discrete in case there was an otherwise reasonable explanation for the drawn blinds, like the possibility Quinn or Skylar planned an intimate moment. She silently stepped away from the door and into the shadows. If Skylar or Quinn had been in a compromising position and noticed her, she could use the excuse that she remembered a legal issue to discuss.

It took a moment for her eyes to adjust. At first, she thought that was just what had happened. Prudence could distinguish Quinn's outline on the floor suspended tenderly above Skylar's face. She heard whispers. Quinn kissed Skylar. Prudence was just about to slip back out when she saw a third wheel totter up from the floor, grab what appeared to be a sword from a wall display, and yowl. At the moment Prudence heard the voice, she recognized Taylor Kerr as the gate-crasher. She understood immediately what was happening and exactly what Taylor intended to do next. Thanks to Prudence, Taylor didn't get the chance.

As Skylar slipped into unconsciousness and Taylor lay motionless in the middle of the floor, Prudence moved to the large front window and pulled back the curtains to illuminate the room. She used her left hand because her right had already begun to throb painfully. It was only then Prudence could finally survey the room.

Her view of Taylor was the least obscured. After absorbing the brunt of her punch, Taylor flipped over the couch and landed on the floor. He was on his stomach, almost perpendicular to the couch. His legs pointed in the direction of the opposite wall, or would have if one of his knees wasn't bent in an unnatural direction. Moving to that opposite wall, Prudence pulled over the curtains on two smaller windows. From where she stood, she saw around the couch Skylar lying on her back. Blood streamed from someplace on her head onto the floor. A little further around was Quinn. His face was covered with streaks of blood. By the time Prudence made her way around the other side of the couch, Quinn had already dialed 9-1-1.

With sinuses swollen from his broken nose, Quinn's voice was paradoxically comical in contrast to the seriousness of the situation as he spoke to the operator, *"Ah deed ah ahbulance and ah police car at..."* Then, Quinn stopped and asked Prudence urgently, *"Brewdince! Bhut's dee ahddress 'ere?!?"*

Taylor's kick sailed over Quinn's head. Quinn didn't know Skylar stood her ground. It all happened so fast. When Taylor pivoted and wheeled for the knockout, Quinn ducked and dropped to the floor. The arc of Taylor's kick sailed over and struck Skylar squarely on the side of her face.

Recently recovered from brain injury, Skylar was susceptible to serious damage that would result from a subsequent concussion. The kick to the head was the first of two. After Taylor struck her, Skylar did not fall immediately. Rather, she staggered before falling backward. When Skylar's body hit the floor, her head slammed down hard in spite of the padded carpet. Her brain had begun to bleed and enlarge even as she regained consciousness and spoke with Quinn for the last time.

Taylor was arrested for a number of charges, including first-degree murder. He couldn't walk and he had a pretty serious headache, so he was transferred to the medical holding cell within the Cook County Department of Corrections. Quinn and Prudence made themselves available to a seated grand jury. Both were credible witnesses, but Quinn's broken nose and black eyes were at least as compelling as anything he said. The assistant district attorney provided more than enough evidence for reasonable suspicion that a crime had been committed, and the twenty-four grand jurists were unanimous in their vote to indict. Taylor was arraigned from his hospital bed via closed-circuit television.

Considering Taylor hired an investigator to locate, track, and report Skylar's movements, waited in her house, and in fact killed her, the outcome of a criminal trial would be almost a foregone conclusion. In spite of his confession and against advice of the second-year public defender assigned to the case, Taylor Kerr pleaded "Not Guilty" to a judge who shared a Sunday morning tee-time at Medinah Country Club with family court judge Floyd Summers.

The bleeding from the laceration to Quinn's head had stopped, and the emergency room doctor set Quinn's nose. Prudence was treated for two broken bones in her hand. After making statements to the police, she and Quinn were allowed to go.

Before she left, Prudence stopped Quinn to explain the real reason for Skylar's visit to her office that morning. "She revised her will. You would have been her husband, Quinn, and she named you as her sole heir."

Quinn was not as much speechless as he was exhausted. His head pounded and he was a little wobbly from his blood loss. Upon hearing the news, all he could do was rub his forehead with his thumb and forefingers.

"And, Quinn," Prudence added, wincing apologetically. "There's one more thing."

CHAPTER 84

The playful puppy in him had long since faded, but the ocean both confounded and energized Dierdorf as each wave encroached further upon the white sandy beach. A warm westward wind pushed down the sun in the evening sky. Dierdorf chased back the receding water and stood proudly for a moment to enjoy his apparent accomplishment. Then, as the water rolled back up, Dierforf scampered in retreat and seemed confused that his conquest had only been temporary.

Quinn walked with the wind at his back and watched with some amusement Dierdorf attempt to solve the mystery of the tide. After a few cycles and the realization of hopelessness, Dierdorf relented and joined his master.

Quinn wasn't met at the airport and that was just fine with him. Weeks earlier, Amelie had arranged for the Triumph to be shipped to the island. Sonny made sure it would be waiting. It would have been a tight fit, but Quinn had planned to bring both Skylar and Dierdorf home in it.

The German Shepherd's ears perked when the phone vibrated. Quinn shifted his backpack from his right shoulder to his left, reached into the pocket of his baggy blue bathing suit, and retrieved his phone. He didn't look at the display before he answered, "Hey, Amie."

"Hi, Quinn," Amelie replied sensitively. "How are you?"

Quinn didn't answer.

Amelie knew Quinn had returned to the island, although she didn't understand his reasons. She suggested he get away from Chicago, considering the inquiry into Skylar's murder had already begun to have unintended consequences.

In their investigation, Chicago police detectives questioned everyone remotely associated with the case, including Quinn, Prudence, Katie, Dean Kerr, and Taylor. Upon hearing the news about Skylar's murder, the investigator Taylor hired came forth to make clear that she was not an intentional accomplice. Detectives stumbled upon Quinn's enterprise, which quickly became a bigger story than the crime itself. Immediately after Skylar's funeral, Amelie started to get calls from standard and tabloid media. She even received a call from a Chicago-based daytime talk show host and contemporary kingmaker. Amelie suggested for his own peace of mind Quinn escape to a quiet place to avoid what he might hear on the radio or read in the newspapers. He did, but for the life of her, she couldn't comprehend the reasons he returned to Antigua.

Quinn asked, "What's happening up there?"

"Everything's fine," Amelie lied. Calls from reporters hadn't stopped and the representative from that talk show was turning up the heat. Apparently the producer thought this would become a huge public interest story and the host very badly wanted the scoop.

"That's good," Quinn answered distantly.

"Yeah," Amelie said.

"Did you take care of the money thing?" Quinn asked, referring to Skylar's will.

"I spoke to Sussman," said Amelie referring to Quinn's personal attorney in New York. "He said there will probably be a tax issue, because, technically, you are the heir, you weren't actually married, and more than one state's intestacy laws are involved."

Quinn shook his head and Amelie could hear the irritation in his voice, "But, it's for charity."

Quinn could never have brought himself to give the money to a group whose purpose he didn't personally support. He decided to give the money to an organization in New York, that helped children and families of children who'd been diagnosed with terminal illness.

"I know, but he said they'd get $35 million in the worst case. That's good, isn't it?" Amelie said hopefully.

Quinn didn't answer but rather wondered about the things the fund would do with that kind of endowment.

"Oh, and Quinn," Amelie added.

Quinn sounded ready to finish the call. "Uh huh."

"I know this might not be the right time considering, well all the stuff happening, but I have another Dream Seeker," Amelie finally found the courage to say. "Her calls started a month or so ago, but obviously I had to put her off."

Quinn disconsolately sighed, "Christ on a cracker, Amie, I just don't know if I can do this anymore. Even if I thought I could, I'm not sure I could do it the way I used to. Considering people will be trying to find me, I won't be anonymous."

Amelie said portentously, "Quinn, it's Luz Marcolino." She heard only silence. Amelie repeated, "It's Luz Esperanza Bonifario."

Without another word, Quinn pushed the "End" button and dropped the phone in the sand. He sat for a few minutes and gazed out to the water and to the drifting clouds above. "If someone wants to, he can see anything in the clouds, a baseball player, a sports car, a castle, a face," Quinn reflected. "The wind blows. The world turns. Clouds are just clouds again, droplets of water condensed in the sky. Nothing more."

Eventually, Quinn stood up. He slung the backpack onto his shoulder and started toward the water. Dierdorf stopped and stepped back as soon as the waves dampened his paws, but he watched Quinn wade into the salty ocean. When the water was deeper than his waist, Quinn stopped, unzipped the backpack, and removed the package inside. Carefully, he detached the protective cover from a box and carefully replaced it back into the carrier. Quinn pulled open the lid and emptied the contents into the ocean water. Dust swirled momentarily in the direction of the sunset before it mixed finally with the water and disappeared.

Quinn stood for a few moments before he walked back out. He rejoined Dierdorf and started back toward the villa. It would be dark soon and Quinn wondered what dreams the night would bring.

Acknowledgements

A few years ago I read a short story in which the protagonist was a sculptor who could only create during a season each year and only when he was unconscious. He'd fall asleep at night and wake up to a new and beautiful, one-of-a-kind sculpture. The artist never knew what he'd create, but he knew the process was extraordinarily exhausting. Each day he consumed tens of thousands of calories, but would still end his creative season emaciated and near death.

The sculptor had previously produced a work purchased by a ruthless crime boss. The boss very much wanted the sculptor to produce a matching piece, but because the artist never knew what he'd make, he could no more duplicate the work than he could fly to the Moon. Understandably, the boss could not relate to the creative process and was humorless about what he believed to be the sculptor's lack of respect.

The boss at last gave the sculptor an ultimatum—either produce the matching piece or die. Already under a significant physical stress from his grueling process, the sculptor was more depleted than he'd ever been. Still, he consumed as much food as he could that day and went to sleep.

When the boss arrived with his henchmen to collect the sculpture or the sculptor's life, he found an incredible work, better than anything the artist had ever turned out. Still, it wasn't what the crime boss wanted, but the artist had disappeared. Neither the boss nor anyone else would ever see him again.

Obviously, the story is a metaphor. The author is the artist in the story while the sculptures are his books. The creative season is the writer's process and the crime boss, of course, represents his publisher or the critics who want the writer to duplicate a previous commercial success. At least from the writer's point of view, he'd been unable to do that and expressed the experience in a short story.

While I haven't experienced an impatient publisher and my own creative experience is not really exhausting, I can relate to one of the author's sentiments: for better or for worse, I never really know what I'm making until I make it.

A few readers of early versions of the manuscript asked whether I was Quinn. Clearly, some of my own personal experience inspired the idea for Quinn and the other characters. Admittedly, there is nothing Quinn has seen that I haven't, but while The Dream Seeker is personal, it's not autobiographical. I'm not Quinn.

About four years ago, I mentioned to author Sharon Linnea my idea for this novel. From that day and before, Sharon has been a friend and mentor, and she referred me to editor Gary Kessler. Gary did a terrific job with the edit, and he taught me a lot about the art of writing. Oncology nurse Wendy Neidich was an indispensible resource as I described Skylar's diagnosis and treatment. Army Lieutenant Colonel William Terhune provided insights relating to life in Western Europe. Zaida Zapata added a great deal of Latin culture to my universe, including the introduction to *el galipote*. Zaida's sister, linguist Clari Zapata assisted with some of the Spanish passages. To make some of the legal proceedings reasonably realistic, Ted Corless, Esquire, provided time when he had it and advised. My book club, including Taylor DiMeglio, Barbara Laino, Chelsea Patterson, and Patty Walker, was courageous enough to tackle a messy manuscript and provide terrific criticism. Other friends to whom I am grateful for reading and providing feedback about an early version of the manuscript are Phyllis Kaminsky and Tina Robbins, who helped in particular with appropriate island footwear among other things. Melissa Albrecht gave me the great name, "Sparvieri," and Lauren Dubuc helped me dress both Quinn and Skylar for many of their adventures. In a previous life, I turned a customer, Alan Adelson, into a friend. Since that time, Alan has shown me the way and encouraged me to take it. Writer/producer Melissa Shaw-Smith, Kerry Lennon, Sandy Lennon, Tami Small, and Dr. Mary Gallert were intrepid readers of a first-time novelist's manuscript and offered enormously helpful feedback. Tom Lennon was a patient, indispensible resource as he designed my image of this book. Of course, thanks to the management and staffs at both the Tuscan Cafe, and Cafe á la Mode in Warwick, who allowed me to sip coffee and work on my project during the past couple of years.

For more than two decades, no matter where I've lived or what I was doing, I've met my "Chicago Research Team," Blaise Cooper, Steve Gordon, Bob Reis, and more recently Joe Cooper, Erik Froehlich, and Rob Rooney, during one summer weekend at Wrigley Field. Blaise and Joe were always available to answer apparently unrelated questions about Chicago, while Bob and Erik provided particularly good opinion about a later revision of the manuscript. Of course, our group has regularly patronized Kirkwood Bar & Grill, Durkin's Tavern, L & L Tavern, Cubby Bear, Murphy's Bleachers, Hugo's Frog Bar, Gibson's, and The Chicago Chop House, although I doubt I can collect any of my twenty-year old receipts and write them off as a business expense.

Most heartfelt thanks for your encouragement and support.

For my children, Jordan, Katie, and Wade, who continue to give me purpose, I love you "until the numbers stop." Finally, Lori, you continue to be my guide and inspiration.